Derek R Payne is a semi-retired entrepreneur and inventor. He is also a poet and his poetry has appeared on television and radio broadcasts. *Letters to Doberitz* is his first novel.

To Ian,

For my family, past and present.

With very best wishes,

Derek Payne

To Ian
All the very best

Derek R Payne

Letters to Doberitz

A Novel Based on a True Story

AUSTIN MACAULEY PUBLISHERS™

LONDON • CAMBRIDGE • NEW YORK • SHARJAH

A CIP catalogue record for this title is available from the British Library.

ISBN 9781528917971 (Paperback)
ISBN 9781528917988 (Hardback)
ISBN 9781528917995 (E-Book)

www.austinmacauley.com

First Published (2018)
Austin Macauley Publishers Ltd
25 Canada Square
Canary Wharf
London
E14 5LQ

My thanks goes to my wife for putting up with my obsessions; and siblings, Anne, Pam and Andrew, for their support. Sincere thanks goes to my Auntie Irene, William and Annie's daughter, who has helped with historical detail and is an inspiration in herself. My thanks to Vincent Brown for painting the book cover, demonstrating that his great-grandfather's talent as an artist is still alive and well.

This book was only possible because my father, Sidney, fastidiously documented old family papers, photographs and stories. Sadly, neither he nor my mother, Lily, are now here to read this. I also thank the writer Nathan Filer, who challenged me to write this story.

My thanks goes to everyone at Austin Macauley for proving that publishers can be good to work with, as well as highly professional; and to my proofreaders, Dorene, Pam, Baz, Liz and Neville

Finally, my thanks goes to William and Annie, and Thomas and Harriet. This is their story.

PREFACE

This novel is based largely on a true story that took place in quite a different world. That is to say, life in the early 1900's was very different to that of today. The motor car had barely been invented, so motorised vehicles were rare. Radio and television were in the imagination of only a few who dared to dream of such things and one wrote with fountain pens or pencils, as the ball point pen had been invented, but was waiting for technology to catch up so that it could be made. The ordinary person in the street read newspapers or books for information and news, so evenings would be spent reading or entertaining oneself and then having an early night to prepare for a hard day's work the following day. At that time, people worked six or sometimes seven days a week with no annual holidays.

The people in this novel are real. They are my family, my grandparents and great-grandparents. They are my ancestors and their story has been written against a background of old documents, letters, the spoken word and a collection of wonderful photographs. I am lucky that my father was a meticulous documenter and collector of family papers and photographs. My family is also lucky that my grandfather developed from an early age a fascination for the new art of photography. With a camera in his hand, he was an absolute artist, with an imaginative eye for composition, lighting and the technical side of working with the relatively new and primitive technology. He developed his own photographs in the spare bedroom at home but his work was never 'discovered' and has lain in a large box in a cupboard for years. Before the advent of colour photography, my grandfather would hand paint watercolours over black and white photographs as good as anything I have ever seen, and it is perhaps no coincidence to see his talent resurface years later through his great-grandson, the quite brilliant Bristol Artist Vincent Brown.

My family is fortunate to have a unique library of early sepia and black and white photographs that are a window into family history and their world, and what a world it was! This is not a story of the wealthy or influential, and there is not a country house or butler in sight. These are ordinary working class people, who were making their way in a tough world where not to work meant not to eat. Their day-to-day lives were probably very typical of their time and possibly of your own forebears. Life was tough. They had setbacks, triumphed, laughed and cried like everyone else, but their lives changed as it did for many millions, when the global events of their time overtook them, the country and the world. There are countless stories to be told of the time around the First World War, but my family's story is unique I believe and I hope, you will later agree, was worth telling.

BUCKINGHAM PALACE

1918.

The Queen joins me in welcoming
you on your release from the
miseries & hardships, which you have
endured with so much patience &
courage.

During these many months of trial,
the early rescue of our gallant Officers
& Men from the cruelties of their captivity
has been uppermost in our thoughts.

We are thankful that this longed
for day has arrived, & that back in
the old Country you will be able
once more to enjoy the happiness of
a home & to see good days among
those who anxiously look for your
return.

George R.I.

The letter written to William by King George V, in 1918

Sepia faces look back from old photographs,
One-hundred-year-old smiles, echo soft ancestral laughs,
Old family pictures that give history a face,
And us a sense of heritage, and one a sense of place

Only the very lucky ones have such photos in a box,
And when we look upon them, our history we unlock,
Marriages in black and white, in military uniform,
Echoes of a previous age, from long ere we were born

Generations of our forebears, alive in cellulose,
Giving one a feeling that they are somehow near and close,
Pictures from a different age, when the world was blown and torn,
Now still gently smiling back, as if as though reborn

I recognise that forehead, that chin, those eyes, that smile,
I see it in their descendants; it stands out like a mile,
And as the camera snaps today, time frozen in a frame,
Wait again a hundred years, for the box to open again…

My relationship to these very special characters:

THOMAS PAYNE   HARRIET PAYNE (nee SIMS)
(Great-Grandfather)   (Great-Grandmother)

Married 11th November 1890

WILLIAM PAYNE   ANNIE PAYNE (nee
(Grandfather)   McGRATH)
     (Grandmother)

Married 4th January 1919

Annie Payne

William Payne   *Harriet and Thomas Payne*

CHAPTER ONE
Bristol, England, 1914

The repetitive beat of the drum in the distance almost matched that of William's pounding heart, the sound echoing louder as he rounded the corner into Queens Square, the boom of the base drum carrying in the still afternoon air as it wafted through the gaps between the buildings. Pedalling harder as he came out of the bend, he overtook a queue of stationary horses and carts, watchful not to catch a wheel in the tramlines as he did, his heart thumping with the exertion of cycling and with the added excitement of what awaited him.

When the bell had rung in the factory for the end of his long shift, he had made a dash for the bicycle sheds, intent on being first to get from Temple Meads to the City Centre and the event that all his workmates had been talking about so enthusiastically during their tea break earlier. William, or 'Will' as everyone called him, had worked in the factory at Mardon Son and Hall, making cigarette cartons since he was fourteen and now, two years later and stirred up by the patriotic posters that he cycled past every morning, he was hungry for change. The talk amongst everyone for months was that war was coming; it was only just a question of when. Old women shook their heads at the prospect but Will's young pal's enthusiasm echoed the press in saying that the Germans were getting too big for their boots. The newspaper headlines had been beating a patriotic drum for months now, gently moulding the mood of the people to a stiffening resolve and there was a growing feeling that something would break soon. Every newspaper raised questions of personal and national morality and right, with Queen Victoria's own cousin Wilhelm glaring out of the pages in rude cartoons depicting him in ever-darker tones.

Will had already made his mind up. As he turned into the City Centre, the sound of the military band hit him full on and his eyes darted left and right, flooded with a euphoric scene of organised mayhem. He quickly dismounted and leaned his bicycle against the wall next to a dozen others. No one would want to pinch the old boneshaker he used to get to work on. It took him a minute to take in the scene before him, and he jumped up onto the back of an empty cart to get a better view of the area. Apart from going to watch the Rovers, he had never seen so many people all together in one place. Over to his left, the baton of the band leader cut through the air to the rhythmic swish of his arm, the sun reflecting from the highly polished brass instruments before him like flashes of lightning, bouncing off the polished buttons of their uniforms and adding to the atmosphere of the thumping beat of the music. A dense crowd of men and women filled the area in front of him and children darted in and out of the edges of the throng. To his right, a large stage had been erected and it was filled with dignitaries looking very important and righteous. Banners were being slowly swung behind them on the stage and a large poster filled the centre, proclaiming loudly that: 'Your Country and King need you'.

Sir Herbert Ashman, the Lord Mayor of Bristol, stood imposingly in front of a large picture of King George V and with a signal from the Mayor, the band brought its rousing song to a neat close. Megaphone in hand, Sir Herbert burst into a rousing speech, telling everyone how blessed they all were to be enjoying the freedom and life that they all have now. Everyone however, from grandmothers to the smallest child, was under a growing threat from the Keizer. Germany was rising. Tensions in Europe were growing and Britain had to stand firm and strong. Sir Herbert was a practised orator and his speech built with each sentence, his words like a rising tide crashing over his audience like a patriotic flood. After ten minutes, everyone listening was filled with patriotism and pride, mixed in with excitement and trepidation. He finished with a rousing proclamation of "God save the King", throwing his fist into the air as he did. "God save the King" reverberated loudly back from the crowd with such a punch that it seemed to echo from every building. Sir Herbert, having now softened up the crowd and got their full attention, handed over the megaphone to Brigadier Townsend whose oration continued in the same vein. Europe was changing and the Kaiser was building up his forces like a dark shadow in the east.

Will scanned the area again from the vantage point of the cart and spotted what he was looking for on the far side of the crowd. Over the entrance to the Colston Hall, a sign had been hastily erected, 'Recruitment Office'.

Leaving the speeches behind, he climbed down and made his way around the edge of the crowd and across the centre, carefully stepping over the tramlines as he crossed the road in front of the Hall. He joined a small queue of excited lads who were nervously joking with each other, friends calling to each other in good-humoured banter. One by one, they went inside and Will took his cap off as he crossed the threshold into the foyer where three desks had been set up. The men moved forwards in turn and Will soon found himself at the front of the queue. He suddenly felt nervous and his throat felt very dry. There was a tap on his shoulder from the sergeant controlling the queue and he was ushered forward to sit at the right-hand desk. The officer before him sat with pen in hand, elbows planted firmly on the desk. With a rugged face and Kitchener-style moustache that was just starting to grey, he looked at Will, emotionless. "Good morning. So you are here to offer your services to your King and Country, young man," the last point being a statement rather than a question. "Please give me your full name and confirm if you are looking to join the army or navy."

"William Ernest Payne, sir, and I want to join the navy, sir, what with Bristol being a seafaring city and all," Will replied.

The officer's heavy pen scribed out the detail as he then asked, "Date of birth and current address?" Will sat straight-backed, with hands firmly planted on his knees and felt a sudden surge of confidence as the thought flashed through his mind, "I'm doing this. I'm actually joining the navy."

Will gave his date of birth and started to give his address but he stopped speaking as the officer had raised his left hand, his fingers and thumb spread out as wide as they could. He stopped writing and looked up at Will.

"Now then, William Payne, I do believe in the excitement of the moment, you've forgotten your birthdate. You see, the date you've just given me puts you too young to sign up and see the world, so here's what we're going to do. I am going to put your papers safe to one side just here and why don't you take a little walk outside in the fresh air and try and remember the right date that you were born? When you come back, we can then complete your papers, alright?"

Suddenly, the confidence drained out of Will in a rush and he stood up nervously, "Yes, sir. Sorry, sir," he blurted, his body suddenly exploding in heat as his face reddened.

Outside, he gulped in a lungful of air and blew it out between pursed lips. "Idiot," he thought to himself. "Why didn't I think!" He went straight to the back of the queue, which had now grown longer by six or seven and stood in silence among the same nervous chatter as before. When he eventually got to the front of the queue, he stepped aside for the lad behind him to take the vacated middle desk as he waited for the right table to be free. In a few minutes, he was sat in front of the officer once more, who looked up with a faint smile. "Ah, Mr Payne, how are you getting on with your memory? Consulted with mother and father, have you?" he said in a smiling sarcastic tone as he placed Will's papers again in front of him.

"Yes, sir. Sorry, sir," he blurted. "Date of birth 17th October 1892, sir."

The rest of the form was a blur to Will. The first and certainly easiest of his wartime ordeals was over. His next one was about to come as he now had to tell Mum and Dad that he had enlisted.

The interview ended with the officer standing up to shake his hand and before Will knew it, he was back out in the sunshine. The first set of speeches had ended and the band had once again struck up a rousing marching tune. People were milling around the centre, filling the area completely, so Will leaned against the wall of the Hippodrome and lit a Woodbine, slowly drawing the smoke deep into his lungs and holding it there for a few seconds before raising his face to the sun and blowing the smoke out towards the heavens. Blimey, he'd done it. Now he had to wait for a letter from the navy and tell his boss at work, Mum and Dad and of course, Annie, his sweetheart.

CHAPTER TWO

The debate at home had rolled around gently for months as developments in Europe unfolded. Will's mother, Harriet, had lost a cousin in the Boer War just a few years back and knew how hard it had hit her family. Many families had been touched by the war in Africa with over 22,000 lost in the fighting and like many people, Harriet wondered what victory had really been achieved against the Boers.

Every evening, she would walk home with her husband, Tom, and after supper, he would sit and read the 'Daily Mirror' out loud to her. Harriet's schooling had been seriously interrupted by having to help her father with his haulage business and she wasn't very good with her reading. Back then, of course, 'Dyslexia' hadn't been discovered or known about. James Sims, Harriet's father, had a slogan hand-painted on his covered wagon, saying, 'All jobs considered,' but a good job for Father was to get a house clearance or removal job and thankfully, there seemed to be more of them in recent times, but it meant his young daughter often had to skip school to help, which she didn't mind at all.

Harriet grew up in the family business and from a child she had been needed to pitch in. When an extra pair of hands was needed, Mother would help and little Harriet would go along, at first sitting quietly in the cart and then starting to help with light work. It had been her job to help her Mother wrap anything delicate being moved in the house in sheets of newspaper before carefully placing them in tea chests, scrunching up more newspaper in between for protection. In some ways, it was fun for a small child and Harriet liked wrapping things up. She had learnt not to break anything though, and in the early years, only Mother packed anything of glass or porcelain. Harriet only ever broke the one glass and thankfully, the woman of the house had taken a shine to the adorable little girl and didn't make a fuss, but she was scalded royally by her father when the job was over and learnt to be ultra-careful in future. Her father, however, soon learnt that when doing house moves where the woman of the house was involved, which was nearly always, having little Harriet along was a big bonus. Her sweet, good nature was endearing, especially to women clients and James always had his story ready about how well little Harriet was doing with her education if the woman of the house asked why she wasn't at school.

Though doing general haulage, the family business had been gaining a reputation for house moves for the middle classes and there was more money in that, which always made father happy. Ever an eye for business, he had put Harriet's education on hold as she helped the business grow. She was, after all, only a girl, so her reading wasn't that important. Harriet's mother, Catherine, could not read or write either, and father ruled the roost, so somehow, Harriet had missed the best part of her schooling. "This is the best place for a girl to learn things," he'd say, "out here in the real world. You're better off knowing how the world works, rather than how a school does."

Harriet could sew better than any of her friends and, by the time she was a teenager, could lift tea chests that some men couldn't. She did feel a bit left out when she played with her friends on a Sunday after church if they started talking about things at school, but then her friends mainly complained about how strict the teachers were, so she felt better off not being there. "You've got to earn a crust like everyone else," her father regularly told her, and being an only child brought up in the family business, she knew no other way. Besides, it was not that unusual and many girls stayed at home to help run the family shop, or work to 'keep the wolf from the door' as they used to put it.

Father did teach Harriet her numbers though, as he wanted to make sure that she knew where the pennies came from, and Harriet discovered that she had a natural head for figures, so much so that by the time she was a teenager, she was better at it than her dad and could tell him how much the business had made at the end of every week.

Now a young woman, Harriet had grown tall and slim, with a face that showed kindness and experience rather than being one of life's natural beauties. The years of talking with people, who were usually stressed because they were moving home, had also given her an easy and reassuring way with people. Everyone she had helped move house had their own story to tell, some of them happy as they moved up in the world, but quite a few sad ones, as people were moving out through growing poverty. She hated doing repossession jobs, even though in most cases, the people had already been moved on by the bailiff, but doing a landlord's forced house clearance pained her, even though it often meant a day of light lifting as there wasn't much to move. But she always had a smile and a reassuring word for those moving up or down in the world and her empathy nearly always softened a situation and although not her intention, often resulted in a tip for Harriet from the better off customers at the end of a job. Father got to spot the signs of any tips coming, to the point where he wouldn't say a word to his daughter, but as the horses pulled the wagon towards home at the end of each job, he would simply extend his open palm in the direction of his daughter, for the tip to be handed over. Harriet didn't mind, as Dad would often give her a big smile and give her a coin or two back, ruffling her hair boyishly at the same time, which used to annoy her as she would have to spend the next few minutes brushing it back as best she could with her fingers.

One spring morning in 1888, she stood patiently by the wagon outside Temple Meads Station while her father went inside to meet a man who was coming down from London with enough luggage to need a wagon. Their two horses were unusually restless this morning, not liking the noise and bustle of the busy railway station and Harriet was standing in front of them, trying to calm them when she met Tom for the first time. The two Shire horses, 'Daisy Deo' and 'Sammy', were tossing their heads and pawing the ground and Harriet was starting to get concerned when from behind her, a soft-spoken voice purred, "Whoa! There boys, nice and steady. No one's going to hurt you." From behind her, an outstretched hand passed her face and gently stroked the horse's faces one by one. She turned to see a fresh-faced young man with dark well-trimmed hair and kindly eyes. He stood there for a minute as if Harriet wasn't there, quietly talking to the horses in almost a low whisper, slowly stroking their faces. The effect was miraculous and both horses quickly settled under his spell.

Harriet turned again to look at the owner of the hand, "You have a good way with horses, sir."

"Lovely creatures, ma'am, horses and dogs. Man has no better friends." As yet, the young man hadn't looked at Harriet, his attention being only on the horses. Now he turned to face her and removing his cap, bowing his head slightly with the wisp of a shy smile, he said, "Thomas Payne, ma'am, and you must be Harriet. Your father told me to find you while he brings my luggage."

Long afterwards, Harriet would tell her granddaughter, Irene, of that moment when she looked into Tom's eyes for the first time. The sounds of the busy station seemed instantly to be lost to silence; the only sound that she was aware of was the soft deep reassuring tone of his voice. His voice seemed to her to be like honey, just at that moment when it melts slowly over the edge of a hot slice of toast. She wanted to scoop up that voice so she could savour it longer. As he turned, she looked into his eyes and all movement around her seemed to stop. The world froze for a moment that seemed to last minutes, the spell being only broken as he extended his hand. Suddenly, sound and movement returned to her in a rush as she nervously thrust a hand out to be shaken firmly but gently.

"Yes, sir, Harriet. Yes, ah, pleased to meet you." She had never looked into such eyes. A young man but with face showing a seemingly greater maturity, his deep blue eyes had a colour and depth to them that she had never seen before, like staring into the bluest of skies on a warm summer's afternoon and all she wanted to do was to look into those eyes and let time stop. But her shyness won and she quickly averted her gaze, contenting herself with nervous glances at him as she felt her face flush red and hot.

"I have rather a lot of luggage, I'm afraid. I've been up to London on business for the shop and bought more stock than I had expected to while I was there." Harriet stood holding the horses' halters, lost to his voice as he explained that he had just been there for two days but that was long enough for him. His older brother and he had opened up a business here after learning their trade from their father.

"When I go to London to see our suppliers, I can't wait to get back. London is too busy now, ma'am, too many people, too many bad smells and too noisy."

The warmth of his voice flowed through Harriet, and his words seemed to wrap themselves around her like a warm blanket on a cold day and they talked easily between themselves for a few minutes that seemed all too short. Harriet's father arrived with several men wheeling sack trucks and trolleys loaded up with large trunks and wooden crates.

Once they had loaded the wagon, they set off for Stapleton Road to find the shop that he ran with his brother. Tom explained that they were Cordwainers and that most of the crates contained leather from London to be crafted in the shop. They made everything from leather; halters for horses through to work-wear boots and shoes. While the men talked, Harriet sat beside her father in silence, lost to a new confusion that she had never known before. There were young men around of her age of course, and she was used to being in their company, but this man was different. In the few minutes that they had together, conversation had been easy and his whole manner exuded a quietly spoken assurance. He just had something very different about him. He carried an air of confident modesty and she felt that she could listen to his deep, soft voice forever and all she could think about was how to steal another glance into those blue, blue eyes as she sat next to her father on the wagon.

On the journey home from London, Tom had sat by the window in the crowded railway carriage as his mind drifted through a maze of thoughts along with the journey. He had read the Daily Mirror from cover to cover by the time the train had made it to Reading and then he sat in silence, gazing out at the countryside as it raced past, his own reflection appearing and disappearing as they passed through shaded cuttings, his face rocking gently with the rhythm of the carriage. Coming home now, he stared out of the window and just marvelled at the lovely countryside. There was so much of it, with fields of cows and sheep dotted amongst lush green pastures of growing crops. His two days in London had been a whirl and now, all he just wanted was to be home. He sat in the carriage, his mind drifted back and forth to his early years as he settled back into his seat.

Life at home had always been full of noise and activity. He had grown up sharing the house with three older sisters and his bother Alfred, with Alfred and him sharing a bedroom. Since Tom had been born, further four younger sisters had arrived, so the house was always chaotic and full of noise. His dad in particular was adamant that their two sons would get on in the world, so life growing up had been a strict regime of school followed by an even stricter regime at home. Father was swift to punish the boys more than the girls for even the most minor misdemeanour, but mother was always there to glide in quietly once father had gone and dry the boys' eyes. She was never allowed to comfort the boys in front of Henry, her husband though, that would have been interference and undermining his authority, but she would whisk the boys away to their bedroom for the comfort and love that only their mother gave them. Schooling and discipline came first in life, but Tom knew that by his nature he followed his mother.

Father was a boot-maker by trade, like his own father and grandfather before him and he had moved down from London and set up a small shop in Lower Ashley Road. His strict manner at home was balanced by their mother's maternal platitudes. If Father had finished a good week and made a few bob, then he would work all day on Saturday and then likely go straight from work to the pub. It was not unusual for him to come home on the Saturday night a little worse for the beer and if the week had not gone so well, then he would come home in much the same state, only often in not such a good mood. That was the time when the kids ensured that they made themselves scarce. Father wasn't a bad man but his mood was nearly always stiffened by a beer or two. His philosophy on his family was simple, that his daughters would grow up and be looked after by their future husbands, so as long as the girls were well mannered and presentable and hardworking, their lives would take care of themselves, or more likely be taken care of by someone else.

His two sons were a different matter. They had to make their way in the world as breadwinners and make their way in the right way. They would only grow into good men of strong character if they knew their place in the family and in the world. Henry Payne was the breadwinner and the family head, and he let them know it. From his earliest memory, Tom, like his older brother, had been made to do small jobs in the back room of the shop where father made his boots and shoes. By the time Tom was eight years old, he was able to put the soles on boots and nail 'blakeys' into them as good as most cobblers could and by the time Tom was ten and leaving school, he could make almost anything that his father could, although not as well or as fast, according to his dad. So, Tom and Alfred spent most of their childhoods locked into an enforced respect for their father. Father ruled and that was that.

But as he grew older, Tom desperately wanted his own business and somewhere else to live. As the boys were growing into men, both he and Alfred increasingly bucked against their father's authority and Henry Payne didn't like it, progressively reverting to small but increasing acts of violence to maintain his authority as head of the household. Tom and Alfred talked together quietly about breaking away and working somewhere else or even getting their own business. They just needed the money to do it. They both worked every hour that their young lives allowed, doing second jobs late into the evening, saving every penny religiously, planning quietly for the day that they would break away.

That day came sooner than they had expected when Father's temper got the better of him once too often. Both boys had been working in the workshop late into the Saturday evening to clear a backlog when Father came back from the pub in a bad mood. Something had happened while he was out and his mood was foul. A row ensued immediately after he burst into the workshop and when Alfred answered his father back, Henry picked up a heavy shoemaker's last and hurled it across the room at him. The heavy metal last span through the air and hit Alfred just above the ankle, the sound of breaking bones reverberating loudly before the metal object clanged against the stone floor.

That act changed many things. Henry Payne was so remorseful the next morning when he had sobered up, that he rarely drank heavily again on a Saturday night. Both bones were broken above Alfred's ankle and the leg took months to recover and when he did, the bones hadn't knitted back well, so he was left with a permanent limp that ever after served to remind his father of his drunken folly that night.

So, six months later when Tom and Alfred announced that they had borrowed enough money to rent a shop in Stapleton Road and start their own business, their father never protested. He had realised that the boys were now young men and that it was the right time for his two sons to fly the nest.

One of Tom's other 'little jobs' to supplement his meagre savings had been to clean out four Shire horses at a coal merchant's yard in Stapleton Road. It meant getting up two hours earlier than normal and cycling over to the yard to feed and groom the horses and clean out their stables. Young Tom's good nature and helpfulness were endearing and Sid Brookman, whose father owned the coal merchants, took a shine to young Tom after he watched him from across the yard, talking quietly to his most difficult young horse. Sid was fascinated, watching from the shadows as the horse clearly responded to Tom's words, the big Shire calming within a minute as he stroked its great head and talked softly to it. The horse's nature changed from the moment Tom arrived in the yard and Sid often used to quietly watch him as he worked with the big Shire horse. He had a way with horses that certainly Sid had never seen before and anyone who is kind with animals is usually a decent person, he reasoned. So over a few years, Sid and Tom got on increasingly well and always had a mug of tea together after Tom had finished preparing the horses for their day. So when in conversation, Tom related the story of Alfred's broken leg and the difficulties at home, it got Sid to thinking and when a shop became vacant just along the road from the yard a few months later, he offered to lend Tom a few pounds to put a deposit down on the rent. Sid made out that he was doing it for his own benefit as much as Tom's, as being close neighbours would always ensure that Tom was on time, but it was an act that was to change many people's lives. The shop was perfect, small, but with a decent sized room out back that could serve as a workshop for Alfred and himself. More importantly, the rent wasn't too expensive either.

Still feeling the guilt of Alfred's injury, their dad helped them to set the business up. The family had continued to grow with nine children of various ages, all crammed into the one small house in St George, so with Alfred and Tom able to live in the two small bedrooms above the shop, it made sense. Henry knew that it would be tough losing his boys' help, but underneath, he was quietly proud that his boys were starting life working for themselves rather than for someone else, which he'd had to do for many years.

Setting up in business was tough for Tom and Alfred, and there were many days in the first months that they went hungry and wondered if they were going to make it. Business had started slowly, then word of mouth gradually started to spread and within a few months, they were making boots and shoes for nearly everyone in the immediate area. Tom found that he had a particular skill in working the more delicate styles of women's footwear, but the female clientele around the Stapleton Road area were not that great, with most local women still wearing hobnail boots.

CHAPTER THREE

Tom's crates were loaded onto James Sim's wagon but the journey to Stapleton Road lasted nowhere near long enough for Harriet. Sat next to her father with this blue-eyed stranger on the other side of her dad, her head was filled with confusing thoughts and when they stopped outside the shop, she climbed down from the wagon in as ladylike a manner as she could and started to take the lighter cases in. Tom stopped her the moment that he saw her carrying a box and insisted that he take it from her. As he did so, both their hands held the box and their eyes met once again and the world around them froze momentarily for them both. Words were spoken between their eyes alone without a sound and a bond was made in silence that they were not to know then, but would last a lifetime. Anyone doubting the concept of love at first sight just needed to have been there for that moment outside that shop in Stapleton Road all those years ago.

Two weeks passed before Tom went to see James Sims under the pretext of commissioning him to collect a delivery of leather from Bristol docks. Harriet was out with her mother when he called and at the end of making arrangements for the delivery, he now somewhat nervously declared an interest in seeing Harriet under more personable circumstances. James Sims carried on writing down the details for the collection like he had heard nothing. He took a few moments that seemed an age to Tom, before James looked up from the paperwork to stare straight at Tom.

"Hmm, alright young man, but before I allow your request, I need a new pair of boots, so I'll come round and meet your brother and yourself at four o'clock next Saturday where you can fit me out for a new pair of hobnails. We can discuss Harriet afterwards."

It was exactly what Tom had expected. No father would consent to allowing his daughter anywhere near any man that showed an interest in her without first thoroughly checking out the man's standing and credentials. After meeting at Tom's shop, James walked away a week later with the finest pair of boots he had ever owned and happy that that this fresh-faced young man would make his way in the world. Tom was invited around for tea the following Sunday.

Their courtship seemed forever to be in the company of Harriet's parents and for months, they only met across a table with usually Harriet's mother and, sometimes, father there. Their conversation was very nervous and difficult at first, with Mother sitting there knitting at the table and they would normally start with talk of their businesses and the world in general. They occasionally touched on Tom's family but when they did, Tom spoke very little about his father other than to say how he had taught Alfred and himself their trade well and helped to get them set up in their own business. He preferred to talk more of his mother but in truth, he diplomatically changed the conversation as soon as he thought he had said enough to satisfy their natural curiosity. When finally after months of Sunday afternoon's tea, Harriet's mother, Catherine, declared that she would have to leave them for a few minutes while she went to the kitchen. The door closed and their short silence was broken when Harriet suddenly burst into laughter, swiftly joined by Tom, who chuckled loudly as he reached out his hand across the table between the empty plates and empty tea cups. Harriet's hand came to meet his and their nervous laughter faded quickly as they gazed into each other's eyes.

"I can't tell you how much I like you, Harriet, and I would like to ask your father's permission for your hand, but I need to know if that it is your wish first." Tom's blue eyes shone brighter than ever, as Harriet gazed at this man who she had grown to love in their chaperoned time together.

"I think you already know it is, Tom. Why don't you talk to my father today? He's in a good mood. I know that as I told him earlier how much money the business had made last week," she laughed. "I think he's expecting you to ask him anyway, sometime soon. He's started talking of bringing in someone else to help him in the business, so I think he's already planning for when I won't be here."

Their courtship continued, still largely chaperoned for over a year before Tom and Harriet were allowed to make their wedding plans. They finally married in Clifton Village Church on the 11th November 1890. The Church was largely taken up by Harriet's family that seemed to be a big family who filled most 'her' side of the Church. On Tom's side of the aisle, only his mum, dad and sisters sat there with a few friends. Alfred stood beside him as his best man, and Sid Brookman and his family had all togged-up for the day, with not a sign of coal dust in sight.

Tom was as calm as he always was and stood facing the vicar, knowing this was the best thing that could have happened in his life. It was Alfred, who had a few nerves as he fumbled in his waistcoat for the ring every few seconds. Tom fixed him a big grin and looked at him with his steel blue eyes. "Calm down, brother. You've checked it a hundred times. You've got the ring. It's me getting married, not you. It will be a good day. Just relax."

It was a typical, cold, crisp November morning when Thomas and Harriet stepped outside the Church as man and wife. After a modest reception back at the Sim's house, Tom and Harriet were hailed away in a carriage for the short trip to Stapleton Road as they started life together above the shop. Alfred had previously had the larger of the two rooms upstairs but with Harriet moving in, he gave up his room for the newlyweds. Life was a little cramped though, and with Alfred in the next room, not perfect for a young married couple, though Tom and Harriet were just happy to finally be together.

The business was going well and the two men soon started to gain a reputation for high quality work and as their clientele grew, so did their modest prosperity. Tom and Harriet saved every penny they could, with Tom still rising at five every morning to feed and muck out Sid's horses at the end of the road. It brought in extra money and allowed Tom some time with the four big Shire horses that he had grown to love. After he went to the yard, Harriet went off to her father's business, so after Tom had groomed and cleaned out their stables, he would nip back home for a quick wash and breakfast before opening up the shop. They decided after some time that while they were making good shoes and boots, they weren't selling them very well, with Tom or Alfred having to pop through from the workshop into the front shop the moment that they heard the doorbell. So, it was agreed that Harriet would join the business 'out front' in the shop area. With Harriet looking after the shop, both Tom and Alfred could devote all their time to producing shoes and boots.

Writing might not have been Harriet's strongest point but she had a good way with figures, so she could measure up the client's feet and overcame her lack of reading and writing by immediately taking the order form through to Tom, where she would tell him who the shoes were for as Tom wrote the name on the form. The two brothers found that their business changed dramatically after Harriet started running the shop. The first thing Harriet did was to put a 'woman's touch' into the shop area and set too by painting the walls a lighter colour and changing the window display. Her easy way with the public was invaluable and she was good with everyone, women customers in particular feeling at ease with her. Before long, more and more ladies were finding their way to Stapleton Road to order quality ladies' shoes and soon, they were making almost as many ladies shoes and boots as men's working boots. Tom was very skilled in making the more delicate footwear ladies demanded and with each pair of finer quality shoes making more profit, they were well pleased with the change in their business. Things were looking up.

Alfred announced that he intended to marry just a few days before Harriet found out that she was with child. When Tom and Harriet had first married, they had put off any thought of children until their finances were on solid foundations, and only after two years did they feel secure enough to try for a family. Night after night, they gazed into each other's eyes, wrapped in a glowing blanket of love, but the expected results of their passion did not happen and their months of trying rolled into years. It was another five years before Harriet fell pregnant and it was just after she had quietly resigned herself to being childless. She made an excuse to Tom about why she was popping out for an hour from the shop, and the doctor confirmed that she was carrying their first child. Back in the shop, Harriet waited until she was closing up. She bolted the front door and pulled the curtain across, just as Tom came through from the workshop, wiping his hands in a towel.

"Are you alright, my sweet?" he asked sprightly. "You've been quiet since you got back."

"Well, I'm as happy as I am pregnant, Tom, and that's very..." she beamed, stopping him in his tracks.

Tom stopped and threw the towel onto the counter. He rushed to her and threw his arms around her and lifted her off the ground, spinning them both around in a circle before stopping suddenly, putting her down ever so gently like he was carrying the most delicate china. "Oh, I'm sorry, love. I'm sorry."

"Don't be silly, Tom. I won't break," she whispered as she kissed his cheek. They stood there then, lost in each other, staring deep into each other's eyes. They kissed, gently and delicately and if love could have been a drum, it would have beaten so loudly at that moment that the whole of the West Country would have heard its sound.

They had spent their first years together in the back room above the shop, saving every penny that they could, hoping to be able to move to their own house one day. With Alfred's impending marriage and their own news, it was time to find somewhere else to live. They had paid Sid back the money he had loaned them and when he offered to help with the deposit on their own house, they gratefully accepted. They moved into one of the new terraced houses in Saxon Road, St Werburges, and were as happy as could be, glorying in their love for each other and in the new life that their love had created.

Harriet worked in the shop until the last minute and her pregnancy seemed to bring them even more women customers, Tom joking that perhaps they should open up a ladies' tea shop out front at the same time. Such was the hubbub in the cramped shop on some days.

They were now making more quality footwear for Bristol's ladies and had a job sometimes to keep up with the demand, the brothers often working long into the night to fulfil orders. Harriet gave the shop the 'woman's touch' as she called it, and turned it into a more comfortable room, fitting for the gentry but leaning ever more towards the tastes of ladies.

When one of their oldest customers, a gruff plumber, came in one day to have a pair of hobnail boots repaired, he looked around in bewilderment before declaring, "Bloody hell! It's like a tart's boudoir." Harriet smiled at him and sat him down to sort his old boots out. Harriet and Tom laughed together later that evening when Harriet recalled the incident, but they needn't have worried, as two months later, the same man was back for a new pair of boots.

Harriet was in the middle of a fitting when her contractions started. She was on her knees with a tape measure in her hand when the first rush of pain overwhelmed her. She winced in agony and her head sank onto her chest for a moment as the second wave hit within a few minutes.

She was fitting shoes for old Mrs Bartholomew from Clifton, who was a regular customer and mother of five. 'Mrs B' as they called her, immediately recognised exactly what was happening and insisted that Harriet be taken home in her carriage, and both she and Tom went with her back to 25 Saxon Road, leaving Alfred to close the shop. Dear old Mrs B took total control in military fashion, sending for the midwife and paying a lad a halfpenny to run off and fetch Harriet's mother. Even though Tom was always the personification of calm, this was a new situation for him and he was happy to let Mrs Bartholomew issue the orders. Even though she fought against it later, 'dear old Mrs B' received her next pair of shoes with their compliments.

William's birth was 'complicated' as the doctor told Tom later. The midwife had sent out for the doctor within a few hours and with encouragement, William came into the world another five hours later. Due to the complications of birth however, William was to be Tom and Harriet's only child. They were both too tired to take in that news at first, and Harriet was confined to bed for a week whilst she recovered.

After going back home with Harriet and Mrs Bartholomew, Tom made sure that there was plenty of coal on the fire and that Harriet was well looked after by her mother before he would go back to work. Though he fretted and worried throughout the afternoon, it had been made plain to him by the midwife that it was not his place to be there, so he had gone back to work and tried in vain to concentrate on working. He left early for once and was pacing the front room of the house anxiously, hours later when he heard his son's first cries from upstairs. Tom was almost tea-total, as seeing his father worse for wear on too many occasions had turned him off drink, but after seeing his son and holding him in his arms for the first time, he was quickly banished from the room while the ladies sorted things out. Exploding with pride, he rushed out into the street, wanting to scream his joy out to the world. He ran to the pub at end of the road and caught last orders to toast his new-born son with everyone in the bar. Although he wasn't that familiar a face in his local, he knew just about everyone there and rolled out two hours later without spending a single penny on drink, despite his first words being, "Buy everyone a drink, landlord. I've just become a dad."

His neighbours were his friends and everyone looked out for each other in the community. When they heard that Harriet had given birth to a son, a cheer rang out and last orders were forgotten in what then became a street celebration. Tom rolled back home gone midnight that night, wearing the biggest smile Harriet had ever seen and stinking of beer, so her mother promptly banished him to the back bedroom to sleep it off!

Tom hadn't told Harriet a great deal about his upbringing and Alfred's deformed ankle was never discussed, but Tom had always sworn to himself that if ever he had a child, it would be brought up true and proper as he had been, only the over-strict violence of his upbringing would be banished and replaced with a firm voice and a hand in a soft glove. Tom and Harriet were devoted to each other and shared a love that was both deep and sincere. They both felt blessed when William arrived and their joy was heightened by knowing that he would almost certainly be their only child. They were determined not to spoil him though and made sure that they didn't, but William crowned both their lives and grew to be the apple of his grandparents' worlds as well as theirs.

CHAPTER FOUR

The sound of the band gently faded as William cycled out of the City Centre and along the side of the old harbour. He pedalled lazily, his mind rerunning the events of the last hour and as he got to the old dock, he stopped and gently laid his bicycle down. He sat on the dockside swinging his legs over the water ten feet beneath. He took his cap off and laid it on the edge of the giant metal mushroom that he leaned against, raising his face to the sun as he closed his eyes, its warmth bathing his eyelids as he contemplated the last hour. His presence drew the attention of a gang of seagulls who swirled in the air above him, screeching loudly until they were satisfied that he had nothing to eat. Instead, Will fed lavishly on his thoughts. Here he was, now to be a Royal Navy Sailor and his heart raced at the thought. He opened his eyes and blinked furiously at the reflection of the sun in the water in the harbour. The afternoon was getting on and the sun was now low enough to explode a thousand ripples into mirrors of sunlight, dancing in the water before him. He looked to the right, where a cargo ship was being laboriously loaded, a large crate dangling precariously from a crane as stevedores waved and guided the crane's master as he lowered it into the body of the ship. Other than that, the harbour was relatively quiet. A couple strolled arm-in-arm walking their dog, the woman slowly revolving her parasol above her, her face bathed in shadow under its canopy, and on the other side of the harbour ships lay tied up like sleeping dogs awaiting a call to life. A Royal Navy Frigate sat motionless in the distance and Will's imagination drifted off into wondering what sort of ship he would serve on and what role he would play in its destiny. The spell was broken by another noisy gaggle of seagulls and Will realised then that time was pressing. He felt suddenly tired. He had arrived at the factory at ten to six this morning and suddenly, he felt his day catching up with him. It was time to go.

Back at home, Will pondered how best to break the news. Deep inside, he was excited by what had just happened, but he guessed that his news would be a shock to Mum and Dad. 'There was only one way,' he thought. So as Mother laid tea out on the kitchen table, he decided to take the bull by the horns. He hadn't needed to. Tom had detected something different in his son's body language as they prepared to sit down and knew that something had happened. Will had an unusual agitation about his movements, like he was sitting on something uncomfortable and although Will was always helpful around the house, this time he seemed overly anxious in helping them prepare the table. Tom's intuition kicked in and an image of Annie flashed across his mind and a momentary thought dashed through his mind that Will might have proposed to her. "How was your day, son? Was work alright?" his father asked him innocently as he passed him a plate of bread that he had just sliced.

"It's been an interesting day, Dad. After work, I went down into town and I've signed up for the navy." Harriet had just taken a sip of tea as the words reached her ears and she spluttered loudly in a short coughing fit. Tom's hand stopped buttering a slice of bread, then after a few moments, slowly the knife moved again and he carried on spreading the butter around the slice. The table sat in silence for a moment, apart from Harriet clearing her throat.

"Will, what have you done, you silly boy?" Harriet blurted. "You're not old enough and besides, you know that there's a war coming. It won't be a game, Will."

"I know, Mum. That's why I have joined the navy. We have the best fleet in the world and the Germans won't be able to touch our ships." Tom stared blankly at the bread he had just buttered without taking it to his mouth. All thoughts of his son talking about marriage dispelled. "I have thought about it, Mother. I would never join the army, it's too risky, but in the navy, I'll be as safe as houses. Don't worry, and besides, if war does come then it won't take us long to sort the Germans out and I'll be back before you know it."

His father looked on thoughtfully. Without thinking, he had now picked up the bread and was chewing it slowly in thoughtful silence. Throughout the meal, he said nothing apart from politeness over passing the butter. As Harriet started to clear up the plates, Tom rose from the table and reached for his pipe. "I'm going out the back for a smoke, Mother," he announced. After a minute, Will followed him. His father was outside puffing gently on his pipe, his eyes fixed on his little vegetable patch, lost in his thoughts. Will sauntered up alongside him and lit up a Woodbine, blowing a great lungful of smoke out eagerly in a huge cloud before him. "I know what I'm doing, Dad."

"I know, William, but you've disappointed me today." Tom rarely called his son by his full name. It was always 'son' or 'Will', William being reserved for when Tom wasn't happy with him. "I would have expected you to have talked with us about this before you put your signature to any paper. Your mother and I have always encouraged you to think for yourself and make your own decisions, I know. We never pushed you into the family business for instance and when you said you wanted to try something different, we respected that but this is different, son. This is a huge decision. War is coming for sure, and I am not happy. I'm really not happy about it at all and I'm very much against any war. Don't forget I've seen it before and I've seen a lot more of life and death than you have, son. I'm not a pacifist, William, but I am a realist. I read the papers but that doesn't mean to say that I believe every line that they write. We are all being led by the nose. Journalists don't really write newspapers. Politicians do, and they led us into a war against the Boers that saw thousands of decent good lads like your mother's cousin lying dead in some bloody foreign field, fighting for something that fed the politicians' personal egos rather than benefiting the likes of you and me."

Will stood in silence, and thought better of interrupting his father when he was in full flow.

"War could be declared at any time, son, and as your mother said war isn't a game and good people die on even the best ships." Will had never seen his father so animated. Tom paced the small garden in anger, stabbing the mouthpiece of his pipe in the air like a sword to emphasise his point. "Bloody politicians," he cursed, "they don't fight the sodding wars themselves. They always find somebody else's son to do it for them while they sit all nice and cosy, tucked up in London. Ask your mother about her cousin and what that did to their family when they were told that he was dead. They didn't even bring his body home, just dug a hole somewhere and threw him in. To this day, his death has torn their family apart." He turned and stared into the sky, exhaling a lungful of air as silence fell for the moment.

"I'm sorry, Dad. I just wanted to do my bit. But I'm not daft. I have weighed it up as I said. Just go down the docks and look at some of the navy ships that come in from time to time. The Germans have got nothing to touch them. I'll be as safe as houses and besides, the Germans need putting in their place, Dad. Even you have said that when you've been reading your newspaper, so if there's going to be a war then I want to be there to do my bit."

Tom reached out and rested his hand on his son's shoulder. "I know, lad. I know your intentions are good, but you should have discussed this with your mother and me before you went off and signed..." he hesitated, stopping himself from finishing his sentence with "your life away" and quickly replacing it with "yourself into the navy".

He paused for a moment, scared by the momentary thought of his son's life having been signed away. "We are all being led up the garden path, William, just like when they wanted us to fight the Boers. For heaven's sake, the Kaiser is the old Queen's bloody cousin. She should go over and sort the bloke out herself."

Tom sucked furiously on his pipe once more, dragging life into the neglected embers until they glowed red once more, smoke filling the air around him. The smoke seemed to calm him though, and his voice lowered to a calmer tone. "Well, you've signed up, son, and when you sign up then you're in I'm afraid. There's no turning back. Just you be bloody careful." Tom turned quickly and headed briskly back down the garden.

It was Saturday the 25th of July and on the Sunday, Will went to see Annie to tell her his news. Annie McGrath was just as sweet on Will as he was on her. They both worked in Mardons and she had caught Will's eye the very first day that she had started working there. She joined the team of girls in the cutting and creasing department and it was Will's job as a printer's assistant to wheel the flat sheets of print through to Annie's department where they loaded the big machines that stamped out the shapes of the cigarette cartons ready to be glued together. He noticed her the first day that he saw her, her bright eyes and shy smile capturing his attention immediately. Every time he wheeled the trolley into her department, he shot nervous glances in her direction. But she was so intent on her work and didn't look up until after a week or two, when the other girls in the department starting nudging each other and then her when Will came into sight. The giggles got louder as they had all noticed Will and where his glances were resting.

Within a month, he had asked Annie if he might see her outside of work, and the ritual of asking her father if he might get to know his daughter better, started. Now, six months later, he cycled round to Mina Road to see Annie and with her mother present, told her of his plans to join the navy. Annie's mother rushed off to find Cornelius, her husband, and tell him, leaving Will and Annie alone. In that moment, Will and Annie had their first kiss. Will had never kissed a girl before and had only ever practised kissing the back of his hand! He wasn't disappointed. The space between them faded as without planning or thought, they gently moved towards each other. They gazed into each other's eyes for a moment before their lips touched and that moment was everything that Annie had imagined. The soft contours of her lips met his and for a brief moment, the very tip of her tongue met his. They both instantly retracted them but it sent a flush of shock and excitement tingling through her body for a brief moment.

Footsteps in the corridor broke the moment and they both stepped back in haste as the door burst open. "Brave lad," Cornelius exploded, grabbing Will's hand and nearly shaking it off his wrist. "The country is going to need good lads like you to teach those Germans a lesson; they've got far too big for their boots." They went through to the parlour and Will felt quite the centre of attention for the first time in Annie's house. Up to that moment, Cornelius had always been polite but slightly business-like towards Will, but now he was gushing in his conversation and waxing loudly at how Britain was the greatest nation on earth and how strong we all needed to be as war was surely coming.

Will cycled back home that evening with his head spinning with it all. He had done a full shift at work, lied about his age to sign up for the navy and been through the emotion of telling his parents. He had his first kiss too, and well, that was quite a lot for one weekend! He laid in bed that night with his head reeling far too much to sleep as it all replayed over and over in his mind. He did like Annie. He liked her a lot. Now he just had to hand his notice in at work and wait for news from the navy. When he did eventually slip into a sleep, his mind churned into dreams of great ships with him standing on deck, trying to maintain balance as waves crashed all around it. He woke up the next morning content and excited.

CHAPTER FIVE

On the 4th of August, the Government announced that a state of war existed between Great Britain and Germany. Whist the announcement was not a great surprise, it was still a shock. In the Payne household, the news had an all too real implication while the nation celebrated in a bout of blind euphoria. A neighbour popped in to tell Harriet, who was washing up at the time but immediately left the washing up half done. She stopped, drying her hands slowly whilst staring into space, deep in thought as the neighbour spoke. She slipped outside into the back garden and walked as if in a dream down the short garden and into the outhouse where Tom sometimes worked on some shoe or other that was a bit special. Tom and Will's pushbikes rested together at the back of the shed and Harriet's hand reached out for the handlebar of Will's bike, her mind churning with the news of war. As she gripped the handlebar ever harder, her eyes slowly welled up as she thought of her only boy sailing into war. The first tear gradually grew and filled her eyes and when the dam could not hold it any more, they escaped trickling down her cheek. She thought about her cousin that was killed in the Boer War twelve years earlier and she knew how much pain and anguish it had caused his family, especially his mother. After a few moments, lost to her thoughts, she started as if from a dream and wiped her eyes with the cuff of her grey blouse. "Compose yourself, girl," she whispered to herself, and strode back down the garden to resume her washing as if nothing had happened.

A week later, the postman delivered a brown envelope addressed: 'To Mr William Payne', with 'Confidential' stamped on it. Will was working the morning shift and arrived home before his parents to find the letter waiting on the mat. He picked it up and walked through to the kitchen without opening it, placing it on the table before putting the kettle on. As the water slowly came to the boil, he carefully opened the letter to reveal the papers he had expected inside. The wording was business-like and brisk. Will was to report to Portsmouth Royal Navy Battalion for intensive training on the 19th of August by noon at the latest. Inside the envelope was an open voucher for a train ticket from Temple Meads to Portsmouth and his papers. So this was it. He made himself a cup of tea and reread the papers four or five times, picturing himself arriving in Portsmouth and the start of his new adventure. What ship would he be on? Where would he be sailing? He sipped his tea with his mind racing with excitement. Yes, this was it. *I'll go and tell Annie,* he said to himself as he gulped down the rest of the cup and dashed out, mounting his pushbike in one easy action, pedalling furiously to get up a head of steam before the end of the cobbled street.

Harriet arrived home and found the letter open on the kitchen table. She sat down, moving the opened envelope to one side as she tried to read the letter. She struggled with the words as usual, but she guessed what it said and her hand cupped her mouth when she read the date. "Heavens," she thought to herself, "the 19th, that's less than two weeks away." She sat in silence, holding the letter but staring into space as the date slowly sank in. She was numb, her Will leaving for war finally striking home to her.

They had been such a happy family unit. Will was a lovely boy and the perfect son, but here he was about to set off on an adventure that he might not return from. She tried not to think about her cousin but she could not stop thinking about the afternoon she had spent trying to console his mother after the telegram had arrived, saying he had been killed in action. She shivered at the thought and put the letter back down, her mind churning as a hundred thoughts flashed through her mind. 'Tea. Put the kettle on.'

Tom had told Will that he wanted to go for a cycle ride on the Sunday out to Queen Charlton. Tom, by nature, was a thoughtful man who whatever he said was usually important enough to be listened to, but for the past weeks, he had been unusually quiet. More than once, Harriet had caught him in the workshop just staring into space over a half-made shoe. The ride to Queen Charlton was one that they had done numerous times in the past, but this day out had more significance somehow. Harriet had made them a pack lunch and the two of them set off straight after breakfast in their best Sunday suits and ties. The sun was rising steadily and they settled into a gentle pace riding side by side, Tom riding on the outside, which was always his way. As they pedalled to the end of the road, they passed Mrs Harris who was sweeping the path outside her house and both men greeted her with a cheery 'hello' as they passed. They rounded the end of Saxon Road and started the steady cycle across the city and out onto the Wells Road. At the village of Knowle, they took a short break and dismounted to check the chain on Tom's bicycle as it had started slipping as they made their way up the steep hill at Totterdown. It was a testing journey with some steep climbs, but they enjoyed freewheeling down a couple of slopes and knew that they would enjoy the ride home more as it was slightly more downhill than up. The sun was high in the sky when they reached Queen Charlton and dismounted, leaning their bikes against a dry stone wall. They sat down on a grassy mound after hanging their coats over the handlebars and opened their carefully wrapped sandwiches. They were hungry and sipped eagerly on the bottle of tap water that Harriet had included before tucking into their food.

Will finished his sandwich first and lay back on the grass, crossing his legs and folding his arm underneath his head to stare up at the puffy, white clouds that hung almost motionless in the blue canopy above. A pair of skylarks conducted an aerial ballet high above them, their sweet song filling the air with its continual melody. Tom leaned back against the wall and loosened his tie, flapping his collar to cool his sweating neck. "You look lost to the skylarks, son, a Penny for your thoughts?" he asked.

"Everything and nothing, Dad. I am excited about joining the navy, but I know that I am going to miss days like this," he said, still continuing to stare at the sky above.

"I understand that, son; it's a big adventure and hopefully not a long one. The papers are talking of the war being over by Christmas. Let's hope so. It would be good to have you back safe by then and all spend Christmas together."

"I know. I don't really want to leave to be honest. I like my life at present. Work is okay. I don't always enjoy the shift work but it could be worse. I am happy at home, though I may as well tell you now than I am getting sweet on Annie. I shall miss it all."

"Ha! I knew that, son," Tom said as he pulled out his pipe and tapped it against the wall behind him to empty the old tobacco out. "I can tell that from the whistling you do after you have been to see her!

"Well, you just remember that we are all waiting back home for you when you climb aboard your ship and sail off." Tom paused, filling his pipe with a wedge of dark brown tobacco that he had taken from its pouch. "Even though I think that this war is wrong, I envy you in a way. While I don't agree with this war, no one is more patriotic that I am and we do have a duty to stop tyrants like the Kaiser from doing whatever he wants."

Will suddenly sat up and looked at his dad intently, "Well, don't you think of ever joining up, Dad. One of us fighting the Hun is enough. You've got to stay home and look after Mother."

Tom tamped down the brown weed with his thumb in the bowl of the pipe. "We'll see, son. I do have a feeling that the papers might be a tad over confident about it being a quick war. You can't tell anything at this stage though, and these Germans didn't start this war without thinking long and hard about the consequences of it, and I wouldn't mind betting they have been planning this for a bit longer than since Frans Ferdinand was shot. This war might not be so quick and easy as they say, son, which is why I'm telling you to be blooming careful."

Will wasn't happy with his father's answer. "You didn't answer my point, Dad. I mean it. Whatever happens, don't you think of joining up. I really mean that, Dad. Mum mustn't be left on her own. I'm doing my bit for the war and one of us away fighting is enough for any family."

Tom struck a match on the wall. "Don't worry, son. You're forgetting that I'm officially too old, just as you are officially too young to leave these shores and fight," he said, cocking a glance at his son as he said it. Will contemplated this for a while and lay back down on the grass. His dad must have guessed that he had lied about his age.

Then he sat bolt upright again. "Yes, but if the war does go on as you say it might, then please, promise me that you won't join up. You have to stay home and look after Mother."

"Your mother and I will both be fine, son," Tom said as he puffed life into his waiting pipe. "You just concentrate on getting yourself home as soon as you can, eh?" Will lay back down, resting his head on his hand and lost himself for a moment to the skylarks above. High above, tiny dots hovered and swooped as they continued their merry song. The sun beamed down and was gloriously warm on his face and for a moment, time stood still as Will reflected on life. Tom tucked his knees up higher and watched his son as he always wanted to remember him. He said a silent prayer to himself for the two of them to be back here soon, but he knew that it wouldn't be until the war was over.

CHAPTER SIX

The morning of August, the 19ᵗʰ, seemed to arrive quickly for the Payne family. Will had tossed and turned all night and had laid awake long before the dawn broke, with his mind racing through a myriad of thoughts. He had been down to Temple Meads after work last week and knew that the 09.27 to Portsmouth Harbour train was the train he needed.

This was the first time he had ever gone away for more than a day or two. He had already discovered yesterday when he said goodbye to his pals at work and then Annie last evening that he didn't like goodbyes. There was an awkward embarrassment somehow and he wasn't one for being the centre of attention, so his parting at work had been a swift one. He had turned down the invitation to go for a last-minute pint from a couple of the lads and had said his goodbyes, clocking off and slipping out of the backdoor quietly before cycling home quickly, not looking back as he pedalled out of Temple Gate. His goodbyes with Annie had not been so easy. Firstly, Anne's parents had been waiting with her to greet him, Cornelius shaking Will's hand vigorously to the point that he thought that he might shake his hand off! Cornelius seemed to talk for ages, enthusiastically going over how the Germans needed sorting out and it would be brave lads like Will that would do Britain proud. Will smiled politely, hardly speaking. He had heard it before almost every time he had seen Cornelius since he told them that he was signing up, and he really only wanted to be alone with Annie.

Mrs McGrath interrupted her husband after a few minutes, "Come on, Cornelius. I'm sure William hasn't come to see us. The outside drain has blocked again and there's still enough light for you to clear it, please." She parted, taking her husband with her and paused in the door to turn and rest her hand on Will's shoulder for a moment. "Good luck, William," she said softly in her warm Irish accent, "I am sure you'll make us all so proud."

Alone with Annie, William rediscovered his acute dislike of partings, especially now. Now he had got to it, he suddenly didn't want to go. Over the past months, he had grown fond of Annie and despite rarely being allowed to be alone with her, their eyes had relayed many silent conversations while Annie's mother had busied herself with her needlework. "Write to me, Annie," Will said as his hands reached out to hold her. They gazed into each other's eyes as they often had done from afar. Will suddenly felt awkward and his tie seemed to cut into his neck. "I have to go," he blurted, kissing her hurriedly on the cheek before dashing out. He paused at the end of the road to light a Woodbine, drawing the smoke heavily into his lungs with a loud inhale. He stared back at Annie's house and wondered when he would see his sweetheart again. No, he didn't like goodbyes.

Tom drove William down to the station on the horse and cart without Harriet. She had hugged Will as only a mother can, watching her boy go off to war, then disappeared quickly back into the shop before she had time to become emotional.

The city was as busy as it usually was at this time of day, but they had allowed for the morning traffic and arrived in good time. "Do you know, son, that it was just about here that I met your mother for the first time," Tom announced, parking up the horse and ensuring that it's nosebag had some hay in it.

"I didn't know that," Will said, suddenly eager to know more.

"Well, it's a story for another time, son," Tom said, picking up Will's small case and jumping down onto the street. "We'd best not have you late on your first day, eh?"

Will suddenly remembered the conversation they had up at Queen Charlton and stopped before the platform, turning to face his father. "Don't forget what we said, Dad. Whatever happens, you will stay and look after mother?"

Tom held out his hand once more, shaking Will's hand firmly. "Son, stop fretting about us and concentrate on yourself now. We'll both be fine. Now, look after yourself. Keep your eyes peeled and remember your port from your starboard," he said, smiling broadly, his blue eyes beaming at his only son as he glowed with pride. They walked together to the train and Tom watched him climb on board. Will's face appeared in a few moments at the carriage window and he gave his father an amateur salute and a broad grin. Tom laughed and saluted back, just as the station master gave a shrill blast on his whistle and raised his flag to signal the driver. There was a loud clang as the heavy engine strained to make the first yard and gave a loud cough from its huge engine, steam billowing from its funnel and filling that part of the station with its sweet-smelling vapour. Tom gave Will one last wave and a reassuring smile before turning sharply. Will wasn't the only one that disliked partings.

The train was over half full but Will found a carriage that was nearly empty and placed his small case on the shelf behind him, tucking himself in the corner by the window facing forwards. The smell of the great steam engine pervaded the carriage, the occasional puff of white smoke billowing outside the window when the old engine laboured up an incline. He leaned his head against the glass and watched the countryside slipping by, his imagination trying to picture what awaited him at Portsmouth and what the next few days would be like. But it was difficult for his mind not to wander backwards as he reflected on recent weeks. He kept seeing the faces of his workmates and smiled at the memory of his 'leaving do' in the pub the week before. Two other men from the factory were also joining up at the same time, though the other two lads were destined for the army. The 'farewell do' consisted of a few beers in the Shakespeare Pub, but there had been a lot of jollity and laughter as they all took the excuse for one pint more than they normally would. He had cycled home in a hazy glow that day, being careful not to look any different as he pedalled past the constable directing the traffic out of Temple Meads Station. He had even held his breath for a few seconds as he cycled past him in case he caught the smell of beer on him, which he realised afterwards was daft, of course.

Annie's face drifted in and out of his thoughts and he regretted leaving her at this time. It was far too early to think seriously as far as marriage was concerned, but she was sweet and well, quite lovely. He had never kissed a girl before and the memory of that moment gave him a glow as he sat there thinking. Several people joined and left the carriage as small stations came and went. He had never cycled much further than Cheddar and Wookey Hole with his dad in the past, and although they had taken rare family train journeys to Weston-Super-Mare for an occasional day trip, he didn't know this part of the world at all.

The train stopped at Eastleigh and a young lad bustled noisily into the carriage and sat opposite him wearing an excited grin. After a sharp whistle and flag waving from the station master outside the window, the train lurched off and the carriage resumed its silence. After a couple of minutes, the lad leaned forwards and grinned excitedly, "I'm on my way to Portsmouth," he blurted, "joined the navy I have, gonna give them Germans what for!" He leaned back again, his grin made more captivating by the absence of one and a half of his top two front teeth. Will smiled to himself as a name for him came into his head. 'Smiler,' he thought to himself, grinning back.

"Then we're going to the same place," Will beamed, thrusting his hand out to be grabbed enthusiastically and shaken by the lad. "William Payne, Will to my friends."

"Harry, Harry Taylor, Smiler to my mates," the lad retorted, living up to his nickname. At hearing his nickname, Will laughed out loud and just knew there and then that they would get on; his character was just so endearing. The short journey on to Portsmouth harbour then flew by, as the two young men exchanged excited introductions and talked as to what they were expecting when they arrived. They were both in for a shock. They left the station and made the short walk to the naval barracks. It was lunchtime and they were both ready for something to eat, but instead of a nice, warm canteen, they showed their papers to the guards at the entrance and were directed to the back of a long queue of shuffling men. They both dropped their suitcases onto the ground and looked around them. It certainly was a barracks, with groups of sailors marching around impressively, arms swinging in unison as they passed. The queue eventually filtered through the waiting door, and Will and Harry went inside in. Their papers were checked and two hours later, they had been through a hasty medical, which Will didn't like at all. Will had never had his private parts grabbed by a man before and he reddened up long before he had time to cough. The queue resumed at the stores, where an adjutant 'sized them up' by eye before giving each of them a neat bundled navy blue uniform with a brown label on top. They shuffled on to the next man who thrust a pair of boots on top of the clothes, though Will didn't have a clue how the man had known his foot size. He discovered afterwards that sizing was done at a glance from the experienced eye and if your uniform or your boots didn't fit, you went back later to ask for them to be changed, though few ever needed to. The whole place had an air of organised confusion, with so many men being herded from one place to another before finally being directed to a room to change into their uniforms. They then had to neatly fold their own clothes up and leave them with the label on top that they had written their names on. They would be posted home to wear when the war ended. Remarkably, Will's uniform fit him well, though his boots were like rock. He had never worn leather so hard and unforgiving.

The next month was a blur of physical and mental exercises mixed in with being systematically shouted at and marched up and down relentlessly. Each day was filled with a combination of exercises and classroom sessions followed by more physical work, often it seemed, involving either getting very muddy or dragging great big guns around the exercise yard. At the end of each day, Will collapsed into the most uncomfortable bed he had ever known, which didn't matter to him at all until the early hours. When he had first arrived, he wasn't keen on the thought of sleeping in a large dormitory with lots of other men, but he was so tired at the end of each day that exhaustion overcame everything and sleep carried him off almost at the moment he had laid down. He habitually woke in the early hours to the noisy springs underneath him as he turned over in an effort to get more comfortable. That was impossible, so he was nearly always awake when the bell thundered its early morning call to start another day. His feet were killing him in his new boots and in his first letter home, he wrote that he had clearly been spoilt with his footwear in the past and just hadn't realised it before.

The daily routine became a big incentive to learning fast to avoid the ear-splitting shouting. The naval instructors had a habit of leaning to within an inch of your ear and shouting at the top of their voices when they wanted to show their displeasure. Poor old Smiler seemed to be the target of one or two of the instructor's venom, though Will couldn't really understand why. It always seemed though that when the squad was getting a shouting at (usually for not being fast enough for something or another), it was Smiler that they picked out for an ear bashing. It didn't seem to bother Smiler that much though, and once or twice, he had finished receiving an ear bashing and turned to Will to flash a big grin at him once the instructor had turned away, giving Will a problem in not sniggering at the comedy. Smiler and Will didn't see much of each other outside of drill and class times though, as Will was billeted in the next building to Smiler, so they only caught up occasionally at meal times.

The classroom sessions were not particularly arduous to Will. The very first thing they had been taught were what the ranks were in the navy and how to address each one in turn. It was all pretty boring and he had a job to avoid yawning on occasions, but as yet had not been caught. They swiftly moved on to instructions on the running of a ship, with every role and tasks minutely described. Three weeks into training and Will didn't have a clue what role he would have on the ship, or to what ship he would be consigned. In fact, they had only once been on a ship in the entire time that he had been in Portsmouth, but the promise was made of firearms training, which he thought was going to be much more interesting.

He had just sat down for the evening meal when someone flicked the back of his ear. He turned to see Smiler grinning at him from ear to ear, balancing his tray of food on one hand whilst he waved for a space with his other. "Budge up, Will. Make room for one hungry man."

They ate and talked about their day. "It's bloody boring so far," Smiler groaned. "I know everything there is to know about command and nothing about manning one of the big ship's guns. Got in early I did, told them what I wanted to do, be a ship's gunner."

"How did that go down?" Will asked.

"Like he was deaf," Smiler snorted. "Got no response other than to tell me to do twenty press ups on the spot, bloody moron. Still, the word is, we're on the rifle range tomorrow. That's a bit more like it."

The word was right. Straight after breakfast, they were all boarded into wagons and twenty minutes later, they disembarked at the Royal Navy Firing Range. For the first time since arriving, Will was quite excited.

"Listen up, you ugly lot. You've had a classroom session telling you about firearms but this is the real thing now, so listen very carefully. We don't want any more accidents, do we?" the training officer boomed. Will wondered what he had meant when he had said 'more' accidents!

"You will in turn be given a chance to fire five rounds of live ammunition at a stationary target and you will get four goes as your turn comes around. Did you hear that? I said live rounds and you will get twenty shots in total each. You are very lucky lads. Your rifles are the very best that the modern military can produce." He held a rifle up above his head. "This is the Lee Enfield. Bolt action, magazine fed, repeat and rapid fire, capable of delivering ten rounds a minute at an operating distance of up to 2000 yards. It has a 303 calibre bullet that will make a rather nasty hole in you, so listen up. We don't want any toes being shot off, do we?" he roared.

He had a captive audience. They each in turn were given instruction on how to load and aim the rifle without ammunition in at first. It was the first time Will had held a gun and he couldn't wait to fire it. When his turn came to fire with a live round, he was surprised how big a kick the gun had into his shoulder. His instructor had warned him, but still his first shot was wild. He laid on the ground resting the gun on a sandbag, but the gun still gave him a wild jolt as it sent the second round somewhere over the target in the general direction of the sea. He did better with his next few shots but he didn't hit anywhere near the centre of the target with his first clip of five bullets. "Okay, lad, take a break," the instructor said, tapping him on the shoulder. Will had to get up and go to the back of the queue. He was really annoyed with himself and his shooting, so when the time came for his next turn, he was determined to do better. Gradually, he improved, and when his last set of five shots came, he was getting the feel of it. "Well done, lad, though I don't think you'll make ship's marksman yet," the instructor scoffed.

The next day, Will's shoulder ached from the experience but he was anxious to try it again. But instead, the morning was spent in the classroom again and in the afternoon, they were drilled relentlessly in marching. Will lay in bed that night and although his body ached from the exertions of the day, his mind was turning. He realised how much he was missing home. All the simple things like having supper with Mum and Dad and having a laugh with his pals at work. There were some good men amongst the lads here but there wasn't much time for anything else other than training, learning and more training and when the day was over, he was so tired at times that it was as much as he could do to eat before falling into bed. He didn't mind the life; he just missed home.

After four weeks, Will felt fitter than he had ever done but had still only actually been on a ship just once. They had been told that their basic training took six weeks, and after that, they would take to sea in a training ship to start specific training in whatever role they were assigned. They had three more sessions on the rifle range and Will was gradually getting the hang of it, though he never felt that they had enough time with the gun in their hand and most of the time was spent watching others shooting. He was getting closer to hitting the centre of the target though, and had made his mind up that he wanted to join Smiler as a ship's naval gun operator. It was hot and dirty work, he knew, but it would feel like he was really getting involved in this war. Unfortunately, many of the other lads wanted to do the same thing, so he wasn't sure what he would be doing yet.

News of the war wasn't good. The first battle had taken place at Mon's and the British and French troops were being given a hiding. The newspapers were full of it and the humiliating defeat had stirred public anger even further, with some of the papers printing graphic stories of how the Germans had shot many British soldiers in the back as they retreated. Being soundly beaten was a shock to most people as the army was thought to be invincible and there were some thoughtful faces in the barracks that night as they read of the Mon's defeat.

At the end of the fifth week in training, the recruits were all gathered in the drill yard and stood to attention. It was unusual that they were all gathered there at this time of day and they stood to attention while a new face arrived before them. By his badges, Will knew that he was a Vice Admiral, although his uniform was different and not one that they had seen before but, the classroom time hadn't been wasted after all, as he knew the badge all right. The Vice Admiral mounted a podium in front of the assembly and slowly surveyed the scene, taking his time to scan the rows of men before him. Finally, he spoke, "Men, you are approaching the end of your basic training and your commanding officer tells me you have done well. Good show. Good show, all of you."

He paused, scanning the assembly again. "Some of you will now be assigned to training vessels to continue your instruction and those of you that have shown an aptitude on the rifle range will be joining the Royal Navy Marines, of which I am proud to say, it is my honour to serve."

As the carefully prepared speech unveiled, Will's mind was racing at the words. Behind him, someone cursed under his breath. The Vice Admiral spoke again, "The marines are a vital element in backing up the army and at this time, the marines are needed to help give the Hun a bloody nose."

Will's mind was racing still, just how well had he done on the rifle range? He knew that he had not excelled. He just hoped that he had after all been a poor shot as the last thing he wanted to be was a bloody marine. The speech pressed on for another few minutes before the Vice Admiral handed over to the base commander who announced that their postings were awaiting them on the main notice board before he promptly dismissed them.

As one, the men turned and dashed off to form a crush around the main notice board but Will couldn't read a thing. He was just too far back and there were too many people in between himself and the notice board. At the front of the throng, there was much cursing and swearing as people found their names on the marines' list. Smiler had been near the front and shuffled back through the crowd towards him for once not smiling. "Sorry, Payney. Your name's on the list with mine, mate. We're bleedin' marines. Fucking great, ain't it? Join the navy and see the western fuckin' front."

Will felt the blood drain from his face. He looked at Smiler with a bemused look and pressed forward again to see for himself. He finally made it and hurriedly scanned the names in alphabetical order until he found it. "Payne. W.E. Royal Naval Marines." *Shit. Smiler was right.*

It was a long list and it seemed that the biggest part of the people in the camp were destined to be marines. Will took a deep breath. 'Well, I signed up to fight the Germans,' he thought to himself, 'so I'd better get back on that firing range and make sure I can shoot them before they shoot me!' He needn't have worried. Their training regime changed dramatically from that moment on, both in the classroom and with more time spent in drilling, marching and on the firing range. Back in the billet, the talk amongst the lads was that the navy had more recruits than ships, and as they didn't have enough ships, the Marine Division was being rapidly enlarged.

The lad in the next bed from Will was Reg Sears from Shoreditch. A likable chap who didn't say more than he ever needed to, but he said to Will that he'd got it from his uncle who worked in Whitehall that the navy had been a bit caught out by the rush of recruits and had quickly formed three new divisions of marines. He was telling Will and a few others what he'd heard when the door burst open and one of the other lads burst in excitedly. "We're going home tomorrow, lads. We've all got leave for the weekend." A great cheer went up and Will's heart soared at the prospect of seeing home and Annie again. He was packed and ready within minutes, even though they could not go until the morning.

Over dinner that night, the mess hall was a buzz of excited chatter at the prospect of a weekend's leave. The chatter ceased instantly as the base commander came in to the mess hall. Everyone shot up to attention and stood in silence.

"At ease, men, at ease. I just wanted to tell you to enjoy your leave and to ensure that you are back here by noon Monday sharp. Anybody arriving one minute after noon will be placed on an immediate charge, am I clear?"

"Yes, sir," the reply barked in unison.

The commander resumed, "You are all now nearing the end of your training. You will receive your specific orders on your return but it is likely that most of you in the Marine Division will be posted overseas on your return for further training in France, so make the most of your weekend but, be sure to arrive back on time."

CHAPTER SEVEN

Will decided to walk from Temple Meads Station to home. He had caught the first train to Bristol and joined dozens of others from the base at the railway station, who then crammed into full carriages bound for home. There had not been time to warn anyone that he was coming home and being Saturday morning, he knew that Mum and Dad would be working at the shop. As he opened the door, his mother had her back to him as she rearranged shoes on the shelf behind her. The bell above the door sounded with its usual resounding clang and Harriet turned expecting to see a customer. The look on her face when William walked in wearing his navy blues and bell-bottom trousers was a picture. She dropped the shoes on the floor with a clatter and gave a low shriek of joy, running around the counter to almost lift him off the ground. "Wow, steady on, Mother," Will gasped in embarrassment, the grin on his face though told her everything.

"Thomas, Thomas, come quickly," Harriet cried and Tom came hurriedly through the door, not knowing what to expect. Alfred came through from the workshop behind Tom, wondering what was going on and shook Will's hand like he might shake it right off its wrist.

"Blimey, I've only been away six weeks," Will cried, "what's the matter with you all?"

"Go on. Push off the lot of you," Alfred ordered. "Get off home and catch up with yourselves. I'll watch the shop." Not needing any prompting, they all headed home. At the end of the road, Tom collared a local boy playing in the street. "Here, lad, run and tell Annie McGrath that her man's come home. Here's a penny and mind you run all the way, won't you?"

The lad's face beamed as he stared wide-eyed at the penny and ran off like the devil was behind him.

"Thanks, Dad," Will beamed. The kettle was on within a minute of them arriving home and Will sat at the kitchen table just revelling in being home again. He had never been away from home before in his whole life and coming back now seemed wonderful but strange. He sat at the old wooden kitchen table, slowly moving his hand back and forwards across a small area like he was caressing his old life in the grain, his mind swimming in joy as he took it all back in. Meanwhile, his mother chatted on and it was just delightful to hear her voice again.

His father sat at the other end of the table, his face beaming while Harriet chatted away as she usually did when she was excited. Eventually, Harriet paused and brought a pot of tea over and their best china cups.

"Take your boots off, son, and chuck them over here." Tom examined them scornfully. "Blimey, Will. I bet these cut your feet to ribbons, the leather is as tough as our toilet door. There's no give in them at all, talk about mass produced, they're horrible."

Will chuckled, "I got used to them, Dad, but they did make me realise that I've been spoilt in the past in the footwear area."

As he spoke, there was a knock at the half open back door and Annie's smiling face nervously peeped around the corner. "Come on in, Annie," Harriet called. "Come on, Thomas, let's take our tea through to the front room and leave these two for a minute."

Annie was now blushing and her pink complexion glowed like the sun to Will. He hadn't seen Annie for six weeks and though they had exchanged letters every week, alone now he felt strangely nervous. Unthinking, he extended his hand and she nervously did the same, and they stood there shaking hands in the middle of the kitchen like they had just been introduced. Will thought a lot about that moment many times later and shook his head to himself in disbelief when he did, thinking, 'What a ninny!'

They sat at the kitchen table and as they started talking, the nervousness melted away. As Annie talked, Will extended his hand across the table towards her and she stopped abruptly in mid-sentence, her hand moving to meet his and for a moment, they held hands across the length of the table. Their stared into each other's eyes and they were like that when moments later, Harriet came bustling back through the kitchen door, talking loudly as she came back to announce their return. Will and Annie's hands shot back across the table and they both sat there red-faced like they had been caught in the act of something much more serious.

Will slept better that night than he had done in weeks. He wasn't constantly disturbed by men snoring or moaning in their sleep and he didn't miss the dormitory late night farting competition that often ensued, setting off giggles amongst those that couldn't sleep. He woke in the morning and just lay there listening to the birdsong outside, in the knowledge that he didn't have to start the day standing to attention or saluting. His uniform hung neatly in the wardrobe and he put his old clothes on that were hanging neatly alongside. 'Blimey,' he thought to himself, 'I've lost an inch around the waist.' And he had to notch his belt one up from where it was before. Harriet had been down to the corner shop for a bit of bacon and a few sausages and they sat down together for a breakfast Royal and as they ate, Will told them just about everything important that had happened since he had left. Everything that was, except for him being a marine. He thought he should save that detail for now as he could imagine their reaction. Tom cut great wedges of bread to soak up the bacon fat and the bone china cups of yesterday were replaced with great mugs of tea. Will was in heaven, and soaked up the picture, savouring the moment. His mother chattered away while his father mopped up the last of the egg yolk on his plate with a piece of crust, his face a study of concentration ensuring that the thin, yellow streak was replaced by a gleaming, clean, white plate.

"I'm going out the back for a smoke, Mother. I'll wipe up the dishes when I come back," Tom said as he rose from the table and took his pipe down from the shelf. He nodded at Will who followed him out into the back garden, picking up his Woodbines as he did. Tom beckoned his son down into the shed, from which he produced a brand new pair of boots, identical to his navy issue ones.

Tom thrust the unlit pipe into his mouth and handed the boots over, "Try these on, son. They should fit." The leather was as soft as a baby's skin and they fit Will a treat. "Blimey, Dad. How did you, or, where did you get these from? They look like military issue."

"Well, son, when you wrote during your first week and said about your awful boots, I thought I had better do something about that, so I went down the docks and got chatting to one of the lads off a navy ship and he let me make some drawings and measurements, so no one will know they are not military issue. They just might help you get a better grip on board when you get your posting. Is there any news on that by the way?"

Will put the new boots on and walked up and down the small garden, enjoying the comfort of his new boots. He couldn't lie. His father had asked him a direct question, so there was nothing to do but answer truthfully.

"Well," he said pausing, "it looks like most of the lads on this draft are joining the Royal Marine Brigade, 3rd division."

"The marines?" Tom snorted. "The marines? Don't say they've put you in the marines, Will. That's foot soldiers with another name. You'll be at the bloody front."

"I don't know, Dad. All I know is that the marines are made up of three branches: the artillery, light infantry and the band section."

"Bloody hell! I knew that we should have got you trumpet lessons. You can't play any instrument, can you? So you'll be up there somewhere near the front lad. Either way, you'll be behind a gun. Bloody hell, Will. I had a feeling something wasn't quite right with you. It's Payne's luck, Bugger." He struck a match and cupped his hands over his pipe, drawing in deeply and sending great plumes of smoke into the air.

"Nothing's certain, Dad. All I know is that when we all get back, most of us are likely to be sent on for further training."

"Your mother won't be happy, son. You'd better say nothing now. I'll tell her tomorrow after you've gone back. I'll choose my moment then, okay?"

"Thanks, Dad. I'm sure it will all work out fine for me. It seems there just aren't enough ships for us all, so some of us have to help the war effort in another way."

"So it's a khaki uniform for you then, lad. Khaki and a blooming gun. Just you make sure you keep your head down, son."

"Sure, Dad, don't worry, I'll keep my head down. They are still saying that the war will be over soon. I'll be back home before you know it."

Harriet's head appeared round the door. "Will, Annie's here."

Annie's arrival broke the gloom that had descended over them and taking a deep breath, they both went back to join the ladies.

The four of them went for a walk in the Sunday afternoon sunshine, Tom and Harriet leading the way arm-in-arm at a slow amble with Will and Annie hanging a few yards behind. Their hands swung by their sides and occasionally their fingers touched. William wanted to hold Annie's hand but with his parents just in front of them, it didn't feel right. He was still shy of such things in public and besides, although Annie was his girl, they were some way away from being engaged, or anything like that. Annie brought Will up to date with the news from Mardons as they walked and he laughed at some of the stories of his old friends. It seemed there had been a steady trickle of lads joining up since Will had gone, mostly men that Will only half knew, but Bert Tann, one of Will's old friends had joined the army, and a few more of his old friends were talking of enlisting. As the sun shone even stronger, the ladies opened their parasols and Annie couldn't resist gently turning hers slowly as she walked. Time was slipping by and the day was slipping with it. Will turned his face skyward and closed his eyes for a few moments, enjoying the warmth of the sun on his face. Relaxed now, he cupped his arm, and Annie threaded her arm through it, beaming at Will as she did. "You come back to me, William Payne," she whispered, "you come back to me as soon as you can, right?"

Will smiled and nodded. "Don't worry, Annie. I'll be home before you know it and you never know; I might even come back with a medal or two," he beamed.

"Don't you worry about no medals. You stay away from trouble, William Payne, and just get yourself back home soon."

The train pulled out right on time and Will found himself in the carriage with another chap that he vaguely recognised from the base, but neither of them felt very talkative. They exchanged pleasantries but then Will could see that the other chap was soon lost in his own thoughts as he was himself. The weekend had gone by in a flash and Will sat by the window with his head pressed against the glass, staring into space as the countryside rushed by. He flexed his toes in his new boots, smiling at the luxury of the soft leather against his feet and wishing he was back in the garden with his dad. He was feeling quite down and he sat there in silence until the carriage burst open and a familiar shout went up. "Hey Payney!" It was Smiler, and Will laughed at the sight of his old mate, broken front tooth and all. Following in behind Smiler came a mountain of a man.

"Shove up, mate. Make room for a little un and a big un," Smiler urged, through a grin as wide as the carriage. "It's a bit quiet in here, ain't it? What's the matter with you?" He introduced his new friend, "Will, meet Terrence. Terrance, meet Will."

"Terry," the man cut in. "Only my Mam calls me Terrence, and then only usually when we've got company or she ain't happy with me."

Will recognised him from the base, but he had been assigned to a different unit and billet, so Will had only seen him before from a distance. Up close, he was even bigger than he looked from a distance. Both Will and Smiler were about the same height at five feet eight, but Terry towered over them by at least six inches and was as broad as a house. He must have created a problem for the naval supplies office as well, as his uniform barely fit him and seemed to bulge in between his tunic buttons and his wrists thrust out from his uniform sleeves by an uncomfortable length. Both men sat down, Terry taking up nearly a seat and a half. "He's a big un', ain't he, Will?" Smiler quipped, as Terry gave him a flash of quiet disdain. "But don't worry. He's a gentle giant is our Terrence. Works on the next farm to where I live and there ain't no one that can lift a sack of grain as easy as he can, but if there's a sick lamb, then stand back cos Terrence will stay up all night nursing it back to life. He will, won't you, Terrence?"

"Terry," he replied, at a slow and deliberate pace to emphasise that he was now a little tired of the joke. Will soon gained the impression that Terry was as Smiler described, a gentle giant. He said little but was polite and courteous when he spoke, but just didn't have much to say for himself, which wasn't difficult with Smiler around, as he could keep a conversation going without any aid or prompting from anyone else.

They exchanged stories of their weekends with Smiler leading the way and it seemed that a good portion of his break had been spent in the pub. *Still Jack, the lad,* Will thought, grinning at Smiler's antics. It cheered Will up though, and by the time they arrived back at Portsmouth harbour, he was feeling less glum.

Back at the barracks, they were given the 'rude awakening' as the navy called it, being drilled and marched from almost the moment that they returned. Only four men were silly enough to be late and they disappeared to spend the rest of the day in cells, peeling potatoes. After marching for most of the afternoon, they were told that their postings were up on the board. This time, Will was straight off the blocks and was one of the first to the notice board. "Payne, William – Light Infantry Marines." It was what he had expected, but at least Smiler would be with him and in the same division.

The following morning was spent on the rifle range again and finally, Will was getting the hang of the Lee Enfield, putting three of his five shots into the central body of the target, which gave him some confidence. Smiler, however, had hit four shots right near the centre of the target and with a grin from ear to ear, he joked with Will. "You'd better leave the shooting to me, Will. You just act as the decoy and I'll shoot 'em when they're having a pop at you!"

Later that morning, they were in for a shock. Drilled and marched once more, they stood to attention to be informed that they were to sail to Ostend in three days. One group at a time, they were called to collect their kit for service overseas. Will queued with the others and filed in to a long hall where he was given a new kitbag that was half empty. The contents were then added, routinely being called out by one clerk while the other one placed it inside the bag. Food rations, clothing, a lightweight coat, two wound dressings, water bottle, jack-knife and more... Will watched the items being checked with mild confusion. All of a sudden, everything seemed to be happening very quickly. In the next room, they were each issued with a rifle and bayonet but when Will looked at his rifle, he was confused.

"What's this, Sarg?" he asked.

"What does it look like, lad? It's a bleeding rifle, and this'll be your best friend in the time to come."

"I know, Sarg, but this isn't a Lee Enfield and I've done all my training on a Lee Enfield. I don't know this rifle."

"Don't worry, son. You will do. This is the Martin Henry. It's lighter than the Lee Enfield and was the army's mainstay of the Boar War, lad, so don't worry. You'll be firing it out on the range very shortly."

The man behind Will chipped in glumly. "They look bloody ancient, Sarg, like you got 'em out from what was left over from the Crimean."

The sergeant's face darkened and he glowered, "Less back chat from the ranks. There ain't enough Lee Enfields and these are perfectly good rifles, so pipe down or I'll see if I can find you something even older, right? If you've got some bloody German bearing down on you one day, you'll be mighty pleased to have this in your hands, believe me!"

Outside, about half of the men had been issued with Lee Enfields and half with Martin Henrys, and immediately, the banter started that the Enfields had been reserved for the best shots, causing enough grumbles to involve one of the base officers.

"Simply put, men, we have been issued from the army stores with what you see, and though the Lee Enfield is the more modern rifle, there are simply not enough in the system, so we've had to issue some of you with Martin Henrys. But don't worry. They are excellent guns. You'll be back on the firing range for the next two days, so you will all get a chance to get acquainted with your own rifle soon enough, so stop your moaning and get on with it."

That little speech did nothing to stop the mickey taking and the disappointment on the men's faces, including Will's, was clear. Will's rifle looked like it had been through the Boar War and more. The butt was damaged in several places with small notches and the end sight looked like it had been filed down on one side, which was disturbing. All the men were looking at their rifles and kit with a mixture of excitement and bemusement. No one had been issued with ammunition but just having their own gun in their hands made them suddenly feel that they certainly were going to war.

The barracks was abuzz with excitement that evening. "Belgium, that's abroad, ain't it? Is that a town or a country?" one of the lads asked.

"It's a country, lad," one of the training officers replied, "so you all just behave yourselves with them foreign ladies. They'll all be too posh for any of you lot and if they're not, then you won't want to get to know them with their nasty diseases."

Will wasn't the only one that struggled to sleep that night. Some men were thinking of foreign ladies but weren't too bothered about their nasty diseases, but Will's mind was a mix of excitement and trepidation. Until a week ago, he had been wondering what ship he would be boarding and now he faced a future on land, doing what? Where? He didn't know. He could not avoid his imagination being invaded by dark unknowns, and the only ladies that he was thinking of that night were his mother and Annie.

Morning came quickly, despite his sleep being broken a dozen times by the noises around him, and two days of intensive firing practice ensued. The moaning of the previous day doubled as the men with the older guns learnt very quickly that they had far inferior weapons. They were slower to load and although lighter, their rapid fire training went out the window with the new guns. Rapid fire didn't exist and Will discovered why someone had filed down the end sight on one side, as his gun consistently fired off to the left and slightly high. He complained to the drill sergeant who wasn't interested, "Well then," his instructor urged sarcastically, "just aim down to the right a bit and Bob's yer' uncle then," he grinned.

After two days' intensive practice mixed in with gun care instruction, they were as good a shot as they could be in the time. However, now that the clock was ticking to departure, everything seemed to be hurried and the pressure on their commanding officers to get them ready quickly was clear.

That last evening in England, Will sat on his bed and wrote home like most of the other men. He kept the two letters to Mum, Dad and Annie short and full of optimism, ending that he was sure that the war would be over soon and to expect him home for Christmas, though as he wrote the words, he struggled to believe it. His dad was right, he thought. The war wasn't going well or looking like it would end in the next few weeks. He sat next to Smiler at dinner and they chinked their mugs together with their daily rum ration, Smiler making jokes about the days to come and the foreign women that awaited his charms.

CHAPTER EIGHT

The morning of departure came and they were greeted with a fine but persistent light drizzle. At exactly eight o' clock, they marched the mile and a half down to the docks in rows of four. There were no throngs of cheering people, no flags being waved at them by enthusiastic locals. They just marched down through the back streets of Portsmouth, the sound of their boots breaking the silence and matching time with Will's heartbeat. As they marched through the gates at the docks, they were greeted by absolute pandemonium though. There were hundreds of men, horses and vehicles milling around and as he looked up at the already full ship and then around him, he thought that they must be due to board another ship. He was wrong. They stood to attention and waited in the rain, all around them were numerous groups of soldiers all doing the same and at different points of the quayside, officers barked instructions to move their group into a different position as boarding slowly continued. Two or three horses neighed out loudly in fear, stamping and swinging their heads wildly as they were walked, pushed and pulled up the gangplanks and onto the ship.

Will shivered in the autumn morning air and his kitbag started to weigh heavy on his shoulders as he stood waiting. His eyes darted to the left and right, taking in the scene. He had never seen anything like it and finally, it dawned on him that they were in fact going to board this same ship. An hour later, he was shuffling up the gangplank, holding on to the rope as his rifle swung awkwardly off his shoulder with the movement. Bloody hell. They got onto the deck and must have been one of the last as there wasn't enough room to put your hand in your pocket; it was so packed. Eventually, the crowd shuffled further in, and Will had the chance take his gun off his aching shoulder and put his kitbag down, but only just. The ship was packed to the gunnels and he just felt sorry for the men and horses that were down under in the belly of the ship. On deck, they continued to get wet, but at least they had some fresh air, Will thought.

October was kind to them as they sailed up the channel on calm waters. Light rain gave way to thin sunshine but the sea air had a sharp nip to it, but Will was kept warm by the body heat of the men around him. There was nowhere to sit down for long though and by the time they reached Ostend, all he could think of was a cup of tea and a sit down. They were one of the first to disembark, which was a blessing, but if he thought Portsmouth had been chaotic then that was nothing to Ostend, the only difference now being that there was lots of shouting and waving going on in a language he didn't understand.

Their commanding officer was Captain Howes and judging by his age, he was a military man of some experience. His grey handlebar moustache was impressive by anyone's standards, and his Khaki uniform was adorned with buttons that shone like gold, almost certainly an old salt from the Boer War. Howes knew what everyone was thinking though, and told them that if they looked sharp and marched in time, they'd have a mug of tea in their hands and some hot food within forty minutes. That bucked everyone up and true to his word, on the edge of town they marched into a farm that had been taken over by the military, with its barns converted into makeshift barracks for the men. They were clearly expecting them and well organised as they could smell the hot food even before they arrived. Before long, they were tucking into meaty stew and potatoes that went down a treat.

As Will ate, he looked around. 'So this was Belgium,' he thought. It didn't look much different from England really. The farm had a different shaped roof and he had heard a few cheers from the locals as they had marched out of Ostend in a language that he didn't understand, but apart from that, he could be somewhere in Somerset, he thought. They had been lucky in being one of the first to disembark the ship and as they finished their meal, they could see troops marching past to stopping points beyond. 'The smell of the food must be killing them,' he thought.

It was now late afternoon and a large map was unrolled and held up, Howes using his cane as a pointer and when he told the men to pay attention, he didn't need to. They were all eager to get an understanding of what tomorrow would bring. Will got the gist of it, but he was some way back from the map, so the detail wasn't that clear. What was clear though was that there were Germans attacking Antwerp and that the Belgium Army was struggling to keep them back. Captain Howes ran through the plans a second time and Will was able to shuffle forwards to hear better. The map showed Antwerp to the south. Howes swung his cane pointing towards the town. They were to position themselves between the Germans and the town itself and beat the Germans back. Howes made it sound easy.

The evening air had a bite to it, so by the time they settled down to sleep, Will was grateful for the blanket that he had carried wrapped over his shoulder all day. He was tired and despite the nervous chatter of some of the men around him, it soon died down, though Will's sleep was fitful and often broken by noises around him.

The morning came with a buzz of excitement and by the time they had marched the short distance back to the railway station, it was alive with people. They halted outside the main station behind a wide queue of army troops, all largely destined for Antwerp it seemed. Will stood there and observed the chaos around him. He didn't need to understand the language to see that the trains arriving in Ostend were full of refugees. Families shuffled out of the station, carrying hastily prepared bundles wrapped in sheets with even the smallest children carrying little suitcases and bags of clothes that seemed far too heavy for them. All the refugees had a common look, one of confusion and fear and it looked like they must have had minutes rather than hours to prepare their bundles of prized possessions. 'Poor buggers,' Will thought. He had never seen such a look of desperation on so many faces, young and old. Tiny Terry, as Will had nicknamed him, and Smiler were stood next to Will. "Poor buggers," Terry said.

"Naw, I don't fink so. I suspect that they are the lucky ones," Smiler replied, for once not grinning. The refugees kept coming, shuffling past in a great, long line five wide, looking this and that way around them, clearly not knowing where to go next.

While they waited, several British soldiers walked passed and grinned at the sight of the Marine Battalion in full naval uniform. One of them looked straight at Will and asked with a broad smile, "Lost yer boat, mate?" Will didn't reply, but for the first time, he felt self-conscious of his navy blue uniform with its bell-bottomed trousers and white trimmings, and he felt a long way from the ship he had been expecting to serve on. He ignored the comment and looked away, but Smiler barked an immediate reply, "F off, army. We're Royal Navy Marines, mate. You'll be glad to have us next to you when the fighting starts." But the man had his back to him and was walking away at that point.

Just about the time that Will's train was arriving in Antwerp, the letter he had written from Portsmouth was falling through the letterbox of 25 Saxon Road. Harriet and Tom didn't get it until the evening when they came home from work and the letter sat on the mat all day, waiting to be opened. As with every letter, it had been read by the writer's commanding officer and 'censored' before it was posted to ensure it did not contain any sensitive detail. None of the men liked that, having to leave the envelopes open so their officers could read everything they had written. It always made Will conscious of every word he wrote. He knew he was not to put in anything like where they were being sent or any military detail, but it also made Will self-conscious about writing any sentimentality, especially when he wrote to Annie.

On the day that Will had taken the train back to Portsmouth, Tom had waited until the evening before telling Harriet that their son wasn't going back to a ship and when he explained what a naval marine was, Harriet caught her breath in shock. "Oh Tom, so Will is no better than a soldier dressed up in another name." Tom tried to soften it as much as he could, but he had never lied to Harriet in his life and he wasn't going to start now, but no kind words could disguise the reality or change the worried look on his wife's face. Her face bothered Tom long into the night as he lay awake thinking about what was happening in the world and to Will in particular. As he lay in bed listening to Harriet's soft breathing, all Tom could think of was a picture of his son running across a battlefield with explosions all around him. When he did eventually sleep, his dreams just seemed to repeat his worries and he eventually woke feeling less rested than he had done before he had gone to bed.

As with every morning, Tom slipped out of bed and dressed as quietly as he could in the dark so as not to disturb his wife, but Harriet had been sleeping lightly and surprised her husband when he heard her moving, fumbling to strike a match and light her bedside candle. "I'll make some tea," she said, gliding past him with her hand cupped around the candle to protect the flame.

Tom still looked after the horses every morning at the coal merchants and didn't normally get a drink until he started work at the shop an hour later. As the shop had slowly become more prosperous, he didn't really need to supplement their income any more by tending the horses, but he loved the big animals and spending an hour with them every morning always gave him a calm start to a day and, as he had told Alfred several times, "shovelling horse shit is good for the soul". He was always smiling softly under his moustache when he said that. Down in the kitchen, Tom slurped hurriedly at his hot tea while Harriet sat at the kitchen table in her dressing gown.

"I'm worried, Tom."

"I know you are, my love, but Will's a bright lad and he's sensible. He'll be alright," he softly replied, resting his hand on her shoulder to comfort her as he spoke. He just wished to himself that he believed the words that he had just spoken.

CHAPTER NINE

Back at Ostend Station, Will's battalion had hardly moved in over two hours. They could work out from the people that filed out of the station roughly where the train had come from, as trains coming from the east had four times the passengers from anywhere else and were nearly all refugees. They all had that same haunted look on their poor faces and no matter how many shuffled past, they all had that same look. Quite a number did brighten up when they saw the troops there and shouted things at them that Will guessed were complimentary. One woman put down her suitcase and rushed over to them, throwing her arms around big Terry who stood out from the rest of them because of his size. She looked tiny against his great, big frame and she was sobbing, "Mercy, mercy, Monsieur," as Terry's face exploded in crimson up above her. All the other lads burst into laughter at his embarrassment. "Bloody hell, Terry. You ain't 'alf gone red, mate," Smiler chuckled.

Finally, they started to move and twenty minutes later, they were loaded tightly into a train with hundreds of other troops and set off. Despite the chill, it was so crowded that they let the windows drop open. The Belgian countryside rushed by and Will noted how flat it generally was. The lucky men had a seat, but most of them crammed into every corner and leaned on the carriage walls, swaying with the train as it chugged along. The mood inside was jolly at first and some wag had set off singing and those that knew the words joined in, but it was a new song to Will, so he just sat there enjoying the sing-song. Several stations came and went but their train did not drop its speed or stop. It was full of soldiers and it knew its destination. After just over two hours, it suddenly came to a grinding halt with a judder and a screech of steel on steel as the wheels bit into the track. There were just fields around them and not a station in sight. After ten minutes, the order barked out to disembark. "Outside, men. This is as far as we'll be going by train."

They gathered outside, forming a neat column four abreast. In the distance and for the first time, the sound of explosions could be clearly heard. The mood suddenly changed on hearing gunfire and Will felt a few butterflies dancing wildly in his stomach. They marched out of the field and onto a dirt road, the sound of their boots stomping in unison against the compacted mud. It seemed that the train would only go into Antwerp under cover of darkness and would take them no further in daylight, as the German guns were now in range of the railway line which had been shelled on previous days. German spotters would see the smoke of the train on the horizon and send a salvo of shells in their direction. So far, they had been lucky and the track had not been hit, but they would not take any chances now and only completed the rail journey into Antwerp after darkness had fallen.

The grey October afternoon gathered around them as the church steeples of the town came into view and as they turned left onto a main road, they met a solid line of forlorn refugees trudging towards them, filling the entire width of the road and blocking their way. Some were driving carts being drawn by already worn out looking horses but most were walking solemnly behind the carts that were loaded up with as many possessions and people as they could load on board. Chickens and ducks clucked loudly from the unwelcome confines of cages and the column of soldiers had to pick its way past the sprawling mass as it rolled its gloomy way, slowing down their progress considerably. Dark plumes of smoke could be seen in the distance and the occasional flash of red broke the darkening sky as they got closer to the town. Their pace quickened. As they entered the western outskirts of the city, the smell of burning could be detected. Ahead of them, the explosions suddenly sounded a lot louder and people were deep in the business of either escaping or rushing to fight fires.

It was the 6th of October, a day that Will would never forget even though he desperately tried to. They continued their way through the town being led by Captain Howes and a Belgian officer who had intercepted them part way. He led them speedily through the streets, occasionally turning to the right or left but moving swiftly with a clear purpose. Shells whistled overhead but in the main, the shell fire was targeted at the defensive forts ahead of them. The clear smell of smoke intensified and flashes of explosions ahead lit the sky with increasing intensity and noticeably, they encountered less people as they headed eastwards. They halted as two army officers rounded a corner to meet them, the first one raising his arm and barking the order to halt with practised authority. Howes and the two officers stood on the corner of the street out of earshot and were soon in deep conversation punctuated by arms being waved to illustrate what was being said. Will could feel his heart thumping and he realised that his mouth was dry. 'It was entitled to be,' he thought. They had not stopped for a drink for hours now. Such had been the urgency of getting to Antwerp to shore up its defences. The conflab over, they followed the officers at the double down several streets, entering a large square which was filled with troops and hastily erected field shelters, where the wonderful smell of hot food suddenly filled the air. They had been expected and with military precision, within minutes their mess tins each contained two scoops of some sort of stew with a great wedge of bread stuffed down the side. It was welcome. Will squatted down on a stack of grain sacks with the other lads and polished off the food within minutes, carefully wiping the last lick of stew from the sides with the bread. The square was full of soldiers in Khaki and the marine brigade in its white braided navy blue uniform and caps stood out like beacons.

As they finished their food, a polished baritone voice struck up in song, filling the square with the first lines of the now popular song 'All the nice girls love a sailor. All the nice girls love a tar', quickly silenced by an even louder and determined bark from an officer, "Be quiet that man." The singing stopped but was replaced immediately by laughter. The officer moved forwards, ready to bark at the offenders, but then realised that the laughter was coming from the marines themselves. They could see how ridiculous they looked in their bell-bottoms and blues and several of them spontaneously started a navy jig to even more laughter from everyone. It broke the tension of the impending battle and no sooner than the laughter died down, they were called to attention. Captain Howes walked down the lines of men taking a headcount as he went. He got to where Will was and stopped between him and Smiler, "Right, men. We are splitting into two groups for now. Payne, you are the last of my group and you will accompany me to the Drake Battalion Position while you other men will join Majors Hamilton and Collingwood."

"Begging yer pardon, sir," Smiler asked, revealing his best toothless grin as he did. "Could I join your group, sir? Only these two are me best mates and well, I'm the best shot of any of 'em and we've worked out a plan like, that they'll stick their Ed's up to attract Jerry an' I'll shoot the buggers first, so they need me like, if that's alright?"

"Go on then, Taylor. One won't make a difference to the numbers," Howes replied, not seeing the funny side of it at all. His face was tensed and the battalion divided quickly amid a sudden air of urgency. Now as they moved out of the square, the sound of explosions increased and plumes of smoke could be seen in a great arc around them. Some of the buildings were already badly damaged and in places people were rushing this way and that, fighting fires. As they walked further, the buildings suddenly thinned out as they reached the eastern edge of the town. To the right of the road, a trench stretched out into a flat ploughed field to a thin line of poplar trees in the distance. The troop gathered round Howes and the Belgian officer. "Right, men. Keep your heads down and follow me. We've to make our way to the front and dig in. We have to hold Jerry back at all costs, so look sharp now."

He hadn't been joking about 'keeping your head down'. The trench had clearly been hastily dug and was no more than four feet deep with shallow sides. They shuffled along bent double like old men, trying not to trip over great clods of soil that lay in the bottom of the roughly hewn trench in the increasing dark and for the first time, Will heard gunfire that seemed uncomfortably close and he realised that the shellfire was aimed at them. By the time they reached the poplar trees, several bullets had whistled uncomfortably close but over their heads, but no one had been silly enough to stand up and investigate despite the temptation. They started to pass weary-looking Belgian soldiers as they left the trench empty for the new arrivals. Their faces dirty and tired-looking, they hardly glanced at the men coming to replace them, but just bent lower to make sure they didn't raise their heads on their way out.

The trench line here wasn't any deeper than before, but a line of wooden crates had been placed to provide some sort of protection in front of the muddy line and one could peep out from the side to view a flat field beyond and another row of trees and hedgerow in the distance. Apart from the odd bullet zipping into the mud around them, it was relatively quiet, but over to their left, someone was copping it big time. Their instructions were clear. Dig in, wait for more orders and keep your eyes sharp. They followed orders and took it in turns to keep watch, the others sliding as best they could into cover for a cigarette, being careful not to expose the flare of the match and lighting as many cigarettes from the one match that they could. Time dragged. Still, the explosions off to their left rained down on the poor sods there. Will pulled up the collar of his greatcoat and watched the night pass, amazingly dozing in snatches until it was his turn to take watch.

There was hardly a moon to give light and your eyes play tricks on you in the dark. Will could make out the slightly darker row of trees in the distance and as his eyes scanned left and right into the darkness, he thought from time to time that he could see some movement. His gun at the ready, his heart thumped as he pictured what might be there, but then he would blink and the movement stopped, and then he wasn't sure if he'd really seen anything or not. This continued throughout his watch and he was grateful to get a tap on the shoulder and take a turn in the bottom of the trench for a while, sucking hard on a Woodbine the first moment that he could. The night seemed to go on forever and Will didn't think that he had dozed but he must have, and as the dawn came, the shellfire suddenly intensified and shifted towards them. Without warning, a salvo of shells whistled overhead and exploded in the town behind them. As more shells fell, they began to creep noticeably back towards them. "The bastards are getting their range on us," Terry quipped, sucking on an unlit cigarette that bobbed up and down in his mouth as he spoke. Several shells landed squarely eighty yards behind them and seconds later, two more just thirty yards away. The ground shook and mud rained down into the trench, and over to the right, two more shells exploded just in front of the trench. A moment later, a shell screamed towards them and landed with a thud just five yards in front of their trench. Will froze, but the explosion didn't come. "Fucking hell," Smiler shouted loudly, "fucking, fucking hell. A bleedin' dud, lads. Thank the Holy Mother for that." He was grinning from ear to ear, "Our luck's in, lads."

The shelling stopped as quickly as it had started. "Eyes front, fix bayonets, lads. Get to your stations," the order rang out along the trench. Will's hand was shaking as he tried to fasten the blade to his rifle. He laid the rifle on the top of the trench and slipped his cap off. 'No point in giving anyone a nice, white target to aim at,' he thought. They waited. Up ahead, he could see movement in the trees and suddenly, a rush of dark figures came leaping out of their cover towards them. Will gulped, but his mouth was dry as sand.

"Wait for my orders to fire, lads, then open fire…"

'Bloody hell! There's a lot of them,' Will thought to himself and he leaned his head down to the sights on his rifle and took aim. His heart was thumping like he had just ridden his pushbike up Talbot Hill. As he looked down the rifle sight again, the figures started to come into focus. They were running like hell itself was driving them and he could see the glint of steel from their bayonets and the spikes on their helmets as they ran towards them. Will froze. Just a few months ago, he would have been at Mardons and now he was going to shoot at a man he didn't know and probably kill him, a complete stranger. It suddenly seemed so strange, but all throughout his training, his shooting at targets and thrusting his bayonet into a straw-filled dummy, it had never really occurred to him that one day it might be a real person that he might be firing at.

They were now shouting. These unknown men were screaming hatred as they ran, waving their guns as they half-tripped at times across the ploughed field. Still, the order didn't come. Will had beads of sweat running down his face now and the enemy was now halfway across the field. 'Legs,' Will thought, 'shoot for their legs.' He suddenly didn't want to kill anyone. Yes, he hated the Germans and yes, he was in a war that he wanted to win but he was looking at young men like himself who clearly wanted to kill him, yet he realised that he didn't want to kill them, but he wanted to stop them for sure. 'Legs,' he thought again and dropped the barrel down, aiming for the man's legs immediately in front of him. When the order came to fire, there was an eruption of noise around him and Will watched the man in his sights fall graciously to the ground. He fell like a drunken man who had just tripped on a kerbstone. 'Legs,' Will thought, 'I'm sure I got him in the legs.' Then he remembered that his bloody rifle fired slightly high and to the right of the sight. He'd forgotten that in his panic and now he wasn't sure if he'd shot him in the legs or in the chest. The thought upset him.

There was no time to be upset. He reloaded, his hands shaking as he did. They were getting closer even though their numbers had thinned. This time, he aimed at the ground to the left of the man's left foot. Once again, his target tripped and fell. To his left, a machine gun had started up, sending lead chattering into the field ahead of them. Like watching a scythe cutting ripe corn, the *Vickers* gun slowly swept from left to right, cutting down men like cutting hay, it was an unreal and awful scene to behold. The onslaught of men suddenly stopped and turned, running back from the fire that had engulfed them, retreating from the certain death that had awaited them. The firing stopped. No one wanted to shoot a man in the back and the only sound pervading the trench then was of cursing and men hastily reloading their guns with the excited nervous chatter of relief that the Germans had not reached their trench.

Sergeant Hewitt came down the line, reassuring the men like he might be their dad. He was one of the khaki regulars and had served a number of years in the marines and came down the line to 'steady the ship' as he called it, patting the men on the shoulder as he passed, reassuring them that they'd done well. "When's the next attack, Sarg?" one of the men asked nervously.

"Attack? That weren't an attack, lad. They were just probing the line, just seeing if there was anyone at home like. Now they know that the navy's in town, I don't expect them back for a while but keep yer eyes sharp. You never can tell."

The day passed without another direct attack, though the bombardment continued unrelenting around them. To occupy their time, they were ordered to dig their trench deeper, which wasn't easy as it had to be done bent low as the Germans still had a couple of snipers keeping activity to a minimum, so throwing a shovel half full of sticky mud out of the trench from a crouched position wasn't easy and made your back ache within minutes.

A ration party arrived from the town, handing out chunks of bread and cheese, giving the men a welcome break and Will squatted down in the trench and ate gratefully. He hadn't realised until then how hungry he was, but too much had been going on to think about it. As darkness fell, you could feel the nervous tension within the trench increasing. A flare would burst above them from time to time, brilliantly illuminating the field in front of them as half of those on watch strained their eyes to look for any movement. The other half on watch had to close their eyes and look down until the flare hit the ground and extinguished. They then had a tap on the shoulder to take over whilst the flare watchers let their eyes re-adjust to the darkness.

At exactly midnight, all hell broke loose. Suddenly, the bombardment that had been going on to their left switched towards them, like an unseen eye had suddenly spotted them hidden in their little hole in the ground. And this time, the guns definitely had their range. The ground erupted in front and around them, with explosions of such intensity that it was like the very door of Hades itself had opened up around them. They hunched down protecting themselves as best they could from great clods of soil that rained down into the trench from explosions in front and behind. Will pulled his hat further down onto his head and prayed silently, not that his navy cap would protect from anything but dust. The ground shook with such intensity that bits of loose soil danced like little, brown hailstones on the ground in front of his eyes.

Word went down the trench that the Germans had broken through on their flank and the Belgians had been beaten back, so they knew then that they were exposed to attack from their side as well as front. The bombardment continued unrelenting and every man in that trench discovered the terror of expecting life to end there and then, not knowing from second to second if that moment was to be their last. Will's heart pounded in his chest fit to burst and he gripped onto his gun for moral support, knowing that it was merely a toy against the howitzers that rained down fire and hell on them. The bombardment was so intense and with their flank exposed, the order was given to fall back, which was a pardon from certain death. They shuffled back down their little trench with as much speed as they could, keeping their heads down and stumbling over great clods of earth still hot and sulphur smelling from the explosives that had wrenched them from the earth.

When they could see the outskirts of the town, the scene they had left yesterday had already changed. Some of the buildings that they had passed were now rubble, illuminated in the dark by the flashes of explosions around them, their twisted roofs and fallen walls filling the streets with chunks of stonework and wood. Will followed the line of men across the last field and was one of the last men to seek the relative safety of the city. Suddenly, the shout went up that German troops were following them across the field. Will glanced behind him briefly but could see nothing in the dark. He tripped and steadied himself, cursing his stupid bell-bottom trousers and wishing that he had been issued with the puttees that the army lads had around their legs. Smiler was around five yards in front of him and to his right and saw Will trip out of the corner of his eye.

"Don't bugger about, William. Keep up for 'Even's sake." 'Smiler never called me 'William',' Will thought to himself. Terry was beside Will and stopped, reaching down to pick Will up when…

Sometimes in one's life, so much happens in such a short space of time that it is impossible for the human mind to take it all in. The brain does its best by working so fast that everything appears for a few moments to be in slow motion, like filming a movie in double time and then playing it back at normal speed. Those brief moments seem to last an age, until the movie stops and normal time resumes.

It took Will many years to recall little bits of the next few fragments of his life and when he did, his mind fought immediately to bury those moments and the memory. His first awareness was of an overwhelmingly loud, high-pitched sound, a sound that engulfed him for a millisecond before being instantly replaced by absolute silence.

He became aware that he was flying, flying in slow motion. 'How strange,' he thought to himself, as he observed the earth moving away yards beneath him as he rotated gracefully in the air in that slow motion, movie time. The silence was then joined by an engulfing darkness. It seemed a warm and comfortable place to be, and he thought later that he remembered smiling as his vision shut down moments before his brain did, but he couldn't be sure. He wasn't sure of anything. The shell had landed at a little distance in front of Will and the shock wave had caught him full in the upper body as he rose to stand up. The blast threw him clear of Terry who had had his back to the blast and who was thrown face down into the earth.

When Will came to, he was half propped up on his side in a shell hole with torn stonework and wood and steaming smoking mud around him. The silence reigned glorious, but now his brain was working at a quarter speed for some reason that he didn't know, and didn't care about. He felt very calm somehow.

He didn't seem to be able to move. Nothing was working. He tried to lift his arm but his body didn't seem to want to do anything. He tried to move his tongue to stem the dryness in his mouth but even that didn't function. His eyes slowly began to work, though the focus was out for some reason. He blinked a long, slow blink, trying to get the focus back before ever so slowly working his eyes from left to right to take in the scene around him. Sat at a strange sideways angle and engulfed in silence, it seemed to Will that he might be in a dream. He wasn't sure. Was this real or not? He didn't know. As his eyes slowly scanned the scene, he saw a shape on the far side of the shell hole. The shape didn't make sense to him. It had eyes and the eyes were open, as was the mouth. The shape had an expression of absolute shock etched into it, frozen as in a mask. Will stared at it again and blinked some more, trying to comprehend what the shape was. The head was attached to a naked shoulder and one arm but nothing else. The blast had shorn what was there from its torso. Will stared, his mind numb to the information that his eyes were trying to feed to his brain. He just could not work out what he was looking at. The eyes worked but his brain just wasn't, just wasn't…functioning.

From almost floating in a calm and glorious silence, his hearing suddenly kicked in like someone starting a motorbike, and when the noise hit him, it sent a shockwave through his body that made him gasp, the sudden rush of sounds causing him to gulp in air like he was drowning. His hand moved to his throat and he could now move his head a little. Smiler stared at him, his mouth wide open, his eyes wide open, his one naked arm laying hand upward by his side. Will stared back, his mind now slowly piecing together what he was looking at, who he was looking at. What was left of Smiler stared back, unmoved, illuminated by the numerous flashes of explosions around them.

Will didn't know how long he lay there, transfixed, staring at Smiler as the flashes lit up their shell hole. The moment seemed to last an age. He tried to move his legs but they objected and as Will stared in absolute shock, Smiler stared back, or what was left of him. Nausea overcame Will and he became aware that he was vomiting, but in the swirling confusion of the moment, it was like he was watching someone else being sick. He passed out.

Time has no clock when one is unconscious. When consciousness flooded back in to fill Will's mind, he became aware of a man standing over him. He was leaning over Will, jabbing the end of a bayonet in Will's chest. "Come, Tommy," the voice said, expressionless. He lifted Will slowly to his feet. He could move of sorts, but his left hand hung lifeless by his side shaking uncontrollably and his head felt like someone had taken a sledge hammer to it. He looked one last time for Smiler as he stumbled out of the shell hole but where he had been was now covered with a camouflage tarpaulin and he stumbled past it in a confused daze. All around, the sound of battle continued, but now he was shuffling back across the fields away from the town, the German soldier occasionally prodding him in the back with his bayonet for good measure.

Scattered in a Belgian field,

Is one who died with no choice to yield,

His smile in life would light a room,

Now a field of corn is his tomb.

He gave his life unselfishly,

So that today we can all stand free.

In memory of 'Smiler'

CHAPTER TEN

The next hours were a blur. Will had such a searing headache that started in his neck and pounded its way relentlessly through to his forehead that just thinking was an effort and he wanted to hide from any light as the dawn rose. He was ordered down into a trench whose exit had been blocked by barbed wire. There were several other disconsolate looking British soldiers there, but no one spoke. Will's head thumped and his left arm shook violently and he slumped down in the trench and slept or passed out. He didn't know which.

His foot was being kicked, and he woke in the middle of a dream where he was cycling down the Wells Road with his dad out in front of him. What he woke to wasn't so nice. The trench had filled with men while Will had lost consciousness and now they were all being moved out. They were herded along a road, a band of around a hundred shuffling silent men, bedraggled and in various states of disarray. Some carried visible wounds, some being half carried by the men around them. Will's arm still hung limply by his side shaking violently and he gripped it with his right arm to try and stop the shaking. The nerves down the left side of his face were also driving him mad as they twitched and ticked with his eye and mouth jumping uncontrollably. His body ached all over like he had been kicked a hundred times by a horse and walking without water or food was difficult. They walked until the afternoon light started to fade, and any requests to stop and tend the injured was met by a rifle butt aimed into the shoulder or sharp prod of a bayonet end. They soon learned not to ask. Eventually, they were carolled into a field where a hastily erected barbed wire pen had been made next to an animal field shelter. There were another fifty men already in the pen and guards appeared from the field shelter, smoking and laughing with each other. One by one, they were body-searched and watches and money were taken from them. The answer to any resistance was a rifle butt in the face or stomach. Will had his watch taken by a grinning sentry who had a disgusting smell of some foreign brand of cigarette on his breath. What Will hadn't noticed until he handed it over was that his watch had stopped at the exact moment of the blast and what the German didn't know was that watch would never work again. Just as he was about to let Will go, the young soldier looked down at Will's boots. He gently pushed his toe into the leather before putting his foot alongside Will's to gauge the size. "*Stiefel,*" he barked. Will looked at him perplexed. "*Stiefel, jetzt,*" he barked again impatiently.

"He wants your boots," the man behind Will said. Will just stood there for a moment too long and the rifle butt hit him mid-stomach, bending him double. He sank to his knees and then onto his bottom on the mud. He was exhausted. The German aimed his bayonet at Will's chest. "*Ous!*" he demanded through clenched teeth. Will reluctantly took off the boots that his dad had made him and stood up, his feet sinking into the cold mud. The soldier pushed him back with the rifle butt again and threw the boots behind him. Later, someone told Will that he saw the man sat in the animal shelter on a bale of hay trying them on, then marching around in a small circle like he was in a shoe shop. Bastard.

They spent a very cold night in the barbed wire pen and with no blanket or coat, Will was freezing. He had lost all feeling in his feet and he spent the night with his arms folded around his knees, snatching short bouts of sleep as best he could. The dawn couldn't come quick enough. More German soldiers had appeared just before light and the smell of coffee filled the air from the field shelter, teasing the prisoners' hunger and thirst. A cart came into the field pulled by a worn-out-looking old pony, half loaded with more soldiers and crates of various sizes. A bucket of water was placed inside the prisoner's pen and two disinterested Germans threw over dark loaves of bread. One shouted "*Petit dejeuner*" in a sarcastic tone at them, like he was calling to his dogs. There were several officers amongst the prisoners and they took charge, counting the men and tearing the bread into roughly equal portions as best as they could. They each had probably what amounted to a quarter of a small loaf and meanwhile, the Germans stood on the other side of the wire drinking coffee and eating chunks of bread, cheese and dark-looking biscuits.

A whistle went up in the distance and the guards hurried into action, grabbing their guns as another party of around forty bedraggled prisoners appeared flanked by half a dozen armed Germans. They went through the same routine of being searched and robbed but then, Will saw something that made his heart leap. The unmistakable large frame of Terry stood in the queue, looking muddy and beaten. Once searched, he came into the pen and Will rushed over to grab his arm. Terry looked shocked and animated. "Bloody hell, Will. You can't be here. I saw you dead, mate. I felt yer pulse and there was nothing. I don't believe it. I swear you was dead, Will. I saw you."

"I don't know what happened, Terry. I really don't. The first thing I can remember is waking in a trench with a lot of other prisoners. I can't remember anything else."

Terry hesitated for a moment. "Smiler's gone, Will. He was led close to you and I thought you was both goners."

Will looked shocked. His hand shook violently and he grabbed his left arm with his right hand and turned away quickly to hide his grief as a momentary glimpse of an image flashed through his mind too quickly for

him to see it. "Oh God, no. Poor Smiler. I didn't know that he was dead."
He genuinely didn't.

'Breakfast' over, they were marched out under bayonet point and started walking again, a column four wide with their captors spread out on either side of them. Of all the things that had gone through Will's mind from the time of joining up to now, being captured wasn't one of them. He had never once contemplated it, nor was it for any of the men in that sad column as it trudged along. One of the other men had been captured with his kit and gave Will his spare pair of socks, which he put on underneath his own as the new socks were dry, but his feet were soon wet again and every step was painful with every stone biting into his feet. Within half an hour, Will was hobbling, despite his feet feeling numb with the cold, and Terry took hold of Will's arm to steady him.

There was a lot of activity on the road, with German troops marching in the other direction and trucks towing guns and troops who jeered and gestured at the prisoners as they passed. Thankfully, they only walked for half the morning before they reached a railway station on the edge of a town whose name Will didn't recognise in his semi-delirium. He was still in a daze, wandering in and out of here and now and nowhere. He just wanted to lie down and get away from the shaking and cold. They were once again herded into a hastily erected barbed wire area and most of the men semi-collapsed on the ground, waiting for things to happen. There was little talking amongst the dejected men and though escape may have been on several of their minds, there had been no opportunity on this open land that would not have quickly resulted in a bullet in the back within yards.

One of the officers asked for water for the men and after a while, a pail was brought full of water that had a strong background taste of petrol to it. Although they protested, it didn't stop them taking it in turns to sip at the freezing cold water. The station was a hive of military activity. The local Belgian population had largely gone to ground now and every train that arrived disgorged hundreds of German troops and supplies, but the prisoners stood in their pen with nothing to do but look on. It had started to drizzle and by the time their train arrived two hours later, they were soaked long before they boarded.

A German General sauntered over towards them, backed by several junior officers, grabbing the chance to practise his English. "Gentlemen, you are prisoners of war and for you, the fighting is over. You will be treated well and with respect, and when we have won this war, you will no doubt go back to your homes." Captain Thayers, the highest ranking British officer captured, pushed his way to the front of his men, stood to full attention and saluted. "Captain Thayers sir at your service. Begging your pardon, but many of my men have been robbed by your soldiers. Money, watches and even boots have been taken and this is not in the conventions of war agreed between our two countries," he spoke firmly.

The General turned to the office next to him and they spoke quietly together for a few moments before turning back. "I am told this is not the case Captain Thayers, but as you say this has happened, we will investigate further and if found, the items you speak of will be returned."

They, of course, were never seen again. The prisoners' numbers had swelled to near three hundred now and they were directed at gunpoint into a train that was made up of cattle wagons. When they thought the first truck was full, the Germans waved them further back with their rifles and forced more men inside. Each truck had over fifty men jammed inside, with Will and Terry being two of the last to be loaded, which later on turned out to have been a mistake. A bucket of water was hastily placed inside and whole lettuce hearts thrown over the heads of the men before the big door slid closed, trapping the men inside in near total darkness. The daylight suddenly disappeared, with the only light entering the wagon being from gaps between the horizontal boarding.

"Bloody hell! Budge up, lads. We're wedged tight against the door," Terry called out. A dozen men replied in unison that there was nowhere to budge up to! The train lurched off, catching the men unaware and a shout went up as they all fell against each other before they could steady themselves. The bucket of water jerked, sending the top third of its cold contents over Will's socks, compounding his misery.

What then started was a day and a half of what many men described later as a journey through hell. Will never talked about it to anyone for many years and only then he did so in small pieces, trying to cut the memory up so as not to recall it in one go and endure its pain as intensely as he had for that day and a half. They were packed in so tightly that it was impossible to sit down or rest. The body is not designed to stand for near forty hours and from time to time, a form of sleep would take over until the knees forgot their orders and unlocked, causing the man to slump and wake immediately and stand up straight again. As the wagons were designed to carry cattle, they had been constructed to deliberately have low light to calm the beasts, but with only slits of light entering between a few of the boards and with fifty men wedged inside each wagon, the air inside soon became stale and foul. After only a few minutes inside, the call went up that one of the men wanted to use the toilet. There was nothing for it other than for one corner of the wagon to be designated as the toilet area, and the men shuffled with difficulty past each other when the call of nature pulled at them so hard as that they could ignore it no longer. The stress of their current situation meant in fact that no sooner than the first man had gone, there was constant flow of men apologising and shuffling through to squat in the foul corner, most gagging as they did. Locked in this wooden box, the stench became almost intolerable and Will, like most men, clutched his tunic to his nose to try and filter out the dreadful smell.

One of the men near the far wall of the wagon called out that he could see the sun through the gap in the wooden slats and reckoned that they were travelling east. He was right. After long hours of stopping and starting through half-sleep and delirium, the train came to a halt and from the sounds outside, Will guessed that they were in a station. He could hear noises outside and some shouting, but it wasn't Belgians but Germans shouting. He gathered that much. The door was slowly wrenched back, flooding the wagon with light that dazzled him and he threw his arm over his eyes to shade its brilliance. There was a wonderful rush of cold, fresh air into the wagon, but as Will raised his arm a little to shade his eyes, he saw a crowd of angry-looking people underneath, men and women, old and young, all with one arm cocked beside their heads. Suddenly, their arms shot forward and Will and the other men in the door area were pelted with stones and abuse. One old woman in particular looked as if she would kill the men if she had the chance. He had never seen a look of such hatred on an old woman's face as a second salvo of stones flew into the carriage, one of them striking Will on the back as he quickly turned to protect as much of himself as he could. After a minute, a group of soldiers waved the crowd back and one of them put a bucket of fresh water inside as they slid the wagon door back with difficulty, plunging the men inside into darkness once more. "Bloody hell," Terry said, rubbing the back of his neck where a stone had struck him. "What the bloody hell was that all about?"

"We're in Germany," another man replied sourly, "and they don't seem to like us and by the way, they seem to have forgotten to feed us. I'm bloody starving."

Will hadn't been thinking of his stomach until the man spoke, as he was still deeply distracted by his searing headache, but then it occurred to him that the gnawing pain in his stomach was deep hunger. Once again, their eyes adjusted to the dim light of the wagon and one wag, who was wedged far inside, called out in triumph, "Lovely bit of fresh air though, lads. It's a bit like being on Brighton Beach of a summer's evening." That caused a ripple of laughter to pervade the wagon and another man called out, "Come on, lads. Let's show 'em who we are," and he started singing 'Onward Christian Soldiers' at the top of his not particularly good voice. Will's thumping head prevented him from joining in, but it bucked up his spirits for a while as everyone else sang at the top of their voices. The train pulled out of the station with the angry crowd being treated to a defiant rendition of not very tuneful British singing. It lasted until the train had cleared the station and then the mood slumped back into reality as someone shouted out apologetically to make way as he needed to get to the toilet corner.

At times, the train came to a halt and would wait there for several hours. They could hear some activity from time to time outside and guessed that they were in a siding, changing the locomotive at the head of the train. Towards the end of one particularly long stop, the door slid open a couple of feet and three German soldiers stood there with guns pointing at them while another soldier threw inside some turnips and lettuces. One of the prisoners held up the empty bucket and asked for more water as between them, they had sipped the bucket dry long ago, but there was no time and the door slid shut on the pleading man and his empty bucket.

Will slipped back into delirium. His legs and back ached so much that only him leaning hard against the door and the pressing of men around him prevented him from falling. The pain throughout his body was excruciating. By the time the train pulled into its final destination, Will and nearly everyone else collapsed on the ground outside when they were let out, one kind German soldier helping them down while a dozen others stood around guns at the ready, should anyone try and slip off. They needn't have been concerned as all the half-starved men wanted to do was lie down on the ground where they were. They were not allowed to sit for long though, and were quickly marched out of the station. Will found that his legs would only move in baby-steps, but by leaning forwards, he could propel himself with great effort forwards. His left arm still shook violently and now his neck twitched constantly, jerking his head in small movements, this way and that. Terry and another man each held Will's arms, helping him along to keep up, but thankfully they hadn't gone a mile when they found themselves walking alongside the tall barbed wire perimeter walls of their next home. As they rounded the corner, a large barbed wire, double-gated entrance appeared and hanging down from it was a large wooden board with the name DOBERITZ emblazoned on it in large, rough, hand-painted letters.

CHAPTER ELEVEN

Harriet had endured a restless night's sleep and woke before Tom. She slipped out of bed quietly so as not to disturb her husband and went downstairs to the kitchen to make some tea. She was just pouring two cups when Tom joined her, pulling his jumper on as he sat down at the kitchen table.

"Good morning, my sweet. You're up early."

"I couldn't sleep, Tom. Been thinking about our Will, wondering where he is now."

"He'll be fine, love. He's a smart lad. I'll bet he's sat in some army camp, bored out of his mind, waiting for something to happen if I know the military." They sipped on their tea in silence for a few moments, deep in thought again before Tom spoke, "Why don't you pop a little note over to Annie's house and invite her over for Sunday tea? She must be thinking about Will as well and it would be nice to see her again."

DOBERITZ – Prisoner of War camp. Germany
October 12th 1914

The first days in the camp were a daze to Will. When the three hundred captured soldiers arrived from Antwerp, they were first given a lecture from the camp commandant that went right over Will's head, as all he could think about was that from somewhere he could smell hot food. Quite a few other men had also caught the same smell wafting across the camp and were also distracted, staring carelessly around hungrily. The 'welcoming' lecture over, they were marched (of sorts) to queue outside a large tent to be processed. Three German officers sat at a rickety old hastily erected desk and one of them asked questions in broken English while one of the other men wrote down each man's name, rank and number. They would be individually interrogated later. The paperwork over, they were led in batches of twenty to queue at another tent and to their joy, to the source of the smell. A huge steaming pot of soup that smelt delicious to the nose but its best attribute turned out to be that it was hot and had a smell of food about it. When Will looked in his tin, it was a quarter filled with grey-coloured water with tiny bits of vegetables floating in it, but it was at least hot, and with hands and feet numb with the cold, it was better than nothing.

Each man received a small bowl with a thick slice of dark, tasteless bread with it, but Will couldn't hold his tin with both hands as he would have shaken most of its contents out, but he sat on the ground with the bowl in front of him and felt the warmth of the hot liquid rush through him like a flood, burning the roof of his mouth in his anxiety to get food inside him. All he remembered of his first day after that was trying to help five other men, including Terry and a couple of other chaps, called Harold and another William, to erect a tent but Will wasn't able to be much help, most of the men were in putting up large tents, but Terry had seen a small bag and decided he'd rather be in a small tent with his mates. They queued afterwards to be each given a coarse, brown blanket after which they all crawled inside their tent and laid down on the ground, wrapping themselves as best they could in their blanket on the frozen mud before crashing exhausted to sleep. The bitter cold woke Will from time to time but exhaustion won that battle every time and carried him beautifully back away from reality. When he finally awoke, he was alone in the tent and it was morning. He was as stiff as a board and ached all over from the hard ground but his waking thoughts were how hungry he was. His head wasn't shaking so much but he was stone-cold though. His feet were particularly cold to the point that he could not feel them anymore, and he rubbed his socks painfully to try and get some life back into his feet. His two pairs of socks had been damp and had frozen hard to his feet. He had walked holes in both socks, and scuffed areas with flesh appeared in several places on his bloodied feet. When he left the tent, he found that he could only take small, painful paces and hobbled out to see what world awaited him, wearing his blanket to protect him from the cold air.

There seemed to be lots of men just walking around aimlessly, all looking like ghosts stuck somewhere that they didn't want to be. There were already many hundreds of prisoners in the camp, some English but mainly French and Russians. They had already migrated to different corners of the camp and the different nationalities didn't really band together but stayed with their own countrymen, nodding courteously to their allies as they ambled past. The camp looked like it had once been a large farm, with lots of outbuildings and a couple of big barns now completely surrounded by two tall barbed wire fences. The other William came rushing towards Will. "Blimey, mate. You've nearly missed breakfast. Hurry up. I'd recommend the bacon, and the sausages are lovely with a couple of eggs and fried bread." Will's eyes lit up until William started chuckling and slapped him on the shoulder. "Sorry, Will. Don't mind me. I'm only joking, mate. It's the same horrible soup again I'm afraid."

Will didn't know whether to laugh or cry; such was his mental state. His brain seemed to be processing information slower than ever for some reason and he put it down to the crushing headache that had not left him. He gave a thin smile in return and nodded as William took his arm and helped him towards the food tent. "You ain't in a good way, Will, are you? I've been talking to Terry and he said you'd both been through the mill and you came off the worst of it. Thought you was dead, he said. You're lucky to he be here, mate. Terry says. Get some food down and we'll take you to the medical tent later. The officers are getting everything organised now and we've got to be on parade in an hour."

The soup tasted as insipid and bland as yesterday, but its warmth helped revive Will's spirits a little and at the parade, he managed to stand to attention, sort of. The most senior British officer stood out in front of the assembly and spoke with the authority and confidence that generations of breeding and privilege had instilled in him.

"Gentlemen. Men. We might be prisoners of war but we are still British, and we are still the king's army and, the best soldiers in the world." He paused to let his words sink in. "We will show the Bosch why we are the finest in the world with discipline and organisation. I am talking now to the camp commandant about providing better facilities and my officers will be coming amongst you shortly to list names and details from you all. We will get ourselves organised, bring some structure to the British side of the camp and ensure that the conventions of war are upheld by the Germans. Chin up, chaps. Our men will be beating a path to our door before long and the war will be over before we get too settled here. Good show, dismissed."

Next to the food tent, a smaller tent had been erected with a Red Cross sign nailed hastily to a post outside. Terry and William helped Will inside where they queued with another twenty men before Will was seen by a medical orderly whose opening words were, "Before you ask, we've got sod all medicine and bandages are as common as hen's teeth. Now, what's up with you?" Terry spoke for Will who was increasingly letting him do so. "He's been blown up and his feet are in a bad way," he said hurriedly.

"Alright. You men step outside and leave me to take a look at him, please."

Will sat on a wooden bench that had once been a door and slowly swung his legs up one at a time, with his feet sticking out over the end of the wood. The orderly removed Will's socks to reveal horrid, deep sores on both his feet. He was patched up as best he could and told to lie back and wait. Five minutes later, the orderly returned with a German Army Doctor who recognised Will's accent immediately and told Will that he had worked in Bath for two years before he had returned to Germany in 1913 to eventually join the army. He was very kind and looked at Will's feet first and then asked him questions for ten minutes about what had happened to sustain his injuries. At the end of the questioning, he told him that he needed to stay with them for a few days in the medical tent.

The tent was heaving with men carrying all sorts of bloody injuries and Will was moved towards the end of a row of beds roughly made out of wood and chicken wire that had hastily been put together. It was better than his first night there though, as he had a blanket underneath him as well as one on top. He was still bitterly cold all the time though and when he slept, he would often wake bathed in sweat and in the midst of a horrendous nightmare. He couldn't remember much about the following few weeks, other than sleeping much more than he had ever slept before in his life. He also remembered being calmed in the night by the medical orderly when his dreams woke him screaming loudly in a blind sweat. He could not recall his dreams though, so horrific were they that his mind closed the door tightly on the memory as he awoke.

When he wasn't sleeping, he had to listen to the painful moaning and wailing of the men around him as they coped with their injuries without painkillers or anaesthetics. On either side of Will were men with shrapnel and gunshot injuries. To the left of him, a soldier lay there not saying a word, just groaning occasionally as the three machine gun bullets across his stomach did their work. On the other side lay a poor chap who hadn't been there long before he started calling out pleadingly for his mother. Will's heart felt for the poor chap and it got him thinking more than ever of home and his own mother. The man's calling went on for an hour or more and got more desperate and loud before suddenly his shouting stopped and he lay there in silence. Both men either side of him died within minutes of each other and were quietly removed to be replaced by two more poor souls who started groaning afresh.

Will couldn't wait to leave. As the days passed, he felt slightly better in himself during the day, apart from his shaking and ticks. He slept a lot at first between which he lay awake, which brought the depression of being surrounded by death and its noises. Terry and his new friend William had been to see him every day but hardly saw him awake during the first week. Will lay there watching the fabric of the tent above him gently flap against a restraining rope above it but he was conscious of little else. Terry and William arrived with a cheery call, carrying a bundle of clothes that was in fact his uniform. He hadn't even realised that it had been removed.

"Room service," William sarcastically called, as he handed over the bundle.

"There you go, Will. Your kits been deloused and washed, mate. It's as good as new and the good news is that they want your bed. You can go, me old mate," Terry cheerily announced. Will didn't hesitate, though he got up more unsteady than he had expected to and was led away by one of the orderlies to get cleaned up. He hadn't shaved for days but the orderly had to shave him as despite feeling stronger. Will's left arm still shook uncontrollably and he was weak and unsteady on his feet. It wasn't easy being shaved by someone else with a cut-throat razor though, and the orderly kept telling him to lie back and relax, but the occasional violent tick nearly caught him out and he ended up with a few nicks. It felt mighty good to get cleaned up, though washing was from a bucket of freezing cold water and after he had put his uniform on, he was given a choice of boots to try on. "Dead men's boots," the orderly chimed, "You've got quite a few to choose from I'm afraid, but go a size up for now, Will. Your feet are still not great and you'll need to stay off them for as much as you can in the next few days."

Due to Will's hospitalisation, he had missed having his photograph taken for the camp records and now had to take his turn for them to be taken. Some, he was told, would be sent home as a postcard. That first postcard turned out to be more important than he could have imagined.

The photographer was a German civilian from the local village, who lined them up in groups as they came, so Will lined up with some French and Russian soldiers as well as another two Brits. He was still in a daze though, and his mind would slip into somewhere else while he waited, lost in thoughts of nothing in particular, but just absent from where he was at that moment in time. Besides, he thought, the photographer spent so much time fussing about behind the camera that Will didn't realise that the photograph was being taken until it was finished. He needed to sit down. He was exhausted.

CHAPTER TWELVE

Dry and bright November Saturdays can be quite pleasant in England, but this was not one of those days. Harriet had made her way to the shop under a large umbrella that had tried its best to turn itself inside out several times as she fought with both hands to resist the gusts. Tom was in the workshop at the back of the shop and had already done a shift at the coal merchants next door. He had been a bit longer than usual as one of the horses had come up lame, so he had spent time with it, applying a hot poultice to its hoof. Now, he and his brother Alfred were working side by side in the cramped workshop surrounded by partially made shoes and boots, hammering away at speed to keep up with the demand. It was Saturday and as busy as ever.

The first customers had arrived literally as Harriet had unlocked the door and the morning had been a constant stream of customers coming in to buy or collect pre-ordered shoes, with sometimes three people sitting there, waiting to be served. They were still doing well with the higher-quality shoe end of the business and there were two ladies waiting in the shop when the telegram boy arrived. Harriet had just not been prepared for it. She was bringing a pair of ladies' shoes through from the workshop when the bell went above the shop door. Expecting a customer, she stopped dead in her tracks when the telegram boy stepped through the door. Telegram boys rarely brought good news since the war had started and he handed over the single piece of paper with an awkward look as Harriet stared down at the letters that meant nothing to her. It was when the lad said "I'm sorry, Mrs Payne" with such feeling that she went suddenly cold, guessing that its contents were bad. For once in her life ignoring her customers and the telegram boy, Harriet rushed through to the workshop, waving the telegram. Her face was torn in horror. "Tom, Tom, we've got a telegram. Read it quickly, please. Read it quickly," she shouted, wishing on her life that she could read and write and not just 'do' numbers. Tom took the one sheet of paper from her and stared at the words. The heading 'URGENT TELEGRAM' shouted out from it. "Hurry, Tom. What does it say?" Harriet pleaded.

Tom read slowly, taking in the words as he did. With every word he read, he felt the blood drain from his face.

I regret to inform you that a report has been received from the war office to the effect that Able Seaman William Payne of the Royal Navy Marine, second division, was posted missing on the 9th October. The report that he is missing does not necessarily mean that he has been killed, as he may be a prisoner of war or temporarily separated from his regiment. Official reports that men are prisoners of war take some time to reach this country, and if he has been captured by the enemy, it is possible that unofficial news will reach you first. In that case, I am to ask you to forward any letter received at once to this office and it will be returned to you as soon as possible.

At the end of the first sentence, Harriet clutched her mouth with both hands and sank to her knees on the floor, her eyes filling with tears as her mind digested the words. "Oh, dear God! Tom, our little boy's dead," she cried out, the tears now flowing uncontrollably. Tom knelt down beside her and picked her up, holding her as close to him as he could to try and comfort her, when his own world had just exploded around him as he had read the words.

"Wait now, my love," he urged quietly, "it says that he is missing. Just that, missing. He could have just got separated from his unit or been captured. It doesn't mean that he is dead."

"He's dead, Tom. I know it," she blurted as the tears flowed. Tom had never once seen his wife cry before, not even when she discovered that she could have no more children and just the pain of seeing her weeping in front of him broke his own heart.

He took a deep breath. "No," he said firmly. "I refuse to think that our Will is dead. I just won't believe it. You wait and see. This will have been a mistake. We'll hear from our Will soon. You'll see."

Tom helped Harriet to her feet as she tried to compose herself. Tom handed her his handkerchief and she dabbed her eyes, trying to gather herself together. "Yes, I'm sure you are right, Tom. You always are on these things," she blurted out firmly, even though her heart remained heavy with the thought that they had lost Will forever.

Tom went through to the shop and explained to the customers that they had a crisis and made apologies to close the shop. Alfred came through and was just as upset as Tom. "Take Harriet home, Tom. I'll carry on here and will pop over later to see you all. Go home, the pair of you." Arm in arm, they clung together under the umbrella until they got home, battling through the wind and rain as they had done earlier. Harriet sat motionless at the kitchen table while Tom made them both a cup of tea, staring at the chair that Will had always sat on at mealtimes, wondering if he would ever sit there again.

The next few weeks were terrible for both of them. Tom must have quietly, and without Harriet seeing, re-read the telegram a hundred times, digesting every word, trying to change the meaning of its content but finding nothing other than what he had read the very first time. The waiting and not knowing took their emotions down a road that neither of them had ever walked before. Normal life stopped the moment the telegram boy had walked through their door. Now, a great pretence surrounded them both, each trying to be strong for the other when inside, the rocks of their very foundations were crumbling quietly beneath them. They both took turns to wander the house in the dead of night, several times meeting in the kitchen in the early hours to comfort each other and talk, each time Tom reassuring Harriet that Will would be alright, and to just wait and see.

Every time the bell sounded above the shop door, Harriet's heart jumped in fear and hope that it would be another telegram boy with good news coming through the door, though her dread was that it would be the worst of messages. Each day passed and only customers came through the shop door, but it didn't stop Harriet's heart jumping every time. The days drifted by with silence in place of news, worry in place of calm. Tom wrote to the war office, pleading for news but no reply came. He went to the recruitment office in Bristol, looking for information but they were so busy dealing with new recruits that apart from one chap writing down Will's details and promising to look, Tom came away disappointed. The worry was telling on both of them and in times of solitude, even Tom started to think that Will might indeed be dead. He never shared that thought with his wife though. Harriet was struggling enough. He could see, covering grief and worry by working even longer hours in the shop, taking this time to 'sort lots of things out' that she had been meaning to get around to. So, every corner of the workshop was tidied and every shelf and corner of the shop spring cleaned in her anxiety to take her mind off her missing son.

It was mid-morning on the 4th of December that the shop doorbell rang and Harriet looked up in slight confusion at seeing the man walking towards her. She didn't often get to see the postman that came to their house 25 Saxon Road as she was nearly always working when he delivered. But now he was in the shop which was on a different postman's round, so seeing him here didn't immediately register with her. It was strange. "Hello, Mrs Payne. I didn't deliver this to your home as I thought you might want to see it quickly, so I've popped over as I've just finished my round."

He handed over a black and white postcard with the photograph of a group of men standing together. Will's face stared blankly out from the card, standing in his full navy uniform on the edge of a group of soldiers. For a brief moment, Harriet looked confused as she tried to understand what she was looking at. The postman spoke again, "These postcards have started arriving at the sorting office, ma'am. They're sent from prisoners of war camps and this one is from somewhere I've never heard of, but it's in Germany. Your son's a prisoner I'm afraid. I'm really sorry."

Harriet turned quickly and opened the door to the shop. "Tom, Tom, come quickly," she turned back to the postman with a look of utter joy of her face. "Don't be sorry. No, don't be sorry. We'd been thinking that our Will might be dead, so now we know that he's alive." Tom had arrived at her side and Harriet handed over the card. "He's alive, Tom. Our Will's alive."

That evening, Tom sat down to write:

Dear Will,

It seems strange, writing to you when you are so far away from us, but you are closer than ever in our hearts, son. Your mother is with me now and sends her love.

We were very relieved to receive your postcard as we had been worrying about you. We have been told by the Red Cross that Doberitz is near Berlin, and from the photograph you sent, you seem to have made some new friends, which is good.

Everything at home is fine, son. The shop has been busy and your uncle Alfred and his family send their love. Annie has been over for tea a couple of Sundays. She is a lovely young girl, Will. You are a lucky chap.

Well, I won't go on, but we have sent you a few things that we hope you like. Write to us, son, and let us know if you need anything in particular and we will do our best to send it to you quickly. Keel smiling, Will. You will be home with us all again soon.

Love,
Mum and Dad xx

CHAPTER THIRTEEN

It felt strange leaving the confines of the medical tent. The camp had changed quite a bit over the ten days that Will had been there. The day after he had arrived, he had been 'processed', though he couldn't remember much about it, giving his name, rank and number to a German official, with a British officer also taking notes as he lay there. The camp now seemed much larger than he had remembered and with a lot more prisoners around with German prison guards marched amongst them, bayonets at the ready.

"Keep out of the way of the guards, Will," Terry said, pointing to a thin line of dried blood that ran in a straight line from beside his eye down to his chin. "They are a grumpy lot and will lash out with the old bayonet if you get in their way. Twice a day, they make us assemble just to bloody count us and make sure no one's popped out for some shopping. It's ridiculous."

Will wasn't feeling too good. His legs felt like lead and his head was thumping like a hammer was hitting it and he felt quite dizzy. "Sorry, lads, but I need to sit down for a minute," he said as he tottered forwards. Terry and William each grabbed one of Will's arms and they sat him down on the ground outside the food tent, standing either side of him. They hadn't been there thirty seconds when loud whistles rang out from around them. "Oh, bloody hell, we've to go and assemble again," William said sounding totally fed up. As he spoke, four German guards came marching through at double pace. They stopped to shout abuse at the three men, "Schnell, Schnell," the first man shouted at them through gritted teeth.

"Hang on, mate. We're coming," William said, "but he ain't very well." The guard didn't understand a word of what William said and swung his rifle butt at Will's head as he sat there. The heavy end of the rifle connected with the side of Will's head with a solid thud, sending him sprawling to the ground. Instinctively and without thinking, William swung out at the soldier, his fist catching him just beneath the chin. For a few minutes, there was complete mayhem. The three other soldiers all turned on William, reigning in blow after blow with their rifle butts, sending him crashing to the ground. The blows continued, and now the soldier who he had punched joined in, kicking William several times in the head and body. Whistles blew out and more guards appeared. There was a lot of angry shouting and William's motionless body was dragged off to the cells. Terry helped Will to his feet and they were pushed and shoved heavily by the guards to join the main crowd that was assembling in the main square. "Shit. William's in trouble now," Terry said. A replay of what had just happened was running slowly through Will's foggy mind. It had all happened so quickly that he found it difficult to recall, especially with his head thumping so much, but Will knew that he felt responsible for what had happened. "I'm sorry, Terry. It's my fault. If I hadn't been feeling so bloody rough, none of this would have happened."

"It's not your fault, mate," Terry said, trying to comfort him. "William should never have lashed out. He's been getting increasingly fed up with being cooped up here these last days and I had a horrible feeling he might do something stupid like this before long. He was lucky they didn't have bayonets fixed or I reckon they would have done for him."

The photograph (right) that first informed Thomas and Harriet that Will, their son, was not dead as they had feared. The Germans photographed every prisoner and turned the photos into postcards for each man to send home and inform their family of their whereabouts. Note the distant look in Will's eyes on the left photo and the uniform he was sent into the trenches with. In Will's group are Russians, French and British soldiers.

That night, they lay on the ground inside their tent and Will wished he was back in the hospital tent. His one blanket would not cover him whichever way he tried, and he lay there freezing, his feet numb with pain and cold until sleep eventually overtook him. In the night, he was roused by Terry to break him out of a nightmare. "Will, Will, your shoutin' out, mate. Keep it down, eh?"

The following morning, they were assembled early and the German commandant marched angrily before them with soldiers either side of him. He called the prisoners to attention, speaking in fairly good English, ladled with a heavy Prussian accent. "Yesterday, a German soldier was struck by a prisoner. This is a very serious offence and a court has found Private William Lonsdale guilty, to which the sentence is death. Wood and materials will be brought, and you men are to construct gallows here in the square, where the sentence of hanging will be carried out when this is finished."

There was a gasp and cries of protest by the prisoners and the line of German soldiers who had quietly made their way around three sides of the ranks of prisoners and raised their rifles, threatening to fire. The noise subsided.

Colonel Russell, who had been standing in the centre of the front row, took three paces forwards towards the commandant, stopped and saluted and then requested an immediate meeting with him. The commandant nodded and the assembly was dismissed, with Russell and two other officers following the group of senior Germans away to their office. Will followed them and waited outside anxiously with Terry until the Colonel reappeared. They saluted him and Will blurted out urgently, "Begging your pardon, sir, but have you been able to talk them out of it?"

"Who are you?" Russell asked sternly in return, adjusting his cuffs as he looked into Will's twitching face.

"Able Seaman Payne, sir. I was with William. Sorry. Private Lonsdale when it all happened, sir. It's my fault."

"Let's not talk here, shall we?" Colonel Russell said calmly, walking so briskly away that Will had a problem keeping up with him as he hobbled after him, with Terry helping. When they were a safe distance away, the Colonel turned and, seeing Will struggling to follow, beckoned him to a bench. They sat together and the Colonel started. "Right, Able Seaman, I have pointed out to the German commander that under the Geneva Convention of war, that the execution of an untried prisoner is not allowed. He however begs to differ, so I have requested time to write to senior authorities in England and suggested that he do the same. I have pointed out that Britain and our allies have a considerable number of German soldiers as prisoners of war, and that any action taken here will create a precedence that will apply to both sides. That, I think, has made him think a little. He is insisting that we still continue to build gallows, but I believe that he will now seek a decision from a higher authority. It has finally occurred to the commander that he might set something off here that has repercussions on

German POWs in France and Belgium. So that's where we are. I have requested to see Private Lonsdale to confirm his current treatment but that has been refused. He is apparently being held in solitary confinement, so there's little I can do about it I'm afraid."

He stood up to face the two men. "Now, I have a letter to write. Dismissed you two, and oh, if I do hear anything then I will ensure you are informed. I guess you're not going anywhere," he said sarcastically, trying to lift the situation. The thoughts of a letter and home struck deep into Will's heart, but with no paper to write on, he was stuck, increasing his feeling of despair.

The days and nights passed slowly. Under their captive's instruction, the prisoners were set to work, making gallows from wood and a limited number of tools that was brought in. Never has a job been completed so slowly, as they mysteriously encountered problems at every stage. The Germans saw through what was happening within two days though, and brought in a builder from the local village to supervise the gallows construction, so afterwards if a piece of wood was cut too short, the man with the saw was beaten by the guards. It made it more difficult to slow construction up and within two weeks, the gallows were finished, minus a rope. The following day, a rope was brought in by a German soldier who took pleasure in tying it firmly to the jib. It was a horrific thing to behold, with its noose awaiting a man's neck to fulfil its function. Every morning when they walked in the camp, the gallows stood there casting a physical and physiological shadow over the British side of the camp. Word had got about the rest of the camp and French and Russian prisoners wandered over in small groups, shaking their heads and muttering as they looked at the stark short piece of rope with its menacing noose hanging beneath it, gently swinging as any breeze caught it.

The gallows cast a shadow over the mood of the entire camp. If it was not enough that their own personal war had been lost with their capture, the gallows served to confirm the desolation of their situation. Will felt it in particular, as a dark depression hung over him. As every new piece of wood was nailed into place, his feeling of guilt increased. He and Terry had asked the Germans if they could go and see William and had been refused numerous times, the last time being forcibly sent packing with the flat edge of the bayonet being thrust at them. Adding to this, the biting cold and wind cut through them day and night. Will had forgotten the last time that he could feel his toes and he hobbled about now, like a cripple waiting to fall. Terry had found him a rough piece of a tree branch outside one of the barns and had one of the men making the gallows cut the end off to fashion it into a rough crutch, which Will clung onto as he hobbled about.

Hunger was a nagging constant in his day. It gnawed at Will every waking minute as it did to everyone else and standing alone or in groups, one was never in silence as their stomachs constantly shouted loudly at them.

When the time came, they queued enthusiastically for soup and bread twice a day, only for disappointment to arrive with each bowl. When asked what was in the soup, the British cook looked glumly back at them. "Lads, before I joined up, I was a junior chef at several big London hotels. I can cook. I could make you a meal you would remember for years, but I ain't got no ingredients. I'll tell you what's in this soup. Every morning I goes to the German kitchens and they give me a big pot of peelings. Potato-peeling, swede, mangle wurzals. That's it. When I asked for salt and pepper or anything else, they laugh at me. I does me best, lads. I scour the edges of the camp for anything that might look like a herb but there ain't nothing growing other than tufts of grass. That's the green bits by the way."

"And what's in the bread?" somebody asked.

"The bread? The bread, mate, is made outside and has got some wheat flour in it somewhere, but take a closer look and you'll see that they add sawdust to it to bulk it out. Nothing gets wasted; I can tell you. I'm doing my best."

CHAPTER FOURTEEN

Tom and Harriet's mood had lifted considerably since the postcard had arrived. The photograph had confirmed that Will was alive and safe; and even the Germans wouldn't dare hurt prisoners in captivity. So Will was safe until the war was over, then he would come home; Harriet continually told herself. They both had a renewed spring in their step and Alfred asked Tom if he realised that he was whistling at his work bench.

Tom had read in the Western Daily Press that the British Red Cross were starting to organise relief parcels to send to POWs. It seemed that there were two types of aid boxes that could be sent, one of food and the other of non-food items. Thinking that food would not be a priority, they set about making a parcel up of different things and included some writing paper and a pencil amongst several pairs of socks and a cardigan, following the advice of the Red Cross. They also added a pack of playing cards, sixty Woodbine cigarettes and two boxes of *Swan Vesta* matches.

"It feels like Christmas," Harriet said to Tom as they carefully packed up the box for Will.

"Well, by the time he receives this, it will damn near be Christmas," Tom replied. That thought plunged them both into silence as they continued to pack in a growing mood of sadness.

"Will's never been away at Christmas before," Harriet said softly.

"I know. We should put something a little special inside for him; cheer the boy up. I'll pop out tomorrow and buy a couple of cigars for him and you can send those handkerchiefs you've been embroidering and we'll pop a few boiled sweets inside the socks as a surprise for him."

The following day, Tom cycled down to the Red Cross Office with the box strapped to the handlebars. As he handed it over, he wished that he could be taking it himself just to see his son again and make sure that he was alright. It was a daft thought he knew. He had at least enclosed some writing paper so hoped that he would hear from him soon. And inside the box, laid out right on the top were two letters, one from him and Harriet and one from Annie. They had both had to write as instructed, and left their letters inside unsealed envelopes for the sensors to read.

Dear Will,

Your mother and I are sat at the old kitchen table drinking a cup of tea and thinking of you son, as we do so many times during each day. All is well here at home and your mother and I are both well, though your Uncle Alfred has had a bit of a cold.

Annie has been telling us that more of your old pals from Mardons have been joining up and that they are now nearly always replaced by women, so that will be interesting. Annie tells us that they are more than capable of keeping your job safe until you return.

I have made the vegetable patch in the back garden larger now and replaced the flowers with things that taste much nicer. You can't beat fresh veg, as you know. The shop is ticking over nicely, so we have no complaints there.

Well, keep smiling, son, and keep your chin up. You will be home with us all again soon; I am sure, and we look forward to that day with all our hearts.

Your ever loving,
Mum and Dad xx

My Dearest Will,

We have been so worried about you and it was such a relief to see your face on the postcard that you sent. It can't be very nice being a prisoner, I know, but at least you are safe and away from the awful fighting, which is a comfort to us all at home waiting for you.

My mother and father send their best, as does everyone at work. We have more girls working at Mardons now than ever before, as more men leave every week to join up. I am one of the old hands now it seems, even though I have not been there that long myself.

I miss you. Can you send me another photograph? Your mum and dad have the one that you sent them on the mantelpiece but I don't like to stare at it while they are with me. Take care, Will. This war will be over soon; I am sure, and you will be home again. I miss you.

Love,
Annie X

The first parcels to arrive at the camp caused a great stir amongst the prisoners and a huge boost to moral as some proper food started to arrive. Will and Terry shared their tent with Alfred who had been a plumber's mate in Southsea before the war and Harold, who had been a clerk in the docks in Plymouth before signing up. The space where the other William had stayed before he had hit the guard was not as yet taken by another inmate and the three men slept closely to conserve heat during the bitter nights.

It was Harold who received the first parcel. A lorry arrived at the camp one morning and the shout went up that it was full of parcels from home. There was a sudden rush as men ran to the camp administration block to see whose name would be called out. The waiting was intense but soon, excited men were walking away with their parcels like they were holding the crown jewels. The disappointment was enormous for the rest of the men when they knew that nothing had come for them, and Will, Alfred and Terry trooped back to their tent with Harold holding onto his box like his life depended on it. They sat around inside the tent trying to keep warm as Harold carefully opened the parcel for them all to see. There was a letter from home which he carefully removed and tucked inside his top pocket and underneath, there were tins of food inside, all carefully packed without a space. He removed the tins almost ceremoniously, reading the label out loud on each item and placing it on the ground in the middle of them as they sat cross-legged in a circle. "Right, lads. Whatever I've got, I'll share with you, okay? And if we all do the same, then we'll all get by together, just like we did in the trenches. Agreed?"

After weeks and weeks of dreadful soup and half stale bread, the sight of tins of 'Bully Beef' and tinned biscuits and tea from home almost brought a tear to Will's eyes.

"Gentlemen, who would like a biscuit?" Harold asked, offering the opened tin to the eager gathering like they were having afternoon tea in Carwardine's Tea Shop back in Blighty. Will never forgot the taste of that very first biscuit. They didn't eat a lot of biscuits at home and when they did, it wasn't anything really special as such, but now he nibbled at its edge for a moment before shoving half of it into his mouth greedily, chomping joyously at it as he closed his eyes to savour the moment, focusing all his attention on its wonderful, wonderful taste. As he crunched the biscuit inside his mouth, he waited for his saliva to catch up with the dry crumbling mouthful, and then its sweetness suddenly exploded on his taste buds. Heaven!

The following hour was a controlled feeding frenzy where the contents of each tin were carefully measured out and cut into exactly equal pieces, all shared out to the hungry assembly. Only the tins of tea, cocoa and milk were left to be enjoyed afterwards and they thanked Harold and all shook his hand profusely. But within minutes, the hunger had resumed, gnawing at near-empty stomachs.

They came out of their tent feeling like naughty schoolboys just as Colonel Russell arrived. Will stood there propped on his staff and saluted the Colonel as best he could.

"At ease, men. I just thought you would like to know that I've just come from seeing the German Commandant who has finally allowed me to see William. In fact, it was the commandant who called for me. It looks like this business has caused quite a big stir at home and even the War Office and Prime Minister himself are involved. The treatment of prisoners is quite a touchy subject apparently, as there seems to be quite a number of us POWs, on both sides. I'm glad to say. The old Kaiser himself has ruled that he will commute William's death sentence to twenty years in prison, just to show the world how compassionate a man he is I suspect, the cunning old fox. So I have seen William and well, he's a bit down as one would expect and like all of us, he's not put on much weight since he arrived, but he is okay. He was pleased to see me for sure, with all that time in solitary confinement."

The relief on all the faces of the men was enormous, but on none more than Will. His legs and feet were killing him and he asked permission to sit down and he buried his face in his hands to hide the small tears that leeched from the far corners of his eyes at hearing the news. It was like the death sentence had also been lifted on him; such were his feelings of guilt still.

Food parcels from Blighty started to arrive once a week, and an hour before the lorry was due to arrive every Tuesday, men started to gather around the administration block in anticipation. It had taken a full six weeks for Tom and Harriet's parcel to arrive from Bristol, and Will could hardly believe it when he heard his name called out. He limped back to the tent with the other men in tow. Alfred, who everyone now called Alfie, also had a parcel, so the four of them sat inside their tent in great excitement at the anticipated feast to come. "Go on, Alfie. Open your parcel first, mate," Will suggested, happy to savour the anticipation of his parcel for a moment longer, as long as he could hold the box on his lap and not let go. Alfie carefully removed the string and opened the sides slowly, but instead of food, a knitted cardigan stared back at him. He rummaged through the box and the excitement grew as he pulled out a small bar of soap and some *Gillette* razor blades. "Gawd! Smell that, lads," he said, holding the soap to his nose. "I'd forgotten what soap smelled like." They each took it in turn to sniff the soap, all enjoying seeing a bar of soap for the first time since their arrival. "You know, I'm going to brave it tomorrow and break the ice on the water butt and have a darn good wash with this soap," Alfie enthused.
"You'll need a hammer, Alf. It's been sub-zero since we got here and the ice will be a foot thick, mate. Go on, Will. Open your box," Terry urged.
Slowly, Will pulled at the string. His left hand still shook embarrassingly, so he wedged it against his leg and asked Terry to tackle the knot with him. But the men's faces were wracked with disappointment as more clothes and objects appeared. They had so been looking forward to something decent to eat. Will was still excited though, especially when he saw the two letters on top, which he carefully removed, tucking them in his tunic before pulling everything else carefully out. He felt bumps inside the socks and guessed what they were. "Hang on, lads. Here's something," he said, as he teased out ten mint humbugs. He handed one each around to the now eager ensemble and they stuffed them hungrily into their mouths, big grins appearing as they savoured their treat.

Will couldn't wait to read his two letters in peace when the lads had gone, and when he had, he read them over and over again, holding onto each word in his mind and feeling the paper between his fingers, relishing in the fact that it had come from home. He sniffed Annie's letter and detected the faintest smell of perfume impregnated on the paper, and he closed his eyes and slowly inhaled the aroma, capturing every thought of her that he could. He looked through the parcel again and found a pair of gloves, which he immediately put on. His fingers had been numb with the cold for so long that he had almost forgotten what being without pain felt like. He held the fresh, newly knitted socks to his nose, trying to remember the smell of home. He caught the essence of his mother's hands and closed his eyes, trying to flood his imagination with images of the old kitchen. The moment was lost when Terry came back in the tent and spoke, "You alright, Will? You look lost in thought there."

"I was just thinking of home, Terry. It's silly, I know, but something so simple as a new pair of socks can take me somewhere else for a moment. I best put them on though and give my old feet a treat. They've been paining me for so long now that perhaps a new pair of socks will do the trick. Give us a hand, would you, Terry? I don't think I can manage the laces, mate."

Will had never had an issue with his new boots being one size larger as his feet had soon swollen up to fill every space inside them. Terry helped him off with his boots but reeled back when Will peeled back each sock to reveal his swollen and blackened feet. Terry cupped his hand over his mouth so as not to gag. "Sweet Jeezus, Will, your feet are terrible, mate. We've got to get you to the medical tent straight away."

When the medical orderly peeled back Will's socks, he also reeled back at what he saw. He disappeared for a few moments before reappearing with an English army doctor. Will's feet had swollen horribly and his toes and heels were a deep purple colour with hues of green and yellow deeply etched into their disfigured mass. Some of the toenails were barely visible, being lost with the dark swelling and the stench from his feet was horrendous. The doctor prodded Will's toes with the end of his pencil before speaking to the orderly like Will wasn't there anymore. "Get this man's feet bathed in warm water and get him cleaned up as much as you can. I'll speak to the German doctor. This man needs a proper hospital and quickly. Both his feet have gangrene."

When the hot water hit Will's feet, the intensity of the pain was unlike anything that Will had ever experienced. It was like his feet had largely been asleep while they had been trapped inside his boots but suddenly, they had woken with a vengeance. He gripped the side of the stool and threw his head back in a muffled scream before passing out, slumping forwards and would have fallen from the stool, had he not been caught by Terry and the orderly. When he came too, he was being bounced along in the back of a medical wagon. A German orderly from Berlin Hospital sat next to him and motioned him to lie still. Will didn't mind doing that. He felt like his feet were exploding at the end of his legs, so he stared up at the ceiling of the ambulance, gritting his teeth against the pain and not daring to look at where his feet were hidden, tucked underneath the blanket. He drifted back into unconsciousness or sleep, he didn't know which, but wherever it was, it was the only place his mind could find to escape the pain.

At the hospital, Will vaguely remembered his clothes being removed and the nurses' look of distain as they dropped his jacket quickly to the floor 'lause' (lice). One of them uttered loudly. He thought he remembered being washed but everything seemed very fuzzy and far away. He heard voices from time to time, though even if they had been in English, he probably wouldn't have understood what they were saying as every word seemed to be reaching him through an oscillating echo chamber before it reached his ears. He wasn't even aware of the chloroform mask as they placed it over his mouth and sent him somewhere where all hearing and senses faded away to nothing.

When Will came to, it took him ages to gradually work out where he was and even longer to work out who he was. The chloroform hung heavy in the corridors of his mind but slowly, he became conscious of lying between clean, freshly starched, white sheets and for the first time since arriving in Germany, he felt warm. The pain in his feet brought him all too acutely back to life and he raised his head off the pillow slightly to look down at his feet, but they were hidden under a frame beneath the white sheet. He moved his feet but nothing happened to the sheet. He had a hammer inside his head and it was swinging violently and he began to sweat as he slipped into delirium again, as his mind escaped the intensity of the pain in the only way that it could.

When the fever broke, eventually almost a week had passed. He became conscious of being enormously thirsty and every part of his body seemed to hurt. His head still thumped like someone was beating it with a lump hammer and the pain from his feet and legs screamed at him again.

"Good, you are awake," a voice said with a heavy German accent. The voice came from a white-coated doctor who took Will's wrist and then stared at his watch.

"Where am I?" Will asked so quietly that the man leaned forwards to catch the last words.

"You are in Berlin General Hospital. My name is Doctor Schultz and you, sir, are a very lucky man. Just tell your family when you get home that we Germans saved your life, yes."

"Can I go home then, sir?" Will's hopes suddenly soaring in his tiredness.

"Nein, nein. I don't think so, but one day, this war will be over and you will go home then for sure. For now, you must rest up and we must get you well again. You will be here for a while as we continue to treat your feet." Doctor Schultz hesitated for a moment and suddenly spoke softly to Will, "You should know now that we have had to amputate some of your toes. Five in fact, two from your left foot and three from the right. It was the only way to stop the gangrene spreading. But the good news is that I was able to save your big toes, and they take most of the weight, so you will still be able to walk in the future. But it will be some time yet before you will be walking properly and you need complete rest while your feet recover."

The news of losing his toes didn't seem to register with Will as much as the pain did. "Do you have anything for the pain, please? My head and feet are hurting something terrible," Will said before remembering his manners. "But thank you for what you are doing," he said, offering his hand limply to the doctor, who shook it slightly embarrassed.

"Nein, Nein. It is my job and I am sure your British surgeons are doing the same for our brave soldiers. We have very little medicines but I will see what I can find. Rest up please, and I will be back to see you later."

Will was in a small room with a huge window looking out across the roofs of several buildings. The nurses attending Will didn't speak any English at all and although they did their jobs and looked after him, he could feel that being English, he was not the most popular patient in the hospital, especially at night when his nightmares woke him shouting and bathed in sweat. His bad dreams had not eased, and night by night, he relived the same moments of horror, though he could not retain the memory or images. When he woke, any memories of his nightmares were vague, but what was there, he wanted to run away from quickly. He just wanted to stay awake now to escape the horror of whatever it was that was haunting him. It got to a point that he dreaded sleeping, knowing that his nightmares stalked the darkness waiting for him. He would lie there fighting sleep for as long as he could before exhaustion took over. The nurses on the night shift were quite severe towards Will, even before his bad dreams had them running to his little room to stop his shouting. And when they shook him awake, they were almost brutal with him, shaking him to the point of bruising his arm.

Doctor Schultz came to see Will most days, and he looked forward to the doctor's arrival just to be able to speak a few words of English with him. Schultz was a kind man, though his demeanour changed when there were nurses present, becoming more business-like towards Will. A week later, the doctor slipped quietly into Will's room and spoke quickly to him. "William, I have been speaking about you with my wife. We have a son. He's a little older than you and he is in France, somewhere with the army." He slipped a small piece of paper towards Will. "Write down your parents' address in England quickly and I will contact them for you. As a parent, I know they will be worried about you. When did you last write to them?"

"I have not been able to write to them since I was captured, but the camp sent them a postcard, I think, with my photograph on."

Will wrote the address down, struggled to stop his hands from shaking, so wrote in block capitals with very shaky edges. The doctor quickly stuffed the paper inside his pocket.

"I will have to write the letter as if I am you, as I would get into trouble otherwise. You are the enemy we are told, and censors will read this letter before it leaves Germany and it would not do for a civilian German doctor to be writing on your behalf. My colleague visits the prison camp twice a week and he will give the letter to one of your officers. They will then send it on to England but this has to be secret, yes? Is there anything you want to say in the letter?"

Will was taken aback and felt very grateful to this man who was a total stranger. He had spent so many hours thinking of home, his mum, dad and Annie, and he could not thank the doctor enough. He thought about what to say and that he would no doubt be back in the prison camp soon. "Can you ask them to send food to the camp please?" Will asked quietly.

Over the next three weeks, Will started to regain his strength with rest and better food. Compared to the camp, the food in the hospital was excellent, although the first few days back on solid food upset his stomach and he had to ask for the bedpan with some urgency more times than suited the nurses, bringing scornful looks from one or two of them in particular. At the end of the third week, they removed the dressings on his feet for Will to see for the first time. He stared down at the scarred missing spaces between his toes. It seemed really strange seeing the gaps where his toes once were, and he realised how little notice he had actually taken of them before. Now, he would never see them again.

A few days later, he took his first steps with the aid of two crutches and a nurse on each arm and only then did he realise how weak his legs were. His knees buckled when he tried to unlock them to take a step and his balance was childlike. The shaking and twitching had become worse since he had arrived in the hospital. His arm was affected most, but his head twitched from time to time, jerking violently to the left. He felt silly not being able to take a few steps without toppling forwards or collapsing like an idiot where he stood, and he would need to be helped back into bed with growing frustration. Not wanting to be beaten, he would wait until the nurses had gone and try again, gripping the side of the bed with his good hand as he tried to get one foot in front of the other. In spite of falling painfully so many times, he slowly began to regain his balance, though the process was exhausting and he would literally fall back into the bed after each attempt. Eventually after days of trying, by using both walking sticks, he was able to get to the window and back to the bed. Triumph.

CHAPTER FIFTEEN

So many weeks were passing without word from their William that Harriet and Tom were getting concerned. It was over two months since they had sent writing paper in the parcel and they were beginning to wonder if their parcel had reached him. When Harriet arrived home after work one day to see an envelope with a 'Doberitz' postmark on the mat, she could not wait for Tom to come home from work to read it to her. Tom looked at the envelope. "It's not Will's handwriting," he said slightly confused, before tearing it open. As he read the letter aloud, he became more confused.

Dear Mama and Papa,

I am writing to tell you that I am well. I have been in hospital here but have been looked after very well and will be back in the camp soon. Please do not worry about me. I have needed an operation on my feet but am recovering and will be well soon.

Can you send some food to the camp please? I will write to you again soon and hope to throw more light on things.

Your son,
William

As Tom read each word out slowly, their confusion grew. "Will didn't write this. He has never called us 'Mama' and 'Papa' and this isn't the writing paper that we sent him. Something's not right."

Harriet went to the postcard on the mantelpiece and brought it down, scanning the picture of Will under the magnifying glass that they kept in the kitchen drawer. "The letter said that he's had an operation on his feet, but his feet look alright here, Tom."

Tom took the magnifying glass and studied the photograph again. "Yes. Yes, they do, but he's not wearing the boots I made for him though. I know my own work when I see it. And look. Look at Will's expression," he said, passing the postcard back to Harriet. "Look at his eyes, Harriet. He looks distant. That's not our Will. There's something wrong."

Tom picked up the letter and studied it again. He read it over and over again, pondering every word. "I don't understand this last bit, where he says, I will write again and hope to throw more light on things. Will doesn't talk like that. Someone else was writing this."

Tom stared at the letter again. It had been written in ink and the spacing between the lines wasn't even, so the letter went onto a second page, though the only part written on the last page were the words 'hope to throw more light on things. Your son, William'. Tom read it again, and then for some reason that he didn't know why, he held the past page up to the light. He could see something. Something pressed into the blank space underneath 'Your son, William'. He moved the paper backwards and forwards to catch the light. Yes, there was something, some words pressed into the paper. He laid the page out on the kitchen table and took a soft pencil out from the drawer. Very gently, he lightly brushed the exposed carbon end of the pencil back and forth across the empty page. The letter 'H' appeared, and then a word, 'Herr'. He pressed on, gently exposing the indentations in the paper and as if by magic, more words appeared. It took all his concentration as he had to press lightly, but within a few minutes, very neatly spaced lines of words had appeared in the blank space.

"Herr Payne, I hope you find this. William is my patient. He has suffered frostbite but is recovering well and will live. He has also some neurological issues from the war and I have asked he be repatriated, but this is not likely. He will recover in time. I am sure. He is in good hands. We Germans are not all bad. Please do not worry."

"Bloody hell, don't worry, don't worry!" Tom said, pushing back his chair and stomping across the kitchen like he wanted to run. He grabbed his pipe and went into the cold night of the back garden, not even stopping to grab a coat. Harriet sat down at the table, trying to take it all in. The cold evening air clung to Tom and a shiver went through him. His face lit up as he struck a match and held it to the pipe, sucking life into its tiny furnace. He had to think.

When the weekend doctor told Will that he was being discharged back to the prison camp, it had come as a shock to him. He knew that he was starting to walk now, but he hadn't seen himself being released so soon. This other doctor was clearly not happy with treating British soldiers and his broken English sounded hard and uncaring. "Dr Schultz is not here," was all he said to Will's question, and within the hour, Will was being taken back to the camp with a German soldier for company. They did let him keep his walking sticks though and he waddled back through the British sector of the camp in abject depression at being back. His left hand shook violently, exaggerating his shaking through the walking stick as he thrust it quickly to the ground with each step. As he walked back through the camp, he noticed that so much had changed. Some new wooden buildings had appeared and another one was still being built, but most of the men were nowhere to be seen. The first person that he recognised was Colonel Russell, who came striding up to Will, wearing a large smile under his huge moustache. "Payne, how are you? I'd heard that you were sent out to the hospital. How are the feet?"

"Fine, sir. Well, what's left of them? Where is everyone, sir?"

"Ah, yes, yes. Lots of changes here I am afraid. Most of the men have been sent into working parties. Look, come and sit down. You look done in." They went into one of the new wooden buildings where the floor was raised off the ground and there were rows of rough beds down both sides, tightly packed against the walls. In the centre was a small wood burning stove and they sat in front of it, soaking in its warmth for a moment. "Special treat, Payne. Would you like a cup of tea?" the colonel beamed triumphantly.

"Tea? Yes please, sir. I can't remember the last time I had a cup of tea. All I had in the hospital was water or the occasional cup of foul-tasting coffee. I'd love a cup of tea, sir. Thank you."

"Potter, two cups of tea, on the double." The Colonel's batman appeared and saluted, placing a metal jug of water on top of the stove to heat up.

"Yes, lots of change here, Payne. Lots of change. We had a visit from a Danish delegation of the Red Cross. Good chaps. Spoke excellent English and damn civilised they were too. Had tea with them and the German Commandant who had to behave himself in front of them for a change, and no sooner as they had gone, the Bosch brought in wood and materials for us to make our own huts and get us out of those damned awful tents. It was good timing actually. Got our chaps doing something positive and gave us chance to get a roof over the men's heads pronto. They're still building them as you probably saw, but I think we can get you out of that old tent of yours tonight Payne."

Potter brought in the tea. It even had milk in it and Will took the mug with his good hand and stared down into it like seeing an old friend again after a long absence. It had been months and he savoured the first mouthful, timing the sip between bouts of head-twitching.

"Still got that damned twitch I see, Payne. You'd better get on top of that one man. We've got to get you up and about pronto. You'll see things have got a little better since you've been in hospital. Not a lot better and the food is still that awful watery soup and sawdust bread that they dish out, but we survive on the food parcels that come from home and the Red Cross. Also, most of the men do some work for the Germans now and get some small payment. Nothing to help the Boshe's war effort, mind you. No, we wouldn't allow that, but they go out on working parties every day, some down the salt mine here and some working the fields or in the local factories. Get paid in camp money, so they can exchange it here for cigarettes and bits and bobs."

Will was enjoying his tea. "Will I be able to work, sir?" he asked.

"Not much chance of that at the moment, Payne. I think you need to get yourself fitter before Gerry will give you a job, but stick at it and I'm sure you'll be running around before too long. Meanwhile, there are always officers here and I am sure we can find things for you to do. As you've probably noticed, our numbers seem to be continually growing here, so we've got to get ourselves organised. The Bosch don't dare ask us officers to work, so most of us oversee the jobs going on here.

"Did you notice that that damn scaffolds been removed? Word came through just a couple of weeks ago that after the old Kaiser had commuted Lonsdale's death sentence down to twenty years, then gave him a full pardon just a week ago. The old commandant wasn't too happy about that, I can tell you, but international pressure, it seems, can come in useful sometimes. You'll see private Lonsdale later, no doubt. He's off somewhere with one of the working parties."

Will's heart soared. He had blamed himself ever since that day months ago and now William was a free man. He couldn't wait to see him again. His tea over, the old colonel suddenly got up like he had somewhere important to go and politely dismissed Will, sending Potter with him to sort out his billet.

CHAPTER SIXTEEN

Ten days had passed since Tom and Harriet had received the strange letter from the German doctor. Since then, they had both gone about their lives in a sombre mood. Tom shared his thoughts with his brother and showed him the letter. Every time Tom reread it, he didn't understand it any better or worry less. The news from the front wasn't as positive as it had been when the war had started either. As Tom predicted, the war was settling down to being far from a quick affair and in December, the Germans had made a statement of intent that they would not give up easily, their battleships slipping up the east coast and shelling Hartlepool, killing 152 civilians with more than 500 injured. The mood of the country was outraged, it being the first attack on British soil since 1066. Conscription had now been brought in and men between the ages of nineteen and forty-one waited for their letter.

Tom and Harriet had been to church as they always did on Sunday morning and had come back for lunch. Harriet busied herself making sandwiches and Tom sat there waiting his moment.

"I have to go, my love," he said, taking out his pipe and placing it in the corner of his mouth, unlit.

"Go where?" Harriet asked, thinking he was about to pop out.

"I am going to enlist. I can't sit here with our son imprisoned somewhere in Germany and especially with him being injured and all. We need to get the lad home, and me sitting on my backside isn't any good. I have to do something. I'm restless."

"Don't be silly, Tom. You're too old for a start. You're forty-three and the limit is forty-one and besides, didn't you promise Will you wouldn't get involved?"

"I did, but things have changed. We will only get our son home when this war is over, my sweet. Now you know that I don't believe in this war and I don't want to kill anyone, but what I believe in doesn't change the facts and me sitting here isn't going to get our son home. I feel impotent. I've got to do something."

"You are too old, Tom. They won't want you."

Tom tapped his fingers on the kitchen table, "Well, our son lied about his age to get in, and I can do the same. I am sorry, Harriet, but I have to go.

I won't feel like a real man if I just sit here and hope that Will might walk in through the door one day."

Harriet had stopped buttering the bread. She knew her husband better than anyone and knew that his often quiet and calm demeanour was not to be mistaken for weakness. He would never be dissuaded on anything once he was sure and had made up his mind. "But what about the shop?" she asked quietly. "Alfred can't make everything we sell by himself."

"It's not a problem. I talked it through yesterday with Alfred and we're going to take on an apprentice. In fact you know him, young Anthony, Sidney's son at the coal merchants. Sid mentioned it a few weeks ago that the lad is coming up to school leaving age and he's not big built, so he couldn't see him lumping great sacks of coal about, so he was looking to get another trade. Anthony helps me with the horses when he's not at school, so I know he's a good lad and he's keen to learn new things. He'll do us fine and it'll give him a trade and keep the shop running. Alfred and Anthony can run the workshop and you can continue to run the shop front, my love, as you always do, and before you know it, I'll be home with our Will, and we'll be all back to normal."

The army recruitment sergeant took a long look at Tom sitting there before him. Tom's wisps of grey hair and the bushy moustache added to the lines on his face, suggesting that he had seen a few winters come and go. "Do you mind me asking your age, sir?" he asked politely. "Only most of the volunteers we see coming through the door are well, somewhat younger shall we say."

"Forty-one, sir, and fit and strong," Tom barked, straightening his back and lifting his chin up as he spoke.

The sergeant leaned back in his chair. He was well past fighting age himself and had a face that had seen a few battles before the desk had finally won. "Thomas, every now and again, I see someone like you walk in through that door. Usually old soldiers thinking they are as young as they once were, all well-meaning, all wanting to do their bit. But we have to be sensible about this. War is most definitely a young man's game and we can't have shall we say, more mature men holding things up cos they're out of breath. Do you understand?"

Tom decided to level with him. "I am younger than I look, sir, and I am fit and strong. There must be something I can do. I am not looking for a fight. I'm not out to kill anybody, but I want to help and I want to be near to the front when we do drive the Germans back."

The old sergeant looked quizzical and took a deep breath, "And why's that then? You don't come across as the big hero type. There's something else going on here. I can feel it."

Tom decided to level with him further. "My son, sir. My son is a prisoner in Germany. I want this war over and to get him back, and me staying here isn't going to help it end. Give me a job, sir. There must be something I can do."

The sergeant leaned forwards and grabbed Tom's hand by the wrist, turning it palm up to see the calluses and lines made from hours of hammering in nails and pulling at leather.

"Pioneer Corp, Payne. The army needs strong and experienced men to make roads, build bridges and dig trenches. What do you do for a living?"

Without thinking and wishing to back up his claims, he blurted out, "Coal merchant, sir." He would work through the story with Sid when he saw him later, just in case the army came checking.

After filling in forms and completing the formalities, the sergeant showed Tom to the door. He stopped to shake Tom's hand. "Good luck getting your son back."

CHAPTER SEVENTEEN

Will limped alongside the Colonel's batman across the camp. "You've got some good Pals," Potter said. "I remember they made quite a fuss to get you billeted with them when their barracks were built. It wasn't easy to keep the space for you when there were so many men waiting in tents to be housed, but they insisted on it. We have to pass the administration office on the way to your billet; do you want me to see if you've had any mail while you were away?"

Will's heart soared when Potter came back with two parcels, one stacked on top of the other. "Who's a lucky boy then?" Potter joked.

Wills new billet was Spartan, to say the least. It had been built with the minimum of materials but like the officer's room, it did have a small wood-fired burner in the middle of the room. Low wooden beds had been made from what looked like old packing boxes that were tightly packed down both sides of the room and each one had a blanket laid out on it, except for one which was Will's.

"I think you'll find that the other men have been taking it in turns to borrow your blanket while you were away, but I'm sure they'll let you have it back," Potter said before shaking his hand and departing.

Will swung himself around on his sticks and sat on his bed, looking at the two boxes. He recognised his dad's and Annie's handwriting. He decided to open Annie's parcel first, but his left side was shaking so much that he struggled with the knots. Without a knife, he couldn't open it and the frustration became too much for him after ten minutes of fighting with the string and he slumped down on the bed, the tears rolling down his cheeks in a silent flood. "This bloody war," he called out alone in his solitude. "This fucking bloody war."

When the first working parties came back, it was dark in the billet and they found Will laid back on the plain wooden slats of his bed, asleep. Exhaustion had eventually overtaken him and the two parcels remained unopened by his side. Terry was the first to see Will laid there and gave out a roar of surprise, the hurricane lamp swinging wildly in his hand. He dropped his coat on the floor and rushed over to Will as he woke with the noise. Will looked up to see his old buddy grinning at him and beside himself with joy, and Alfred, Harold and William gathering behind. The reunion was complete. Will hardly got a word in over the next half an hour as they all excitedly gave him their individual and collective news. He sat there nodding at his friends with a faint smile across his face, but was conscious that an occasional tear was finding its way to the corner of his eyes. He tried to ignore them but had to discreetly wipe them away from time to time with the back of his hand. The men pretended not to be aware of it. Seeing William again was wonderful. Will got himself up onto his feet with the aid of one of his walking sticks and thrust his hand out as William came forward grinning at him.

"I'm sorry, William, for the shit I got you into. I really am."

"Sorry for what? It weren't your fault, mate. I were a bit hasty with the old right hook shall we say, but that's all behind us now. We've all got ourselves top jobs down the salt mine. It's lovely, they bring us tea and cakes at eleven in the morning and there's an hour off for lunch and proper coffee in the afternoon, all served on their finest bone china."

They all laughed, but once the joy of seeing them had subsided, Will could see how exhausted and grimy they all looked.

"Hey, who's been getting parcels?" Terry quipped, prodding one of the boxes with his finger. "Every time we get a parcel, it's like our birthday, mate. Come on, open them up then. You've been away so long. You've got two you lucky sod."

The five of them sat on the edge of Will's bed and Terry did the honours untying the knots, pushing the first box back to Will to unfold the cardboard lid. 'Annie's box first.' Will tucked the envelope quickly inside his jacket to the banter of the other lads. "Hey, hey, who's got a love letter then?" they joked, but the banter stopped the moment Will took out a bar of *Fry's* chocolate. They sat around the box like excited little boys around a Christmas tree as Will carefully took out each item. Three cartons of Woodbines, two bars of milk chocolate, two boxes of matches, a pair of hand-knitted gloves and a round tin. Will opened the lid to reveal a *Victoria* sponge that was a shade slightly darker green than the grass outside the prison camp. They removed it and carefully broke it apart to see if there was any tiny part of it that was edible. Sadly, there wasn't. It had been awaiting Will's return too long. To compensate, Will handed one of the chocolate bars to Terry to divide up amongst the hungry gathering. They groaned in turn as they worked the chocolate in their mouths. "I'm not going to swallow it," Alfie quipped, grinning with pleasure. "I'm going to keep it in my mouth for as long as I possibly can." He talked through a lump of milk chocolate, making the others chuckle as they took on the challenge of seeing who could keep the melted chocolate in their mouths the longest without swallowing it.

Both parcels had been sent long before Dr Schultz's letter had arrived back in Bristol but by luck, the second parcel from mum and dad was full of tins of food taken from the suggested list of the Red Cross. Tins of Bully Beef, biscuits and now mouldy cheese were removed to the delight of the waiting men. Split between them, it would not make a meal, but it would sustain their spirit as much as anything. The Germans had got even stingier with their daily bread ration, and now every man in the camp was reliant on their food parcels to avoid starvation.

Will realised, as he fell back onto the bed, how spoilt he had been in the hospital. The crisply starched white linen sheets and mattress were replaced by one rough-haired blanket, and the wooden boards beneath him pressed into his hip and back whichever way he laid.

He had read and re-read his two letters over and over again, holding onto every word from home as he digested their news, so desperately missing the normality each word suggested. Oh, how he missed home. He knew that he needed to write home tomorrow. His mum and dad had sent more writing paper and another pencil, and he would have to face up to writing back to them in the morning.

"Quiet, Will. You're waking the entire camp, mate." Terry was shaking him awake. Will was running in sweat and his last image had been that of an ashen white face surrounded by darkness looming towards him. The mouth was wide open as were the dead eyes, staring at him underneath a great blotch of red congealed blood where the hairline and forehead should have been. The image disappeared in a flash as he woke. What was it? Who was it? He couldn't remember, and his head was pounding fit to explode. His throat was parched and he was vaguely awareness that he had been shouting.

"Sorry, Terry. Sorry, mate," he whispered, rolling onto his back and wiping tears of despair and sweat from his eyes in the near darkness. Sleep eventually took him away again but then the activity in the billet woke Will early. He had tried desperately to stay awake after the nightmare to avoid it returning to haunt him, but exhaustion had taken over not long before the other men woke up to go to work. All the men seemed to disappear very quickly and Will was suddenly alone in the hut feeling left out, exhausted and now depressed at his exclusion. He would write to mum, dad and Annie and get the letters done now, as he had not been looking forward to the task. He felt really low and alone in the world. As he sat down at the one table and laid the writing paper out, anxiety flooded through him, and his shaking seemed to increase in intensity. His left side jerked and jumped about as he exploded in a sweat, and he knew it was no good. He put the paper away underneath his bed in one of the boxes and laid down again to rest. He woke unexpectedly an hour later, shivering with the cold but knowing that he had to try writing again. As his pencil touched the paper, the emotion of his situation overtook him. He wanted to lie, wanted to hide his despair but found himself pouring out his heart as his tears fell. Even though he wedged his left side against the table as hard as possible, it still shook. He could not afford to waste one single sheet of paper and he realised that he would have to write in block capitals or they would simply not be able to read his scribble:

DEAR MUM AND DAD.

I AM SORRY. SORRY THAT I DIDN'T LISTEN TO YOU AND SORRY FOR SO MANY THINGS SINCE. I HAVE HAD A DREADFUL TIME OF THINGS SINCE I LEFT ENGLAND AND AM MISSING YOU AND HOME DREADFULLY. I AM SO SORRY TO BE THE CAUSE OF SO MUCH WORRY TO YOU.

I HAVE NOT BEEN WELL AND HAVE BEEN IN THE HOSPITAL WHERE FIVE OF MY TOES HAVE BEEN TAKEN AWAY. I AM CONSTANTLY IN PAIN AND MY HEAD HURTS SO BADLY THAT I CANNOT THINK STRAIGHT AT TIMES AND HAVE A LOT OF HEADACHES. SO I AM NOT HAVING THE BEST OF TIMES. I WISH THAT I HAD LISTENED TO YOU BOTH.

PLEASE SEND ME SOME FOOD IF YOU CAN. I DO HAVE SOME VERY GOOD FRIENDS HERE AND WE SHARE EVERYTHING. THEY HAVE LOOKED AFTER ME AND ARE A STRENGTH THAT I STRUGGLE TO FIND IN MYSELF SOME DAYS. I DO NOT KNOW WHAT I WOULD DO WITHOUT THEM.

I CANNOT WAIT TO BE HOME. I KNOW THAT IT WILL NOT BE EASY FOR YOU. BUT CAN YOU PLEASE SEND ME A BLANKET FROM MY BED? IT WILL BE LOVELY IF IT HAS THE SMELL OF HOME ON IT. SO ONE FROM MY OWN BED WOULD BE VERY NICE. I NEVER REALISED HOW MUCH I WOULD MISS MY OWN BED. AND CAN YOU SEND ME SOME WARM SOCKS PLEASE? FOR SOME REASON. THE TOES THAT WERE CUT OFF PAIN ME MORE THAN THE ONES THAT I HAVE. THAT IS DIFFICULT TO UNDERSTAND. I KNOW. I DON'T UNDERSTAND IT MYSELF.

I AM SORRY TO CAUSE YOU SUCH PAIN. BUT I WILL BE HOME ONE DAY. I PROMISE.

I LOVE YOU BOTH VERY MUCH.

WILLIAM XX

He folded the paper and placed it inside the envelope, addressing it to 25 Saxon Road. He didn't seal the envelope as he knew that one of the officers would have to read and censor the letter. He suddenly felt embarrassed at his words. *Fuck it, and fuck them.* They would have to read it. Will never normally swore, even to himself.

He took the next sheet of paper out to write to Annie. The girl he had not been going out with for that long and had only ever kissed once properly suddenly loomed so longingly in his mind that he felt a surge of love and emotion sweep over him. In truth, had he stayed at home and not been in a cold, lonely prison camp and not felt so desperate when he sat down to write.

Annie would probably have received a much more reserved letter. Instead, when she opened the letter at home back in Bristol, she blushed profusely. She had not realised that this man, who she had shyly grown so fond of and admired for going off to war, had felt the way that he now expressed:

MY DEAREST ANNIE.

I AM SORRY THAT MY WRITING IS SO BAD BUT I HAVE NOT BEEN WELL I AM AFRAID. I AM RECOVERYING NOW FROM AN OPERATION BUT THE THOUGHT OF COMING HOME ONE DAY AND SEEING YOU WILL MAKE ME FEEL BETTER. THANK YOU SO MUCH FOR YOUR PARCEL AND LETTER. IT WAS WONDERFUL AND THEY CHEERED ME UP VERY MUCH.

I DID NOT TELL YOU BEFORE I LEFT THAT I LOVE YOU. YOU ARE VERY SPECIAL TO ME AND I LONG TO COME HOME AND BE WITH YOU AGAIN. PLEASE SEND ME ANOTHER PHOTOGRAPH SO THAT I CAN HOLD YOU TO MY EYES AS WELL AS TO MY HEART.

IT MUST BE VERY DIFFICULT FOR YOU. I KNOW. AND I KNOW THAT THERE WILL BE OTHER MEN THAT WILL LOOK AT YOU WITH AMEROUS EYES. I CAN ONLY HOPE THAT YOU WILL WAIT FOR ME. I DID WONDER IF THE GERMANS MIGHT LET ME HOME WITH MY INJURIES BUT THAT DOES NOT LOOK LIKELY. I NOW JUST WANT THIS WAR TO BE OVER SO THAT I CAN BE WITH YOU AGAIN. I AM SORRY THAT I DID NOT TELL YOU THAT I LOVE YOU BEFORE I LEFT HOME BUT I DO WANT YOU TO KNOW THAT MY HEART I KEEP FOR YOU. IF YOU WANT IT.

ALL MY LOVE.
WILLIAM XX

Annie's blushing continued in the confines of her bedroom as she read the letter a second time. She finished reading and heard a noise on the stairs outside. She stood up briskly and hid the letter under some summer clothing at the back of the top shelf of her wardrobe. The word 'love' had never been suggested in any context before Will had left and now reading such unexpected emotion made her blush, like pulling back heavy curtains to be suddenly bathed in hot sunshine. She stared out of the window for a moment to distract her thoughts, but her hot flush continued and she sat down on her bed again, her mind reeling. His words frightened her a little, but they also excited her. Will was nice. She liked him a lot, but he had never shown such feelings towards her before he left and he always seemed, well, so reserved, a gentlemen. He must have been hiding his true feelings all along. She smiled at the thought.

When Tom opened Will's letter, the first thing that struck him was the handwriting. It was in uneven block capitals and almost childlike. It frightened him. It certainly wasn't Will's normal hand from his schooling, which was flowing, with the letters slightly leaning forwards. Tom read Will's letter aloud to Harriet. As he read, he could find no way to soften the despair so apparent in his son's words. Will was normally such a steady and happy lad who quietly got on with things and never really made a fuss or let his emotions show. He had long reached the age where Will would blush and disappear quickly if his mother ever gave him a quick kiss on the cheek, and amongst his friends at work, Will was known for his quick wit and humour. This letter just wasn't like the son they had nurtured from a baby, and his obvious despair cut Tom to the bone. It just wasn't like him.

Tom felt helpless as he read. He had heard nothing back from the army since he had enlisted and Will's letter only confirmed what the coded letter from the doctor had suggested, that Will had some 'other' problems. Tom had recently read an article in a newspaper written by a Welsh civilian doctor who was working in France, who wrote about a new phenomenon that they were seeing out in the trenches that the doctor had referred to as 'shell shock'. It had not been seen before in any war and the article was a plea from the doctor to the military and to the establishment in Britain that this was a genuine medical condition and not cowardice or malingering. It was an article that Tom read but did not share with Harriet, but after reading Will's letter, which was just so out of character, his mind wandered back to the doctor's article.

Harriet paced the kitchen as Tom read. "We have to get our boy back Tom," she said quickly as he finished. "There's something wrong. It's like someone else is writing to us. It's not like a letter from Will. I'm really worried.

"I know, my love, but let's stay calm for his sake and do what we can at this end," he paused for a minute, staring into the darkness outside the kitchen window. An age, that was only half a minute, seemed to pass before he spoke again. "Let's send a food parcel as he asks and I'll write to reassure Will that everything is well here and waiting just as it was for him to return to, just as it was. We need to do everything that we can to try and keep his spirits up. That's important I think. If things are not good with Will, then we need to give him something positive to hold on to, let him know that home is his rock and that he'll be coming back one day soon. Give him some hope to cling to and as much food as we can afford. We'll send them as often as we can and keep his hopes up in the only way that we can. Stay strong, my love. We need to stay strong for Will's sake."

The next day, they went to work and started making up a food parcel when, as with cruel timing that seemed designed to give the Devil a smile, they got home to find a brown envelope waiting on the mat for Tom, with instructions to go to Sutton Veny in Wiltshire to start his military training. Tom sat there reading his instructions. He needed to think.

CHAPTER EIGHTEEN

When Annie came over for Sunday lunch with Tom and Harriet, she was still flushed with the thought of Will's love letter that had made her realise how much she missed him. Annie had taken Sunday tea with Tom and Harriet a few times now, and she felt increasingly at ease with them. They finished their sandwiches together and were sipping tea in a moment of silence when Tom spoke, unveiling his plan.

"Annie, we all know that Will is not having a good time of it in captivity. In truth, he's having a tough time, and while he's locked away from us, we need to do what we can to keep his spirits up, let him know that all is good here and waiting for him when he gets back," he paused, composing his next words carefully.

"Now, Annie, I made a promise to Will before he left that I would always stay here and 'look after mother', as Will used to say, but things have changed. I've been called up and will have to leave soon for training but I don't want Will to know that. He's got enough on his mind and I don't want him worrying about me or anything going on here. He's got enough to think about. What he needs from us now is reassurance that his home is waiting for him and that everything is fine here. That's all he needs, along with the food parcels, that is. As you know, Annie, Harriet isn't good with writing, so William will be expecting letters from us to come from me, but I am not going to be here, so we will need to come up with another plan to keep Will reassured. Our letters need to be as normal as possible and tell him what's going on here and give him the local news, just as we would do normally. I think that it'll do him good to know what's going on here. Keep him focused on coming home.

"So here is my plan, and here's where you come in, Annie. I'm going to be training in England somewhere for probably six months and hopefully by that time, the war will be over. If you and Harriet can write to me and tell me what's going on here, I will rewrite your letters and post them back to you so that you can post the letter off to Will with the food parcels with a Bristol postmark. Hopefully, the war will be over soon and we'll both be home before we know it. He will be none the wiser and the poor lad won't have anything to fret or worry about while he's over there."

Tom had already talked through his idea with Harriet, who had agreed. Annie now sat there sipping her tea politely, listening intently. "What about the dates on the letters?" she asked, thinking it through.

"No dates," Tom replied. "We know that it should take just a few days from Sutton Veny to Bristol but it can take anything from three weeks to three months for letters to get to Germany, so they say, so we won't complicate things by putting dates on."

"I think it could work," Annie said with a smile, "and I agree there is no point in worrying Will when you staying at home was so important to him."

They sat in silence for a moment before Harriet spoke, "There is something I need to ask both of you. Firstly, dear husband, when you do write, please don't forget to send us two letters, one to be sent to Will and one to tell us how you are getting on."

Tom chuckled, "Of course, my dear. I would never forget that. Just be sure that you send the right one on to Will.

Harriet then turned to Annie.

"Annie dear, I have two special favours to ask of you in addition. Firstly, I will, of course, need you to read Tom's letters out to me. Remember that, Tom, when you are writing!" she said briskly, looking quickly at Tom who started smiling as he fumbled in his pocket for his pipe. "My last request, Annie, is a slightly less personal one but probably more difficult. Could I ask that you might help teach me to read and write? It's silly, I know, but it's become a bit of a mental block for me, but I realise that I do need to learn now. I just feel frustrated that I can't do something that most people take for granted. So if you could find some time to help me, I would be very grateful."

It had taken all of Harriet's courage to ask. While there were still quite a lot of women of her age that couldn't read and write, it was still an increasing cause of angst for Harriet that she was included in their number.

When Private Thomas Payne arrived at the army training camp in Sutton Veny, he quickly became aware that he was one of the older men in the group, though he was relieved to see that at least half of the pioneer brigade was over thirty. They were quite a mixed bunch of men but nearly all big and rough chaps, largely having come from backgrounds of manual labour. Tom's platoon contained quite a number of ex-coal miners from the Radstock and Midsomer Norton Area. In the main, they seemed to be glad to have a change in career, what with many of the coal seams running out and work being more difficult to find. So using their skills in the military suited them well, giving them a steady wage to send home whilst using some of their base skills. When Tom shook hands with the men as he met them for the first time, he could tell from their handshakes what their backgrounds were. The ex-miners had fists like rock and their handshakes felt like you being gripped by a human vice. They all seemed friendly enough, though most of them dwarfed Tom in height, and he felt quite lithe and relatively compact against his new pals.

At the induction medical, Tom stood in a queue stripped down to their underpants and he felt quite short compared to most of the men around him. Two officers interviewed them to assess their background skills, and the miners were quickly grouped together afterwards. Tom kept up the pretence of being a coal merchant, though he realised that his body would not substantiate that story for long, so he stressed that he worked more on the administrative side of the business.

"I didn't think you had carried too many sacks of coal about," one of the officers said sarcastically. "So what other skills can you bring to the pioneers then, Payne?"

"Well, sir, I do have some skills working leather from a previous employment and, I am good with horses." The officer scribbled furiously before dismissing Tom, who felt that they had not been too impressed with his credentials.

He found the first few weeks very tough. They seemed to be subjected to endless square bashing and physical exercise and Tom discovered that cycling to work and making shoes did not make him the fittest man in the platoon, neither were the ex-miners though, when it came to running. Give them something to lift though and that was different. Tom wrote home at the end of the first week and waited for the reply from Annie and Harriet. It came the following week.

Dear Tom,

Please find paper and envelopes enclosed. We hope that you are settling into the camp and making new friends. Alfred sends his best and is going to write to you separately. Anthony is doing well 'for a learner' as Alfred calls him, but he is having to work longer hours while Anthony is learning, but we are all coping well. The shop has been particularly busy with ladies this week, and we have taken orders from some new customers, one of them who caught the train in from Bath, especially to buy our shoes. Our fame is growing it seems, but Alfred still has a few concerns as you were particularly good at the better quality ladies' shoes, and he's better with the hobnails as he often says when he's shaking his head. You know what he's like! No doubt he will cope.

Back at home, Mrs Williams at No 22 opposite has broken her leg. Poor old thing! She's not that steady on her feet, as you know, and caught her foot on the kitchen rug and fell heavily, so Mr Williams is having to wait on her for a change, but everyone in the street is rallying round to help where we can.

That nice Mrs Bevin at No 39 gave Mrs Williams a nice bottle of stout to cheer her up, which made us laugh as we suspected it might have been a tot of Gin being to blame for her falling over in the first place!

Everything else is fairly steady here, and we are looking forward to when you get some leave. Have they told you when that might be yet?

With love from home,
Harriet and Annie xx

As soon as their letter arrived, he set down to write to Will and get it posted back to Bristol as soon as possible.

25 Saxon Road

St Werburghs

Bristol

Dear son,

Your mother and I are sat in the kitchen having a nice cup of tea, and guess what? It's raining outside. We are all well and of course missing you, but I am confident that the war will be over soon and you will be home again. Things then can return to normal, son.

The shop is doing well and your uncle and I are making more ladies' shoes than ever, though there is still plenty of work for boots; I am pleased to say. There was some excitement in the street last week when Mrs Williams at number 22 tripped over the kitchen carpet and broke her leg. Poor thing! Mr Williams isn't happy as you would imagine, as he's had to get out of that chair of his and look after her. Everyone is rallying around and your mother baked an extra pie yesterday and took it over for their dinner. If it had not been so painful for the poor old girl, it might have been funny. You know how Mr Williams likes to be waited on hand, foot and finger, so now the boot is on the other foot.

I oiled your bicycle along with mine on Sunday and look forward to jumping on them together and taking a ride out around Bristol. I still remember our last ride out to Queen Charlton and thought of taking a ride out there recently, but have decided to wait until you are home so we can ride out there together.

We have put together a few things to hopefully help you there, son. Write back when you can and let us know if you need anything in particular and we will do our best. We think of you every day and look forward to the day when you come home. Stay positive, son. I'm sure it won't be long now.

Your ever loving,

Mum and Dad xx

The kindest of deceptions had started. Although no one liked the thought of lies or deceit, Tom, Harriet and Annie all knew the importance of giving their boy something solid to cling onto. Will needed a rock to cling onto as his own sea churned wildly for him in captivity.

With each new letter that they received from Doberitz, their understanding of the conditions and difficulties that Will faced in captivity grew. He was not their Will. He was clearly suffering mentally and each letter served to strengthen their resolve to continue with the deceit. Lying was not in their natures, but because of the circumstances, this lie did not feel wrong at all; it felt justified. Will clearly needed to hold on to the thought that everything at home was unchanged and waiting for him. Home was his rock, his island in his personal maelstrom. Having him home again was the final silent prayer each night that all three of them made before they closed their eyes.

CHAPTER NINETEEN

Will sat outside in the sun, reading his last letter from home for the umpteenth time. The summer of 1915 was being kind and it felt good to feel the warmth of the sun on his face again. He laid his head back against the wooden hut and stared at the light of the sun through his closed eyelids, letting his thoughts drift back to that day in Queen Charlton with his father. The moment didn't last long though; moments of solitude or privacy rarely did here in Doberitz. There was always someone close by, always people in a crowded space.

"Payne, what are you doing sat there? Haven't you got anything better to do?" It was the voice of Potter, doing a mock impression of his commanding officer, Colonel Russell. He boomed at Will, who immediately rose from the ground and stood to attention mockingly. Both men grinned at the humour but Will lost his balance as his left side shook and he leaned back on the hut. "You're popular it seems, Mr Payne. There's a German doctor asking for you up at the medical centre." Surprise wasn't the word, and Will made his way immediately to the hut with its large Red Cross hanging over the door. He had guessed it would be Dr Schultz, and it was. When Will entered the hut, Schultz was examining a nasty head wound on a soldier. Will waited until the chap left with his head in a paper bandage. Dr Schultz beckoned Will to sit down on the examination table and then told the British medical officer he could take a ten-minute break if he wanted, leaving Will and Schultz alone.

"How are you, William? I have volunteered to spend some time out of the hospital at the camp. It's not a popular position with my colleagues, you know. As this war goes on, you prisoners of war are becoming less popular in Berlin hospital, it seems. Let me look at your feet please," he asked, waving Will to take his boots off. Will carefully removed his boots and socks, revealing the gaps where his five missing toes had once been. Doctor Schultz bent down and examined the now healed stubs where his toes had been. Will's left side still shook and jumped and Schultz steadied his left foot as he examined it. "You need to wash your feet more, William, and ensure you have a clean pair of socks each day. This is important. I am pleased though. Your wounds are healing nicely. We just don't want any infection to get in and undo the work done to save your feet."

Will was still using one walking stick to steady himself, but that was largely to ward him against the tiresome shaking. If he held the stick in his good hand, he could grip has tunic with his shaking hand and hold his arm closer to his side, taking the emphasis away from the jerking limb.

Will spoke for the first time, remembering his time at the hospital and the letter that the doctor had sent his parents. He had never had time to thank him properly. "How are you, sir, and how is your son? I wanted to thank you again for writing to my parents. I know they got the letter and they have been sending me parcels ever since, which is a blessing. Thank you."

Schultz sat in the chair opposite Will and leaned forwards. "Well, William, I am fine, and thank you for asking. And my son, well, he is now spending some time where you would like to be, in England. He was captured, so thankfully taken alive but it seems that my poor son, Gunter, is troubled with a similar affliction to yourself, with what some Germans are calling 'hysteria' or 'neurasthenia'. I like neither term. I understand some of your English doctors are now calling it 'shell shock'. This I understand.

"This is a new condition for us all and to be frank, it troubles us Germans. Many men are being sent back from the front as the war drags on and they are labelled as cowards by many, an embarrassment to the army and to the German people. Me. I don't think it is cowardice at all. You're not a coward, are you, William?"

"No, sir," Will replied quietly, the suggestion alone hurting him.

"No. Neither do I see you as a coward. And my Gunter is certainly not a coward. He was. He is," he said, quickly correcting himself, "a strong man with as much courage as two men, and more life in him than most, yet his English doctor has written to me and informed me that his mind is paralysed and he spends his days in the hospital just staring into space. This is most upsetting to my wife and me, most upsetting." He paused for a moment, lost to a picture of his son staring out of a window into an English sky. He quickly resumed however, the picture broken by this skinny boy sat in front of him with his left side jerking and shaking. "I should not be telling you all this, William, but you will understand now why I have a renewed interest in you, and in your condition. This, this illness of the mind, is new to us all and as a doctor and a father, I want to understand it better myself. You want to get better, William? You want to stop these tics and shaking, yes?"

"Yes, sir," Will replied, trying to take everything in that the doctor had said but not understanding what 'getting better' might entail.

"Good. Then if you are in agreement, we will make a start next week. I still have my duties at the hospital but will spend part of my day off with you, sometimes here and sometimes at the hospital. As yet, I have no official sanction to conduct this work but I shall do so in my spare time, what little I get, that is. My Gunter is more fortunate than you, I think. He is in an army hospital where many such cases have been gathered to be studied by doctors. I am pleased at this. An English doctor is no different from a German doctor.

We all serve to help people and make them better. For now, we Germans are still trying to understand that this condition exists at all. But as more of our men return from the front, there is a growing understanding that we have to do something."

He stopped as abruptly as he had started and stood up, taking a deep breath as though he had got something off his mind. "William, I shall send a car from the hospital for you next Sunday morning, eight o'clock sharp." He extended his hand to shake William's, turned and was gone in a moment, striding across the room and out of the door.

Will spent time on Saturday afternoon carefully going through the seams of his clothes, picking off the lice that were everyone's companion in the camp. From time to time, the Germans would have a purge and have everyone's clothes fumigated in a huge boiler, but within ten days, the lice were back with a lot of new friends. Despite their billets being kept meticulously clean by the men, the lice seemed to find a way back after every purge.

As expected, a horse drawn cab arrived at exactly five minutes to eight, with a driver and one guard, who sat opposite Will in complete silence on the journey to Berlin hospital. Occasionally, Will could feel him staring at him from the other side of the carriage. He guessed that he was the first British soldier that he had encountered. Will ignored the glaring and stared out of the window, just enjoying looking at something different, though his shaking made him self-conscious with the guard staring at him. As the months had worn on, camp life had become a daily grind of familiarity and monotony. Men got sick of pacing the same wire, seeing the same people, keeping the same routine, so it was a tonic just to stare out of the cab and see Berlin's streets, even though it was quiet in its Sunday morning inactivity. People strolled to church in their Sunday's best clothes but this early in the morning, there was little else going on.

Dr Schultz greeted Will enthusiastically. With him were two other men in crisply starched white coats who Schultz introduced as doctors, Blokkmann and Oppenheim. They were introduced as having different expertise in psychiatric medicine by Schultz, while they glanced somewhat hesitantly at each other. They were both in their fifties and had an understanding of English, though Dr Oppenheim occasionally interrupted loudly in German to ask for a translation of something.

The morning was spent with Will being prepared. He changed out of his clothes, which the nurses then handled with disgust; clearly, his de-licing yesterday had not been totally successful. He was weighed and his height measured by the nurses and he was then asked to change into a white medical gown. When he returned, the two doctors sat in front of him behind a large table. Will had his walking stick taken away from him by the nurses and found it difficult to stand in front of them without wobbling horribly as his left side shook more violently than usual. Dr Schultz sat to the side of the room, observing proceedings. Clearly, psychiatry was not his field, but he was keen to learn and gain an understanding. For a few moments, there was an uneasy silence while both men stared at him. Dr Blokkmann sat with his hands clasped under his chin, just looking at Will in deep thought. Dr Oppenheim said nothing, but took copious notes as he too stared at Will over the top of his half-moon spectacles.

"So, William, please tell us about yourself, starting with your early life in England, your family etc. Take your time."

Will was thrown by the question and for a moment, he didn't know where to start. He suddenly felt quite naked, despite his white gown, but he started talking about his parents and where he had been born. "Your voice," Blokkmann interrupted. "It is not affected by your shaking, no?"

"No, sir, I don't have a stutter, if that's what you mean."

"Continue. Schultz, can you find this man a chair? If he shakes anymore, he will fall over and I think we have seen enough."

Will sat, glad to take the weight off his legs and in particular, his feet. Since the amputations, he had not found standing for long periods easy and his missing toes pained him as if they were still there and just damaged. The questioning continued, with Dr Blokkmann going over every point in detail with so many questions that it felt to Will that he was going around in circles, answering almost the same questions than he had been asked before and Will felt like the questioning was turning into something like the interrogation he received when he was first captured. But instead of being repeatedly asked about how many men were in his unit and where they had been, the doctor seemed to be fixated with Will's early years as a child. Will's headache suddenly resurged in protest and when a break came for lunch, he was grateful for the break away from being questioned. He also eagerly looked forward to eating something other than camp food. He was disappointed when a bowl of soup was brought to him with a chunk of dark brown bread not dissimilar to that in the camp. The soup did have a few more lumps of potatoes and thinly cut vegetables in it and the bread tasted less of sawdust, but clearly, the war was beginning to bite into the lives of ordinary Germans too.

The afternoon session started again, but thankfully did not last more than an hour, with Dr Oppenheim looking at his watch every five minutes for some reason. Dr Blokkmann switched the questioning onto how Will was feeling now and when he told them of his dreadful nightmares, they became even more interested.

"Describe your dreams, please. Are they the same? Are they always different? Where are you, and what is happening to frighten you? What is it that gives you these nightmares?" Blokkmann asked each question in a rush, leaning forwards in his chair and suddenly talking in a softer tone with a great deal of interest.

"I don't know, sir. Every night is the same. I wake up aware that I have been shouting and am usually running in sweat but I can't remember the dream, although I am very aware I have been dreaming. It doesn't make me popular in my hut, sir, and often someone wakes me up to tell me to pipe down." The doctors started talking amongst themselves in German, having at times a quite heated debate between them. Will had picked up a few German words from being around the camp, but hadn't a clue what they were arguing about. Dr Schultz said little, but interjected between Blokkmann and Oppenheim from time to time as they discussed Will's condition. It was clear that they were at odds as to what to do next and the argument was clearly about a disagreement in treatment. The discussion ended abruptly. Dr Oppenheim was the more forceful character and it was he who suddenly stood up and left the room. Dr Schultz walked Will to meet his guard at the waiting car. "William, as you probably understood from the discussion, my two colleagues are suggesting different courses of treatment to be able to help your condition. For now, my colleague Dr Oppenheim has won the day, so we will make arrangements for you to stay at another hospital for a few days while we look into this further. I will not be able to join you there I am afraid, my other duties prevent this, but please, always remember that whatever happens, we are trying to help you."

That last sentence ran uncomfortably through Will's mind repeatedly on the journey back to the camp.

CHAPTER TWENTY

Tom was becoming an expert at digging trenches. In fact, he was having enough practice digging and filling them in again that at times, the area around Sutton Veny was starting to resemble the front line itself, he thought. Later, he was to realise just how far away from reality that really was. At first, it started in the classroom, with a burly sergeant drawing the side profile and then an aerial view of a trench. He drew different shapes on the chalk board that started to resemble the teeth of a giant saw. There was, it seemed, more to digging a trench than it being just a hole in the ground.

The sides had to be angled from the vertical so that they would not collapse too easily and then reinforced with wood if necessary. It had to be levelled out to make a flat seat shape known as the 'fire step'. Then, they dug again until they had a hole deeper than a man's height and at the bottom of the trench, a wooden framework was laid to keep any gathering water underneath and give an even track for the men to walk on. Immediately in front of the trench, sandbags were laid and everything had to be just right or the sergeant would throw a fit and have them running around the yard with their rifles above their heads until the pain in their arms screamed at them. Tom was getting tired of holes in the ground.

Several platoons had been formed from those with coal mining experience and they disappeared soon after basic training was complete. Tom remained with most of the men and the spaces left by the departing miners were soon filled by another bunch of enthusiastic recruits who all came in full of youthful bravado. Tom's platoon continued its more advanced training, learning everything from how to make emergency road repairs to laying a barbed wire defence. The barbed wire was something that nobody liked to work with, but like the trench digging, there was an art to it. Without fail and no matter how careful they were handling the wire with thick leather gloves, it would almost always 'get you' somewhere on your body at least once during each training sessions. Laying wire was one part of their training that they preferred to learn about in the classroom, as the practical side of it was hardly ever without pain.

Tom certainly had no trouble sleeping at night. At the end of every day, he was physically exhausted and if they ever had a lighter day, which was very rare, all the platoon would be sent out in full kit and marched around the training ground or out through the village into the Wiltshire countryside for miles on end. Yeah, Tom slept at night alright. The letters kept coming from Harriet and Annie, sometimes with a letter from Will enclosed. He read them all hungrily, missing home and his family with every sentence. Annie and Harriet had clearly grown very close over the last months and Annie had, in a way, become the daughter that they had always wanted but never been able to have. Sales in the shop had dropped a little, partly because so many men had left their jobs and Bristol to go to war and partly because ladies orders were also down, reflecting the general air of austerity that was running throughout the country. The Germans efforts to cut off supplies to Britain with 'U' boats had intensified, with regular and well-publicised sinking of merchant ships. In truth, the main reason why sales of ladies' shoes had dropped was that poor Alfred struggled to make the more delicate shoes with his big, stubby fingers. Young Anthony was doing alright though and learning the art of shoemaking through a gradual increase in responsibility as his mistakes lessened. As Alfred told him regularly, "We all made mistakes when we started, lad. It's just that leather is too damn expensive and scarce these days to mess up, so you've got to watch and learn rather than try it and get it wrong." He was right about leather becoming scarcer; the drop in demand was matched by the lack of materials as the blockade bit.

With every letter from home came more blank paper and an addressed envelope. Tom used to smile that Annie had addressed the envelope for 25 Saxon Road, like he didn't remember where he lived. As always when a letter came in, as soon as the evening came and his duties were over for the day, he would sit down and translate all the news from home into a letter for Will, writing everything afresh like he was sitting at home at the old kitchen table. Then, he would write his own letter to Harriet, always remembering that he could not write anything intimate as Annie would be reading it out to her.

It was a hot August's Thursday afternoon when news came out of the blue that they all had leave for the weekend. It was their first leave since arrival and Tom's heart sang when he heard the announcement. The excitement was short-lived when in the next sentence, they were told that soon after returning back to camp, they were being posted to France.

There was no time to write and warn anyone of his three-day leave. Friday morning, they were all marched in groups to the railway station and before Tom knew it, he was on a train bound for Temple Meads. When the train arrived, he went straight to the shop, putting his kitbag down gently outside and peeped around the corner of the shop window, waiting until Harriet had her back turned as she moved shoes around on the shelf behind her. Ever so quietly, Tom opened the door, reaching up to slide his hand inside the crack of the door to stop the bell above from ringing. Gently, he slid inside and closed the door behind him, tiptoeing to the counter as best he could in his army boots. When Harriet turned around, there was her Tom beaming at her with his arms wide open. She rushed to him and he picked her up off her feet and spun her round in the centre of the shop. Their kiss was long and passionate and as Tom put Harriet down, he was awash with the joy of being home. "Do you remember, Tom, when you spun me around in the very same spot once before, a long time ago?"

"How could I forget, my love? It was the day that you told me you were carrying our Will inside you and do you know what? You've not put on an ounce of weight since," he joked, picking her up again and swirling her ever faster around as they laughed together. As he stopped spinning and came to a halt, she stared deep into his eyes that were still as blue as the sea. "I've missed you, husband of mine," she said quietly.

Tom gazed back, his eyes beaming in the sheer joy of the moment. "And I've missed you too, my love, more than you'll ever know." Their embrace was cut short however, by the bell above the door clanging as a customer came in. Tom quickly put Harriet down and left her to the customer as he slipped through to the workshop to spring his next surprise. Alfred was stretching a piece of leather over a shoemaker's last and Anthony had a large piece of leather that he was cutting a shoe shape out from a template, so both had their heads down when Tom quietly slipped into view, booming loudly in military style as he entered, "Come on, you lot, let's get those boots made double time!" Alfred grinned from ear to ear and they greeted like the best friends as well as brothers that they were. They shook hands and then Alfred held his brother's hand by the wrist and looked at his palm. "What's this, little brother? Do I feel callouses on your hands? Don't you ruin those delicate little pinkies, will you? You've got some proper work waiting for you here when you've finished playing soldiers," he said, grinning all over his face.

Harriet shut the shop half an hour early that day, and she and Tom walked hand-in-hand back home, stopping at the grocer's shop on the way to buy something a little bit special for supper. They didn't stop talking all the way home. Despite writing every week to each other, there was so much to catch up on and of course, with Annie writing Harriet's letters for her and reading Tom's letters back, neither of them had written anything of a personal nature to each other more than the basic formality of signing off with a 'love xx' at the end. When they reached home, Harriet placed her shopping basket down and Tom kissed her tenderly and led her upstairs by the hand. He needed to hold her, needed to feel her warm body in his arms and for an age, they did nothing other than lay naked in each other's arms, gazing into each other's eyes. When their passion met, it was caring and delicate, savouring each other's caress, each kiss, every moment.

The light of the late summer sun was starting to fade when they dressed and went down for supper. As Tom made a cup of tea, he broke the news to Harriet that he had not been looking forward to.

"I've been posted overseas, my love. I leave for France next week."

"I did wonder, Tom, the moment I saw you. I guessed that they would be sending you sometime. So now, I have two of you to worry about."

"Well, you won't need to worry about me, my love. I shall largely be mending roads and building bridges a long way behind the front line and what is important to us both is that I shall be so much closer to our Will, so the moment we win this war, I shall be up to Doberitz like a flash. I'll get him back safe. Trust me." Harriet did.

Tom decided that now would not be a good time to talk about his weeks of training of digging front line trenches. Harriet was worried enough about Will without needing to be worrying about him, and he had no intention of getting himself killed or captured. She nestled her head on his shoulder and they stood there in silence for what seemed too short a time, just happy to have her man back and enjoying each precious second that they now had together.

The three days' leave went remarkably quickly. The shop had to stay open on the Saturday as they could not afford to let customers down and business had to go on, so Tom went with Harriet to open up, then he made boots in the workshop with Alfred and Anthony. For a day, everything was almost just like it had been before. They gave Anthony the afternoon off as a treat for the lad and worked together just the two of them. Alfred was grateful that Tom took to making several pairs of intricate ladies' shoes and it gave him chance to catch up on a small backlog of orders. They had sent a message to Annie to come for tea on Sunday, but it seemed that word had got out that Tom was home. They had a constant procession of friends and family knocking on their door all morning to say 'hello'. When Annie came in the afternoon, she brought some tins of food to go in Will's next Red Cross parcel and a letter. She had guessed, or hoped, that they would write to Will again while Tom was home.

Without saying a word, they all knew that communicating with Will was about to get much more difficult. Harriet, through Annie, would write to Tom. The army postal service would then have to find Tom wherever he happened to be, in France or Belgium or wherever. Tom would have to rewrite each letter again as if he was sat at home at the kitchen table, and also write the envelope addressed to Will in Doberitz. Then that letter would go inside a bigger envelope with his own to Harriet to be read to her by Annie. The army postal system would have to get the letter back to Bristol, where Annie and Harriet would take it out and post it once again to Will in Germany, fresh with its Bristol postmark.

It was Annie that broached the question first as she finished her sandwich. "Do you know where they are sending you, Tom?"

Tom shook his head and smiled, trying to soften the question. "France I suspect, Annie. No one is told in advance and we will only know ourselves when we arrive. The papers say there's a lot going on across a wide front now, so I guess I could be anywhere in France or Belgium. It would be more important than ever now that we send the letters undated though. The postal system is supposed to be very good to our troops, but it might still take a while for some letters to find me if I'm moving about. But don't worry. It will be fine. We've got a system in place now and it works. Will doesn't suspect a thing. I'm sure of that from reading his last letters."

Tom took advantage of being home and he had already sat at the kitchen table in the early morning light and written his next two letters and a spare envelope out to Doberitz. His writing was helped by being at home again, recharging the realism of his words. He sat for a moment when he had finished the second letter and tried to hold on to the moment. Somehow, he had to write letters from abroad as if he was still sitting here at the kitchen table. That wouldn't be so easy to do. He wrote his two letters as if they were about a week apart. Now, they would send the first one off straight away and Harriet would hold on to the second to send later while Tom was travelling. It would work. It had to.

CHAPTER TWENTY-ONE

The car was very punctual as expected and Will sat in the backseat with a different guard this time, noticing that before long they were taking a different road out of Berlin. Will tried to stay awake and take in every part of the trip, but he had slept even worse than usual last night after being woken forcibly to be told to stop shouting, so before long his head had gently slipped down onto his chest and he had drifted off to sleep. He woke with a jolt after how long, he didn't know, but the car had turned sharply and suddenly stopped. They were in the courtyard of what Will guessed was a military hospital, with more men marching around in uniform than in white coats.

Will noticed straight away that there were quite a lot of men there with similar issues to himself, walking often assisted by male nurses, as they shook and gyrated in awkward steps along the corridors. In a strange way, Will found some comfort in knowing that he was not alone in his torment. Back at the Doberitz camp, there were a few men that had some 'issues', but nothing as bad as Will's. Here, some of the men had clearly been very badly damaged and several carried grotesquely contorted faces, whilst others just sat and stared into space as if completely lost in their own distant thoughts. Then there were the 'rockers', as he later called them, sat lost in a different world while their upper bodies rocked violently back and forth, never ending or taking a break from their tormented movements.

Will was taken again through the process of being de-loused and made to take a bath and change all his clothes. Although there was only about three inches of lukewarm water in the bath, it was heaven to Will. He had had nothing other than a strip wash in usually cold water for months and although the bar of soap was tiny, while he was washing himself, he could not help putting the thin bar to his nose and sniffing deeply. The smell reminded him of washing his hands back at work in Mardons, and for a brief moment, he closed his eyes and was transported back there. It felt good to work the soap into his scalp with his good arm and wash his hair and by the time he had been prodded firmly in the back to tell him to finish quickly, the surface of the water was a grey, scummy lather with dozens of nits and lice floating on it, some swimming forlornly for their lives while others looked as lost as some of the patients here. Will was delighted to say farewell to his unwelcome guests and was happy to don a bug-free grey jacket and trousers to wear. At least for now, he might be free from the scratching that the little blighters brought on.

He walked shakily down the middle of a long ward with beds either side of him to a room at the end. Inside was one bed, a bedside cabinet and a large, lightly curtained window with bars on it. The door was locked behind him and Will tried to make himself comfortable inside the bare room. It wasn't large and it had stark, white walls that were devoid of any clock, paintings or anything. Will lay on the bed and closed his eyes, trying to close his ears to the noises and occasional shouts and scream that came from beyond his door. Sometimes, the noises sounded more animal than human, and he pulled the blanket up around him and tried to shut the sounds out.

After a long while, the door was unlocked loudly and Dr Oppenheim came in with two senior-looking military men in uniform. "You have been locked away for your own safety, William. You will understand that the other patients here are German soldiers and we are unsure how some of them might react to having you here. So when you are in the presence of other patients, please refrain from speaking in English. It is best that your nationality is not known. Treatment will begin tomorrow." That was it, he left as fast as he had arrived and was gone, the door locking with a loud click behind him.

Despite having already been through some tough times, Will suddenly felt very apprehensive. He tried to gather some comfort by pulling the sheet and blanket up around him as tightly as he could, but little comfort came. Alone in his little cold room with its stark white walls, with the enemy outside, locked in apparently for his own safety, he suddenly felt quite small and alone. His body continued to shake and jerk as he lay there, and it seemed worsened by his new fears. Though his journey from being captured to arriving in Doberitz had been frightening, it had been something of a blur at the time, but this suddenly felt different. He pulled his knees up as he did every night and curled up into as small a shape as he could but sleep took a long time to come. That night, Will's nightmares haunted him as every night before, only tonight, no one came to wake him and tell him to pipe down, and outside, a dozen other nightmares raged, as the hell of war relived its own personal story inside the tormented minds of the German patients. The horrors of war, it seemed, had no boundaries and stalked its victims on both sides of the barbed wire.

Will discovered that the treatment was both experimental and painful. He was marched in silence the next morning, back through the wards of troubled men to a room at the far end of the hospital. After he had been examined, he was asked to walk up and down in front of a group of military doctors who observed him closely. His body still shook down his left side so as he walked, his leg trembled violently and he had to forcibly put it down hard to the ground and lock his knee before moving his right leg, as his left arm also jerked and twitched. Although he was used to walking with his disability, it looked rather odd as he slapped his foot to the ground, locking his knee to avoid falling. He was led to a wooden bench where his wrists and ankles were strapped down, and a leather strap fastened across his forehead and buckled tightly at the side. Will's pulse quickened and his mouth went dry as fear suddenly exploded inside him. A rubber bung was placed in his mouth to stop him from biting his tongue and for the next thirty minutes or so, electrodes were attached to various parts of his body and he could hear the doctors playing with a machine that was by the side of the bench. The first electric shock that hit him was very mild, sending a light tingling sensation from his wrist right through his body to his ankle. As the power increased, Will became uncomfortable, and by the time the fifth shock came, it hurt to the point that he let out a scream as the current surged through his body. His requests for them to 'please stop' were ignored, and his heart raced and then almost stopped when the sixth shock was administered. The rubber bung in his mouth had a smell and taste to it that he abhorred; it was foul. The next electric shock came right after they had moved the two electrodes from his wrist and leg to his head, the two damp pads being positioned either side of his head between his eyes and ears. He knew nothing after that.

Even when the foul rubber gag had been removed, Will could still taste and smell it when he came back to his room. He was parched dry but he was strapped down to the bed and felt totally exhausted and sick. With the foul stench of rubber still invading his nostrils, he slept deeply until the sun was low in the sky. When he woke up, his bindings had been removed while he slept and there was a mug of water and a plate with two slices of dark rye bread and some slices of cheese next to the bed. What he wanted most though was the water, which he gulped at greedily. His body ached like he had been doing hard labour but as he sat up drinking the water, he realised that his shaking had almost gone. He transferred the glass to his left hand and held it in front of him and the joy of seeing his left hand not jerking so violently was the best feeling that he had had in months. He didn't know how, but whatever the doctors had done had worked.

Nobody came to the room during the evening and when he woke next morning, the empty plate and mug were still by his bed. His clothes were damp from sweating and he had a vague recollection of another nightmare but he could not remember anything. He heard the key turn loudly in the door and Dr Oppenheim marched in with two orderlies. Will was asked to walk up and down the room for a full five minutes, getting him to stop and do different bending and stretching exercises while they chattered enthusiastically amongst themselves. Will couldn't understand what they were saying but they were clearly pretty pleased with themselves as they left. For the first time since he had known him, Dr Oppenheim gave Will an awkward smile and handshake as he left the room.

By mid-afternoon, Will was thoroughly bored. A severe-looking nurse in a heavily starched uniform brought him a small tray of food at breakfast and lunchtime, and he tried to eat each piece slowly to pass the time, but he was so hungry that he found that difficult. He had not been expecting his next visitors, who burst in the door without notice and marched him down the corridor briskly to the same room as yesterday. Without examination or discussion, he was strapped down again to the leather couch and before he had time to comprehend what was happening or protest, the dreaded rubber gag was thrust between his teeth. He remembered little else until he woke drowsily back in his little room hours later. As he regained consciousness, his head was filled with a high-pitched whine accompanied by a feeling that he had been hit by a very large hammer. The severity of his headache dominated everything other than the feeling of utter exhaustion.

He slept or passed out, he wasn't sure, but it was dark when he awoke, sweating profusely and gasping for air. The remnants of a nightmare slipped quickly from his consciousness. His headache had lessened but he shot bolt upright in the bed in an effort to get more air in his lungs and his every movement was painful. He found thinking difficult. There were thoughts there, but they seemed to be blocked as he tried to conjure them up into words. His neck ached as did his arms and legs, and when his hands moved up to the sides of his head, he could feel a circular callous like scab which was tender to touch. Slowly, the memory of yesterday evening came to him in small pieces, a flash of memory here, a fragment there, until he could assemble enough of the pieces together to recall that dark little room again and the electric shock that tore through him before he blacked out. That was confirmed and nailed into his brain by the foul rubber taste in his mouth still. As his tongue ran over his front teeth, he was sure he could feel tiny fragments of rubber embedded deep in the gaps. The hours passed and his mind began to slowly reassemble itself. It dawned on him that he must have been given a hell of a high dosage of electricity to melt the rubber into his teeth and burn holes on the side of his head. It was a long time until the dawn came, but slowly, piece by piece, his memory found the connections to put at least part of what had happened together. What he did know was that he dreaded ever going back to that room again.

Harriet's nephew was in the Cavalry (note his spurs). He was unfortunately crushed underneath his horse and died.

Harriet, Tom and Harriet's nephew.

Private Thomas Payne. Taken before he set sail for France

CHAPTER TWENTY-TWO

Tom had seen large ships a hundred times moored up in Bristol dock over the years, but he had never actually been on one. Like most of the men boarding that day, he had never been to sea. Crammed on deck in the middle of the English Channel, he could see nothing but the grey ocean and the other ships in the tightly packed convoy. Knowing that 'U' boats might be in the area made him feel strangely vulnerable. They were a real threat to shipping in the channel now, so he was very happy when the convoy reached Calais and they disembarked. He had just about held himself together against seasickness despite several of the men around him pushing past with urgency to be sick over the side. He had decided by the time they landed though that he was an old land-lubber, and couldn't wait to step onto firm ground again.

It was September 1915. Already the France that Tom stepped onto had markedly changed in the year or so since his son had disembarked onto the same soil. Tom couldn't help but look around him and wonder if his son had seen the exact same scenes when he had landed. In actual fact, the engines of war ran much smoother now, and Tom's unit was marched away from the port with urgency and precision. All Tom could think of as he marched in step with the men around him was that he was now on the same soil as Will. There was no water between them, so walking far and fast enough and within a few days, he could be with him if there was no damn war going on. It was strange how having crossed that little strip of water, he somehow now felt much closer to his son. It made him feel good and more determined than ever to survive this war and be reunited with his family back home.

As he marched, his mind flashed back to the life that he had left behind and he realised how he missed Harriet dreadfully. He thought about his old life and missed Alfred working alongside him in the workshop. 'Enough of that though,' blocking his thoughts before they made him too sad.

They were billeted overnight in farm buildings and settled down for the night. He was confused when he was counted by the farmer as he came amongst them late evening, counting the number of British soldiers that were on his farm. Tom walked over to a sergeant, "Excuse me, Sarg, but what's the French guy doing counting us. Is he spying?"

"No, private. He's counting us because the British Army will get a bill in the morning for every soldier staying on his land."

"A bill," Tom snorted. "We're here trying to save his county surely? And he's charging us?"

"That's about the sum of it. He won't feed us or find us beds other than let us use the straw in his barns, but he'll be paid per head, so that's why he was counting, to make sure he gets the bill right in the morning."

Tom shook his head and wandered back to the barn to bed down for the night. The word was that they were heading off to a place called 'Loos' in the morning, and some of the lads had joked about it sounding like a toilet. Tom was just happy that they were heading in the general direction of where his son was.

Before Tom had left Bristol for his training in Wiltshire, old Mike Harris from number seven in Saxon Road had taken him aside to give him some advice from an old soldier. Mike had been a veteran of the Crimean war. "Your mates are your mates, Tom, but don't get too pally with any of them cos it gets very hard if they cop it. You'll need your mates and they'll need you, but my advice is to keep a little distance from them on a personal level."

Now they were getting close to the front line. Tom understood the advice. His age made him more of a father figure than a pal. He was old enough to be their father in most cases, and he realised that he looked at the world in a slightly different way than most of the other men. While they were full of bravado and enthusiasm for the fight, Tom was more intent on making sure he survived it rather than win any medals. He took quiet comfort from his pipe and largely kept himself to himself, whilst being a warm and almost paternal figure to the others in the unit.

It had been a long and uncomfortable night when they were roused at 4 am. Tom was grateful for his blanket as despite it being the end of September, there was a chill to the night. Little did he know it would be absolutely nothing compared to the cold that he would endure in the months to come. The unit was on the march before five, and Tom marvelled at the beautiful sunrise that they seemed to be walking directly into as he marched in step on his first morning in France. They didn't have far to march and were soon loaded into lorries to head towards Loos.

No amount of training can fully prepare anyone for the first sight of the realities of war. They had driven to within two miles of it when they were forced to stop in front of a deep shell crater that had recently taken half the road out. Tom guessed what their first job would be and he was right, to fill the hole in and repair the road. The ground was still hard and a dozen men set to work with shovels, repairing the road. They had to work fast. It was tough going and they had nearly finished it when a loud, whistling noise signalled the start of a German bombardment. Their target was the front line ahead of them, but several of the shells overshot to within five hundred yards of where they were, and it accelerated the efforts of the men who largely worked in silence as they grafted to get the job done. The poor devils in the front were copping a pasting for sure. Tom thought to himself, as the bombardment continued for several hours.

The next days were a blur to Tom as they literally hit the ground, or rather underground, running. His first experience of the front line trenches was very different to what he had imagined. Within minutes of their arrival, they were digging furiously to repair the sides of a trench that had been hit by a shell. Every half spade full of the sticky clay had to be dug from a semi-crouched position within the trench, as to stick your head up over the level of the parapet itself would be lethal and probably your last action in life. Snipers watched every flicker of movement through telescopic sights with such a speed of reaction that the merest glimpse of the top of a cap would be met by the instantaneous release of a murderous bullet. But digging shoulder-height from a crouched position, ever conscious that you mustn't forget for one tiny moment that you had to keep your head down, was difficult. Very difficult.

Tom saw his first casualty of carelessness within an hour of arriving and it gave him an unwelcome memory that he would always carry. Five yards away on the other side of the damaged trench and without a hint of warning, a young private was thrown to the far side of the trench by the force of the bullet as it hit the top of his head. Two memories from that moment stayed with Tom for many years. Firstly, the sound of the bullet as it struck its target with a dull thud and secondly, the amount of blood that suddenly seemed to cover half of the trench. The intensity of its colour was shocking to Tom. It reminded him of the red lead paint that he had used to undercoat his pushbike at home. It was everywhere, like someone had taken the lid off a new tin and thrown it right across the trench. The bullet had clipped the top of the man's head and torn half of his scalp off, sending hair, fragments of bone and blood everywhere. Amazingly, the man wasn't dead, but writhed in agony, screaming for all his worth as everyone around him leapt to his aid. For everyone else, that was the most dangerous moment as Herr Sniper now had his sights firmly trained on that exact spot, waiting for the next careless head to appear in the frenzy of activity surrounding the wounded man.

The medics arrived fairly quickly, thank God, certainly before the man's screaming stopped. Tom discovered many months later, from letters sent to one of the chap's friends in the unit, that the wound was in a way less than it looked as it had spared his life, whilst being far worse than it could have been, as the man was, from that moment on, turned into an imbecile, just a millisecond after the sniper's finger had squeezed ever so gently on the trigger. The family of the poor man would spend the rest of his relatively short life visiting him in a mental institution until his early demise. He was to be just another casualty that appeared on the statistics of the war as 'wounded in action', without giving detail or hint to the years of tragedy and tears that his brief moment of carelessness would lead to for him and his family.

Tom's first weeks at the front were a time he would never forget. Sleep was like an old friend that had been misplaced by activity and for the first three days and nights, from before dawn to dusk, they were constantly on the go with hardly the time to grab any proper rest. Then the nights took on their own routine of noise and activity that drove any thought of sleep deeper than the trench that sheltered them. By the third night, Tom was so exhausted that he squashed himself in the corner of the trench, crouched up on the fire step with a piece of tarpaulin over him and became unconscious rather than slept, exhaustion taking him through all the noises of a bombardment overhead into the silent world of sleep. He only had around three hours sleep but went out so deeply that when he awoke, he was disorientated. He had been dreaming of home and was at a loss to work out where the hell he was for a few seconds as he came too, realising that a large rat was running over his legs. He woke confused and in a sort of hell, with shells bursting around, shaking the ground violently.

Everything he seemed to do now was backbreaking. He was just relieved that he was not part of the mining teams who were digging deep below no-man's-land, burrowing like rabbits under the German positions. He didn't fancy that at all, trapped deep underground working in total silence to avoid giving the game away.

What he did everyday was hard enough but at least, he could breathe in God's air. That was until the first gas attack came. When it did, there was a mad panic amongst the troops to put their masks on quickly. They had practised doing this so many times before, of course, but it wasn't as simple to do it when it came to the real thing. They had practised putting the horrid cloth bag with glass eye holes in it on snugly numerous times, but this time, when the officer's whistle shrieked, there was an air of wild panic in the noise. The shout "Gas! Gas!" rang out with great urgency but when it did, the first thing Tom had to do was remember where his mask was. He was repairing the sides of the trench with wooden slats, so had put his kitbag and mask to the back of the trench. It only took him a matter of seconds to unclip the poppers on the container and get the mask out, but by the time he had thrust it unceremoniously over his head and flattened it out over his shoulders, the slowly tumbling mist of the grey-green chlorine gas silently and insidiously spilled down over the front of the trench and dropped down to the bottom, as if it were a living creature seeking out its innocent victims. It clung low to the ground and found every nook and cranny as it half filed the trench. Tom's heart raced and inside the crude mask, the glass eye pieces steamed up within seconds, making vision almost impossible, but the faint smell of the gas through the mask's fabric made it clear that poor vision was better than poor breathing. Stuffed inside his mask had been a pair of woollen gloves that Harriet had knitted him before he left and he hurriedly thrust his hands into them to avoid any contact with the dirty, yellow-green gas. A man groped about past him like someone escaping Halloween, feeling his way by the walls of the trench as he stumbled past, cursing loudly under his mask. Sitting there trying not to breath hard through the mask wasn't easy. Tom could hear men coughing and retching further down the trench so clearly; some poor sod had failed to get his mask on in time.

After half an hour or so, a cheer went up as a breeze suddenly, picked up from nowhere and changed direction, slowly carrying the deadly mist back to its rightful owners. Tom couldn't wait to escape the dank air from inside his mask but when he removed it, the horrid smell was fetid and unnatural as it lingered in the air around him. Lined up along the length of the trench, men crouched now, guns at the ready, expecting the usual post gas attack. Tom was primarily an engineer first, so he was not expected to pick up a rifle unless the call went up, so he continued to repair the trench with a sharp ear on activities before him. Herr Sniper continued to ping the odd shot at any wayward cap that came into vision but the awaited attack never came this time.

CHAPTER TWENTY-THREE

Will eventually drifted back to sleep, but when he woke, every muscle still ached like he had been wrestling with a bull and lost. The foul smell and taste of rubber still invaded his mouth and he sipped slowly on a glass of water in a vain attempt to remove it. His head pounded and he struggled again to think clearly, grasping at fragments of memory through the fog surrounding the last few days. His memory returned gradually, the electric shock treatment, the blacking out and the dread of going back for more. He had already had three sessions, with each session clearly using a higher voltage than the last and judging by the coating over his teeth from the rubber bung they had wedged in his mouth, and the round calluses of singed skin on either side of his head, the last session must have used a really high dosage. He held his hands out in front of him and they both stayed pretty steady, which was wonderful, so at least the treatment had worked. His left side no longer shook uncontrollably. It, like the rest of him, was just too tired to move.

When the key turned in the lock, he shuddered, dreading to see the white coats of the doctors that might drag him off for another session of treatment, but it was a stern-faced nurse, who brought in a tray of cereal that was supposed to be porridge he guessed, but tasted like something else, but he couldn't quite work out what. He was grateful nevertheless, and the sight of food made him realise just how hungry he was.

One of the junior doctors came half an hour later to check on Will's condition. His English was very good and it felt good to talk to someone at last. The chap was very business-like at first, as he asked Will to stand and walk about. The young doctor seemed to enjoy the chance to practise his English on someone and after a few minutes, the questioning and conversation became noticeably lighter and Will wondered if he would ever shut up, rabbiting on about how he had learnt English in school from an English teacher who had moved to Frankfurt from London.

"So how do you feel in yourself? It must be good to be cured of this shaking you had, yes?"

"It's wonderful, doctor. Though I still feel very shaky inside, sort of starting from my stomach, but not outside, which is good." Will sat back on the bed and the doctor noticed the singe marks on the side of his head, examining them closely with his fingertips and exclaiming quietly to himself as he did. It was over the following conversation that Will realised that they had thought that the last treatment had come close to killing him.

"You are very strong, Will, and between us two I can tell you that I think you easily hold the record now for this treatment and we will not be using such a high dosage in future on our other patients."

"What happened then," Will asked quietly.

"Well, technically you died for a short while when we increased the dosage, and it was only down to the skill of our doctors that they managed to revive you. As I say, Will, you are clearly a strong fellow," he said, smiling and slapping him on the shoulder.

"You must understand that this treatment is very new for us all and we are driving our knowledge forwards at this hospital, so you have been very lucky to have been brought here and we have cured you, yes?"

Will nodded but said nothing, thinking to himself that yes, it seemed to have cured his shaking, but it had clearly almost killed him in the process. He didn't say it to the doctor, but the thought struck him immediately that they had used him to see how high a dosage they could deliver without killing him. Now they would know how far they might go to safely treat their own soldiers. He didn't care too much now though. He just wanted to get out of there.

Will dreamt of home that night. He was cycling up the Wells Road out of Bristol with his dad and it was summer. He could feel the heat of the sun on his face and he closed his eyes against the glare. Then the dream changed instantly without notice. It was now inky dark. He was lying in a muddy crater with just enough of a glimmer of light to make out where he was, but for some reason, he was unable to move. In his dream, he wanted to move but his body seemed rigid and locked. He was not alone. There was someone with him on the other side of the crater, but he could only just make out that it was a person in the thin light. The man opposite was staring at him, staring with his eyes and mouth wide open as if screaming at him. Only, no sound came out. It was difficult to see clearly in this light, but the person was clearly staring at him. Then suddenly, the face seemed to rush towards him, coming across the trench at him at speed. There was a huge bloody hole where the left top half of its head should have been. The face seemed to leave its body and rush at Will from the other side of the trench, with its eyes still fixated on Will. The screaming woke Will, but it was his own screaming. He sat bolt upright in the bed, gasping for air and drenched in sweat. The face had gone. He no longer saw its gruesome image and lost its memory as the spell broke, chasing its hideous face back into the deepest recesses of his memory to be locked away by his conscious mind once more, waiting to be released again perhaps while he slept on another night. Now he just fought for air and gasped for it noisily as the sweat continued to pour from him.

After a day of being examined and walking up and down in front of numerous doctors, doing sit ups and exercises, Will was dismissed amid a lot of self-congratulations and back-slapping amongst the doctors. An hour later, he found himself being driven back to the camp. He must have appeared as more of a threat to them now that he wasn't shaking, as not one but two armed guards were used to accompany him back to Doberitz. But he didn't care. He was just relieved to be away from the hospital. He still couldn't get the foul taste of rubber out of his mouth though.

As he was driven through the German countryside, he tried to recall how long it was that he had been away from Doberitz but couldn't. It couldn't have been more than a few weeks or a month at the most. It had been difficult to keep track of time there, but on his return to the camp, things seemed to have changed. The camp seemed bigger for a start and as he walked through to his hut, there were a lot of new faces. He went straight to the camp office and his heart soared when there were two letters and a parcel waiting for him from home. He clutched them to his chest with a joyous anticipation as he marched the last yards to his hut with his prizes, swinging his walking stick as he did.

He poured over the letter from his dad and mum and then the second one from Annie, drinking in each word and rereading them at least three times until he had totally absorbed the pictures of home that they conjured in his mind. He could visualise his dad, sat at the kitchen table with his mum sat next to him, prompting his dad not to forget this or that and his dad telling her to slow down and give him a chance to write. Will smiled at the thought of that. As he read, he could almost smell the kitchen at home, and pictured his mother cooking supper for the three of them. He closed his eyes as he finished the letter for the third time, still picturing his dad crouched over the end of the kitchen table, writing. What Will didn't know was that his father had been crouched over a table, writing alright, but not the one that he had imagined so sweetly in his mind. Tom had been just ten miles behind the front line outside of Loos when he wrote the letter, carefully capturing the picture and flavour of Annie and Harriet's letter into his own words, painting the image with his mind, recreating the picture of Bristol and what was happening at home at that precise moment in time.

Will reread Annie's letter, seeing images of her in his mind, picturing her walking to work at Mardons, but then he had to fight hard to remember the fine details of her face. He sighed as he realised that her image was not as clear to him as it has been months ago, and it dawned on him that the months he had been in captivity were slipping by and turning into over a year. He went to his little box of possessions and carefully took out Annie's picture, tracing her face with his finger tip and gazing longingly at the tiny image. 'She is my girl,' he whispered to himself, reassuring himself. He must ask her for another photograph when he writes to her next time, he thought. With his prize possessions, a few sheets of writing paper, he eagerly set about writing to his parents and Annie. It was a boost to his confidence that he could write without having to wedge his shaking arm tight against the table and for the first time, he wrote with ease.

Dear Mum and Dad,

Well, I hope that you will be able to read my writing a little better than the previous letters I have sent. Since I last wrote to you, so much has happened here and my apologies for the delay in writing. I had not said too much in my previous letters as I did not want to worry you, but I have been suffering with some problems with shaking as a result of the fighting before I was captured. It was a blooming nuisance to be honest, but the Germans have been trying to help me. I had some time away from the camp at a military hospital where I was treated for my shaking and it has worked. So you would recognise me now more as your son than you might have done before. I have to say that it is a great relief to me.

I have only just come back to the camp and am looking forward to seeing my friends later. They are out working and I am hoping to be able to do the same shortly and get out of the camp a bit more. I miss home terribly and hang on to the thought that this war will be over soon. We get little news here on real events as you would imagine. The Bosch tells us that they are winning and the only other news we receive is from newly captured men who bring us up to date with our side's version of events. The camp is full to bursting now, so we tend not to see too many new faces and the news is a bit sketchy. We do okay though, and the British part of the camp is well organised. Before I went, they were starting to organise a concert here, so that will be something to look forward to.

Well, I am running low on paper, so will have to finish here. If you can send me some more writing paper, I would very much appreciate it.

Your ever loving son.

My dearest Annie,

Every time that I write to you, it brings joy to my heart as I think of my sweet love waiting for me at home. It is a picture in my mind that I cling to longingly and I cannot wait to be home and see your smiling face once more.

Much has happened here since I last wrote, and I apologise for not writing earlier, only I have been away at a hospital and I am pleased to say that I am more like my old self now. They have treated me to cure a tremor that I had down my left side. It worked. I am pleased to say so. Your Will looks much more like his old self again; you will be glad to hear.

I really miss you, my sweetheart. Can you send me a photograph of yourself please? I only have the one here and I am wearing it out with my eyes! I am always thinking of you and cannot wait to be reunited with you. Goodbye for now but please remember that one day, I will return to your side.

Your ever loving, Will.

It was long after dark when the other men started coming back to the camp from work and when Terry, Alfie and Harold entered the hut, Will was quite taken aback. The months working under near slave conditions down the salt mine was clearly taking a toll on them. Any of the autumn's sunshine had clearly passed them by as they looked pale and even gaunter than before Will had left. They were delighted to see Will back though, and they had a small celebration, each bringing some small article from their last food parcel that they had saved up for a such a special occasion. Some tea, a small pack of digestive biscuits etc. But Will could tell that behind the effort, all the men were exhausted. Terry, in particular, was putting on a brave face. "Blimey, Will. You look a different man. I do believe that you've put on a little bit of weight and blow me down, that blasted shaking has gone. What did they do to you?" Will told them his story, and how he had been kept away from German patients but that there were a lot of their soldiers suffering in similar ways to himself. He told them about the electric shock treatment, and how at first, it had made his arms and legs tingle and not done any more than that. Then, he relayed how they had upped the voltage to the point where he had blacked out with the intensity of the pain on the last two sessions, and had come around feeling near dead but with the shaking gone. He held his hands out in front of him again for all to see and they nodded in admiration before gently taking the mickey out of him as friends do.

It wasn't until 2 am the next morning that the entire hut realised that Will wasn't in fact totally cured, as he woke nearly the entire camp with his nightmarish screaming. All of his demons, it seemed, had not left him.

CHAPTER TWENTY-FOUR

Weeks merged seamlessly into months and Tom's perceptions of the war before he had joined up were being realised. Whether in the trenches or behind the front line, everyone started each day with a feeling of exhaustion. If Tom was lucky, sleep was grabbed in stints of two hours at the most, as there was always some sudden noise that tore through the unconscious mind to wake him suddenly. An explosion or a donkey braying loudly and fearfully, that's all it took for sleep to be broken. So if he had four hours sleep at night in total, then he considered that a good night. They all got used to functioning in a constant state of tiredness, so when sleep did overwhelm him, it was through near exhaustion. All the men were the same, and when they chatted together in the rare quiet times, the subjects of conversation were always either of home, food or tiredness. All three dominated their minds at different times of the day.

The mud was unrelenting. It stuck like glue in great clumps to your boots and clung to your hands and coat sleeves when you put a hand out to steady yourself, which you had to do all the time when navigating the slippery trenches, so keeping clean was horribly difficult. But military standards were enforced rigorously, so when Tom wasn't reshaping a trench or filling in mortar or shell holes, he would be cleaning furiously. It was impossible. After what seemed endless days of routine, fear and exhaustion, the time finally came for a break from the front line. Tom's unit slipped back through the line of trenches to a village about eight miles back from the front. They moved at night, marching under the cover of darkness, safe from a short burst of shellfire that illuminated the night sky behind them. They were to take a 48-hour break, but although it meant they were away from imminent danger, the men were almost as busy as they had been in the trenches. After a slightly better night's sleep and a morning of cleaning their kit to be meticulously inspected, they were sent off to repair a road that had been hit by a rogue shell. They then spent the afternoon cleaning again, including themselves. Just the simple luxuries like taking a hot shallow bath were becoming lost here, so it was quite uplifting to be able to have a bath and have a proper change of clothing.

No letters from home had caught up with him, so in the evening, Tom wrote a personal letter to Harriet (and Annie) bringing them up-to-date with his own time there. He was always careful to keep his letters home upbeat, knowing that Harriet had enough worries thinking about William, so he painted a more relaxed picture of his life than it was in reality, being careful to miss out too many references to the front line. He then wrote a letter to Will. Without news from home, he had 'to wing it', inventing life at home without too many specific references to actual events. He addressed Will's envelope, then left it open before carefully placing both letters in the one envelope back to Bristol. As he licked the gum of the envelope, he just wished that he could be carrying them back personally. He missed home more now that he was away from the front for some reason, perhaps because he had more time to think about it.

The morning wake-up call greeted them early with an order to look sharp. There was a 'flap' on, and their leave was being cut short. That usually meant that either they were expecting a major German attack or were about to launch one themselves. Just as they were assembling to march back, word went out that the post had arrived, and Tom's heart soared when his name was called. With no time to read the letter, he thrust it inside his tunic and set off with a renewed spring in his step. When they reached the trenches, the word was that the British and French were going to mount an attack the following morning at dawn and that every man possible, including Tom, would be going over the top. Tom had only been involved in direct fighting once so far and had approached it in a 'kill or be killed' manner. He remained sceptical that the war had any true merit other than to satisfy the egos of the politicians and he had no grudge against the Germans personally, other than they had incarcerated his son. But if faced with anyone trying to kill him. He knew that he would naturally defend himself.

After a full day of hectic preparation, Tom found twenty minutes over a mug of hot, strong tea to read the letter from home. Will's last letter had been read by Annie to Harriet and then sent on to Tom. He noticed immediately the different handwriting. This was much more like the old Will's hand. He read eagerly of the treatment his son had received to cure his shaking and when he read Will's words that the Germans had "been very kind and treated me", it made him less eager to point his gun at anyone tomorrow morning and pull the trigger. He reread the letter but he had no time to ponder it anymore as a barrage of German shells rained in, sending everyone into corners to pray and wait to see if any of the shells had their name on them.

Morning came following a near sleepless night of being constantly disturbed by the lights and noise of almost constant allied shelling. They prepared for the attack down the line, shuffling forwards to take up their positions. The dreaded whistle would sound at first light and if the wind direction held, they were using gas first. Like everyone else, Tom hated the stuff and took no joy from the fact that it was the British using it against the

Germans. Whichever side's gas it was made no difference. It was awful stuff and Tom had now seen on too many occasions, men gagging for air, their enlarged pleading eyes staring out from ashen faces, their hands gripping their own throats like they would strangle themselves rather than endure the burning acid engulfing their lungs. It was dreadful stuff, inhumane.

Smoke grenades were set off to check the wind direction then the order barked to put their masks on. The cloth hood had been impregnated with something that made it resistant to gas seepage which made it smell most unpleasant and as before, the crude eye pieces fogged up within seconds, making visibility difficult. They had been instructed to spit on the inside of the glass and rub the saliva over each eyepiece to reduce the misting but it didn't really work. Along the front line, gas cylinders were cranked open, and their evil contents slowly drifted eastwards towards the German lines. There wasn't much of a breeze, so it moved slowly, but at least the low lying cloud made it impossible for Bosch snipers to pick out any heads to target. There was nothing to do now but wait. The order went up to fix bayonets and all around Tom, men struggled to see through the fog of their masks to fix their bayonets securely. It was tricky enough with clear vision. Fear coursed through the line, making hands shake and adding to their difficulties. Tom gripped his rifle, trying not to think of the coming attack when suddenly, a barrage of shells opened up, reigning down on them from a German battery to the north east.

Tom looked back weeks and months later and realised just how very lucky he had been. The air was alive with the whistle of incoming shells and without warning, one landed on the lip of the trench just fifteen yards away, the explosion ripping deep into the belly of the trench. The blast killed everyone within the first ten yards of its impact, with two men instantly vaporised and eleven more decapitated or mutilated beyond recognition. There were five more men between the explosion and Tom, all waiting for the gas to subside and the whistle to blow. None of them heard the whistle that day. Tom was thrown backwards by the body of the man who had been stood next to him and who had taken the full force of the explosion, protecting Tom from its worst. Tom landed in a heap against the far wall of the trench with the man on top of him and as he tried to push the body off of him, despite the trench being a maelstrom of noise and confusion, he could hear nothing. The percussion from the blast had knocked him senseless and it took him a few moments or minutes, he wasn't sure which, to regain his senses, at which point he realised that he was struggling to breathe. A man's body straddled Tom's chest and face and moving his dead weight was at first impossible. He tried to twist his head to the side but his gas mask made it difficult. He could not move his right hand at all. It was wedged under something and with the body on top of him, he couldn't see what. Using his free left hand, he slowly managed to shift the man's body off his head and neck. Trying again, he was able to shuffle out from underneath the body and break free. Tom's gas mask had been half blown off by the force of the blast and he completed its removal with his left hand, sucking in air gratefully as he tore it from his face. He looked over to his right hand which was still gripping his rifle, but the rifle butt was wedged under the torso of another dead man. The top half of the poor wretch had been blown clean off and the stomach and legs now lay across the rifle, its intestines dripping out over Tom's arm. With his left hand, he eased the body away from the rifle barrel with difficulty and pulled his right hand out, still griping the gun. He could see now that a nine-inch shard of metal had impaled his hand to the rifle shaft, pinning his hand to the wooden butt like a huge nail. For a moment, he just stared in shock at his hand, trying to take it all in. He could feel no pain at first, and it only hit him the moment he managed to prize the rifle away from the blade that impaled his hand. The pain then was excruciating and as he pulled at the blade, three large flaps of flesh pulled back from the palm of his hand. He gasped in agony and stared at his right hand, still trying to take the last few minutes in. Carefully, he folded the three flaps of skin and flesh roughly back in place still around the blade and reached inside his jacket for his field dressing. He started to shiver violently as a wave of shock rippled through him. He could see that what had gone through his hand was the broken end of the blade from another man's bayonet that had been sheared off in the explosion. He didn't want to remove it there and then, so he roughly wrapped the field dressing around his hand and the shrapnel as best he could. With the blade still in and the bandage holding tightly around it, the worst of the blood flow was stemmed. He stumbled out from the trench cradling his injured hand like a baby, taking care to take the weight off the blade as best he could to ease the pain.

The following few hours were near lost to confusion and mayhem. Men were shouting and stumbling over the wounded and dead. In other parts of the line, dozens of whistles had sounded the order to attack and men had obeyed their commanders and disappeared towards the German line. Left behind them were the British injured, who were carried or led away from the front line, back through a zigzag maze of trenches. Tom was following a medic who had an injured soldier slung over his back like a sack of coal. Tom was shaking violently, and every jolt and stumble sent a bolt of pain through his injured hand and he bit through his bottom lip trying to stem the agony. His hearing started to return gradually as silence was replaced with muffled noises and eventually, Tom and the other wounded were led to a field dressing station in a partially bombed-out barn. One of the injured men was making a hell of a row and Tom started to wish that he had still been deaf. Laid out on a stretcher, the poor lad (for he didn't seem old enough to be called a man) shouted for his mother through blood bubbling uncontrollably out of his mouth. He took one last shout before his breathing changed into frantic panting for a minute and then abruptly stopped. Tom hoped then that the poor chap found his mother waiting for him where ever he was now.

Tom sat on the damp ground in silence, cradling his injured hand, the blade sticking through his hand looking almost surreal. The doctor who eventually saw him looked at the blade sticking out from both sides and was straight with Tom. "All the anaesthetic has been used up already I'm afraid. This really needs to be removed now though. Do I have your agreement to remove it?"

Tom took less than a moment to answer. He knew removing it would be painful but he was in agony now. "Get it out," he replied briskly. Four orderlies held Tom's legs and shoulders and without any hesitation or fuss, the doctor grabbed the thick end of the blade with a cloth and pulled it out in one movement. The pain took Tom's breath away and in a moment, the wound was doused in vodka and tightly dressed with wadding and bandaged.

"Looks like you might have been lucky," the doctor said as he bound the hand up quickly. "It looks like the blade went in straight and in between the main tendons, so with luck, you might be able to keep your fingers crossed, if you get my meaning. The good news is that a one-handed soldier isn't much use out here, so I'll be recommending you go back to Blighty for a bit. The bad news is that I suspect you'll be coming back again in a month or two," he said, grinning limply.

CHAPTER TWENTY-FIVE

And so it was. A week later, with his right arm in a sling and his back pack slung over his left shoulder, Tom walked briskly into Stapleton Road and noisily sprang the bell over the shop door. As he stepped inside, the stunned face of Harriet looked back at him in shock. She rushed past her bemused customer and he pulled his arm out of the sling as she jumped into his arms. He cradled his beloved as best he could with one hand bandaged and they kissed before the moment was drowned in the reality of them having a customer standing in front of them. They parted quickly, embarrassed at the show of affection in front of a stranger, but the woman beamed back at them both, guessing what was happening. While Harriet went back to serve the woman, Tom slipped into the workshop to see Alfred and Anthony. Alf was delighted to see his younger brother again and they exchanged a joking handshake with their left hands after Tom held up his bandaged right hand in a mock salute. "I hope you can still grip a hammer when you get back," Alfred said concerned, looking at the bandage.

"Don't worry, brother. I'm told I've been very lucky, so I shall be fully functional in a month or so. They've given me ten days' leave and I have to have the hand dressed at the hospital every day while I'm here, but they reckon I'll be as good as new and have a rifle in my hand before a hammer I'm afraid."

When Tom got home that evening, a surge of joy almost overwhelmed him when he stepped into the hallway again for the first time in many months. 'It's funny how your own place has its own peculiar smell,' he thought. He hadn't noticed it before, but its familiar smell brought a moment of sheer joy to him as he drank in the familiarity of his home again. Harriet had gone through to the kitchen and put the kettle on, but he gently leaned past her and switched off the gas tap. He held out his good hand, which she took with an almost shy smile as he led her out of the kitchen and upstairs.

There were boiled eggs and toast for breakfast. "Lovely," Tom beamed. Alfred and Anthony were opening up the shop this morning and Anthony was becoming a dab hand with the customers when he needed to. He had settled well into the business and was learning the skills of shoe-making fast as well as being good with the people out front. So for an hour, Harriet and Tom enjoyed a leisurely breakfast together that Tom would remember for the rest of his days. "It's my right hand, Harriet, so I can't write for a while I'm afraid, so we've got to come up with an excuse and ask Annie to write to Will for us for a few weeks."

"We'll say you've hurt your hand at work. I'm sure Will won't suspect anything," Harriet replied.

Tom had to eat with his left hand and spreading the butter on the toast wasn't easy, and he ended up getting the butter over his once white bandage. He made light of the war as much as he could without lying to her. "It's not very jolly, my love, but it is war after all and we get by. I've seen some things that I'd rather not talk about and it's a world that only those that were there would understand. I just hope that we can make the breakthrough soon so we can all get back home." He crunched on his toast, savouring every mouthful as he enjoyed the moment. It was nice just to sit there with his old clothes on and not be in uniform.

He walked Harriet to work before setting off for the Bristol Royal Infirmary where he eventually had his hand redressed, making a joke about the butter on the bandage. The doctor looked carefully at the wound and encouraged Tom to slowly move his fingers into a semi-grip. "You were very lucky, Mr Payne. The angle that the shrapnel went through your hand was kind to you. Another quarter of an inch either way and you would have likely had a gammy hand for life."

Tom walked back through the City Centre, enjoying the images that he knew so well and logging it to memory once more. Back at the shop, he awkwardly made a cup of tea for everyone and started the process of catching up on all the general news. It seemed strange that just a few months out of the job could make everything so distant to him. The business was getting by, but the effects of the war were beginning to bite and without Tom, they had lost some of their higher value ladies' shoe sales. Anthony was doing a good job though and learning the ropes well, progressing from just cutting out the leather from templates to starting to make some basic shoes. But the business missed Tom for sure, and he couldn't wait to get back to it.

Annie came for lunch on Saturday after working the morning shift at Mardons. Tom noticed quickly how close she and Harriet had become as they chatted together while they carried tea and sandwiches through. Annie was like a daughter to Harriet he thought, so relaxed and at ease and Annie clearly loved her company as they talked through the events of the last days since they had seen each other. "We've got a surprise for you," Harriet said, smiling at Tom. She sat down at the table and opened up a writing pad and, with a pencil, started slowly and painfully to write. The letters were uneven and she had to pause in between the letters to think through the spelling, but she finished the first sentence before stopping, looking with slight embarrassment to Tom for some reaction. "Well done, my love," he beamed, looking at the line of words and quietly thinking to himself that it reminded him of his own first writings at school. "And it's good to read that it is 'nice' to see me home again," he joked.

"I can spell 'nice', Tom," Harriet chipped back. I would struggle to spell 'lovely' or 'wonderful' yet, but then I think you're teasing me, Mr Payne, and you are fishing for compliments!"

Tom laughed and as their eyes met, he realised just how much he loved and missed her.

"Annie's a good teacher," Harriet said, breaking the moment and Tom snapped back into joking with them.

"Well, someone had better be writing to our William for a few weeks while I get my hand back together because I certainly can't hold a pen at the moment."

"I can write your letter, Tom," Annie said. "You can dictate it to me, starting with how you've hurt your hand in the workshop."

And that's what they did. Tom made up a story about how he had cut his hand unloading a delivery, so he was only doing light left-handed duties around the shop and workshop, getting frustrated at only having his left hand to work with. Harriet sat there, listening for anything that might sound unconvincing as Tom dictated slowly and Annie wrote, keenly listening for any part that might sound unconvincing. It didn't. Harriet sat across the table from Tom as he spoke. It was lovely to have him back home, she thought. As she gazed at him dictating the words for Will's letter, she thought just how much she had missed him while he had been away. 'The blooming war,' she thought to herself. Firstly, she had lost her son to it and now her husband. She stopped though, when she thought of those wives and mothers who had already received telegrams with the worst of news. She shuddered at the thought.

When Tom had finish the opening passage, Annie read it back and they congratulated themselves on how it sounded before Tom continued to dictate more mundane events of life around him in Bristol. This time, he felt easier about writing from things he was actually seeing, rather than being sat in a trench somewhere in France, reading letters from home and rewriting them with his writing pad balanced on any flat surface he could find, from his lap to the bonnet of a lorry.

"She is such a lovely girl," Harriet said to Tom after Annie had left. "And she really is fond of our Will; you can tell. Will writes to her and she tells me bits and pieces but doesn't show me any of his letters. I think they are stronger as a couple now than when Will was here. That's the impression I get anyway." And her impression was right. Will's letters to Annie were becoming more personal over time and, as he received her replies, had become more from the heart. They were both aware that their letters were always read by British and German officers, which made them conscious of their words, but the bond that had been there when they had kissed their goodbyes in 1914 had developed into much more than just a friendship, as the months had drifted into now almost two years. Annie missed him more as each day passed. The solitary photograph of him in his navy uniform stood alongside some other prisoners in the camp was becoming worn at the edges; she had taken it down to look at it so much. It was dusk when she walked home after seeing Tom and Harriet, and she took the photograph out once again as she went to bed, staring again into Will's distracted eyes and wondered when she would see him again.

Tom's leave was passing fast. He loved every minute of being home but each day when he woke, he was conscious that this precious time in his life was slipping by. He got a tram to the B.R.I. hospital every day to have his dressing changed and the doctor was now getting him to flex his fingers as the risk of the wound reopening was reducing. He still had limited movements and the palm of his hand itched intolerably, but the doctor reassured him that this was a sign that the wound was healing.

He walked home, taking a small detour alongside the river, taking in the sights and sounds of what he loved, his hometown. He stopped to awkwardly light his pipe, and leaned back on the wooden fence while he enjoyed the moment. Two more days and he would be reporting for duty again at the Ashton Gate barracks and from there going to who knows where.

Between them, they had prepared the next food parcel for Will and with Tom being there, they wanted to make it special. He had bought two hundred Woodbines for the parcel, and carefully opened one of the packets, slipping inside a tiny photograph of Harriet and himself, taken a week ago to be right up to date. Harriet was seated and he had hidden his bad hand behind as he stood by her side. With the letter safely inside the box and another one from Annie, they carefully wrapped the box up with string and addressed it to Doberitz POW camp, Doberitz, Germany. 'Soon," he thought to himself with determination, 'soon, I hope I'll be breaking the doors down at that camp and getting my son back.'

When Tom left for the barracks, he did so quickly and without fuss. He had come to hate goodbyes, and thought it better to say a quick farewell rather than draw out the anguish for everyone. For every one soldier at the Ashton barracks, there seemed to be twenty horses. It was chaos, with men running everywhere holding on to the halters of confused and frightened-looking mules. To his frustration, he spent two nights at the barracks, with nothing better to sleep in at night than bell tents. 'I've got my own bed not twenty minutes away,' he thought to himself, annoyed at just having to kick his heels for two days amid the malaise. On the third day, he was finally examined by a military doctor. "Your hand is another three weeks away from being of any good to the army yet, private. We'll send you for recuperation at a hospital in Southampton for a fortnight and take it from there."

"Begging your pardon, sir, but could I not recuperate at home? I live not fifteen minutes from here and can have the wound dressed here or at the B.R.I. without need to take up space in Southampton where there are probably more needy cases than me, and I can be well looked after at my own expense rather than the nations." The doctor looked like an old warhorse himself, his main feature being one of the bushiest white moustaches that Tom had ever seen, over which bright, clear, blue eyes rested above a large, wide nose.

He looked at Tom for a few seconds before snorting briskly. "An argument well put, sir. Can't see anything wrong with that." He scribbled a few notes and his signature on two forms and handed them to Tom. "Report to the B.R.I. in one week's time for dressing, then back here to me in two weeks and we'll take it from there. Dismissed."

Tom stood to attention and saluted as best he could with his bandaged hand before slipping it back into its sling. He walked out of the Ashton Barracks with a real spring in his step and he felt like singing. When he walked into the shop, the look on Harriet's face was just as surprised as it had been when he had walked through a week before.

CHAPTER TWENTY-SIX

"I'm really sorry, Will, but you are going to have to go, mate. Just for the nights. Come back during the day and evenings, but your screaming is making us all lose sleep and we're knackered, mate." Terry was really apologetic as he spoke.

Alfie and Harold both chipped in, "It's just for nights, Will, but with working down the salt mine, we're desperate for sleep, mate. It's nothing personal."

They were accompanied by a Welsh Doctor who Will had not seen before, "You can sleep up in the medical centre, William. We can keep an eye on you there, lad," he said kindly. Will was already aware that his nightmares were causing the others in the hut a problem. Since he had returned from the hospital a week ago, almost every night he had been woken sweating and shouting by bad dreams. He was still unsure if it was the same dream every night. It was difficult to tell as it left him the moment he woke. In a way, he was happy to move out as he didn't want to upset or be a nuisance to anyone else. Dr Morgan walked with him to the medical billet as he wanted to check Will over. "You're new here," Will enquired as they walked back.

"I am that," Morgan replied in a warm Welsh accent. "I was captured tending the injured outside of Loos just two weeks ago." What neither of them ever knew was that Dr Morgan had been within a mile of Will's father just before he was injured.

"How is the war going? Who's winning?" Will asked eagerly. "The Germans in the hospital were boasting that they were pushing us back and that they would win the war within months."

"Well, that's a question of who you talk to then, because the opinion of our newspapers is that we have got the Bosch pinned back now. Certainly at Loos, we were gradually getting on top, though to be honest, laddy, the war is turning into a bit of a stalemate from what I can make of it."

Dr Morgan examined Will and noticed the burn marks on each side of his temple. "What caused those?" he asked, quizzically. "They look like burns, and they're fresh injuries for sure." Will explained the electric shock treatment that he had received, and how it had taken his shaking away. Morgan listened with interest and then examined the burn marks again. "I don't know the first thing about electro therapy, boyo, but I do know that it must have taken a hell of a voltage to do that to you. I'd say you're damn lucky to be alive."

"Well, I think I was a bit of an experiment. One of their doctors told me that they had taken the voltage up to see how much a man could take. Apparently at one point, I had technically died but they managed to revive me. I don't remember anything though."

"What!" Morgan bellowed. "I should say they did. Bloody war crime that is, Gerry using British soldiers to test how far they could go with a treatment. I shall make a serious complaint. I will. It's totally against all conventions of war." Will noticed that as he got angrier, his Welsh accent seemed to get stronger.

"Please, don't make a complaint, doctor. They did stop my shaking and if you had seen me before the treatment, you would understand why I don't want any fuss made. I'm still a prisoner of theirs after all. We all are."

The doctor paced the room in anger at the thought of what Will had been subjected to but after a minute, he sat down again. "But they didn't cure you of everything though, did they? These dreams of yours, these nightmares, they are part of the same problem, boyo. The same trauma that caused the…"

The doctor's sentence was cut short by two gunshots. Both men ran outside to see what was happening. As they rounded the corner of one of the buildings, two Germans were awkwardly dragging the body of a Russian prisoner away. A small group of British and French prisoners had quickly gathered. "What's going on?" the doctor asked one of them.

"It's one of the Russians, sir. He started raving at one of the guards, sir, who was taunting him with bread he was taking through to the German kitchens. Poor buggers! Most of the Ruskies are half-starved. When he started waving his arms and looking violent, one of the other soldiers shot him, sir. Twice, sir."

The Russians were indeed half-starved. While the British and French supplemented the awful camp food with food parcels from home, the Russians received nothing other than what their captors fed them. To the British and French, food from home made the difference between just surviving and starving. Camp food largely consisted of very thin and watery soup with a hint that the water had once contained a vegetable or two, largely mangle wurzles and turnips. Chunks of bread made from rye wheat helped to bulk it out, but that over time noticeably contained an increasing amount of sawdust in it to bulk out the mixture. It was dark and heavy and was really hard and dry unless you held it down in the soup or drank water with it. If you were lucky, a little butter might be sent in a food parcel from time to time, and this was scraped on to the bread before being carefully scraped off again to impart its buttery flavour and make the butter go as far as possible.

The camp had formed into three main sections with British, French and Russians. There were no barriers, so they were free to walk between the sectors, but whilst each nationality was very polite and always nodded with a friendly acknowledgement to the other, language was a barrier, especially with the Russians. So, each nationality tended to mix with their own and keep themselves to themselves. After more than a year in captivity, the British and French prisoners looked thin whilst the Russians were looking half-starved. Senior British, French and Russian officers had met to try and help each other where they could; after all, they were all allies with a common enemy. It was clear that the Bosch held the Russians in particular contempt for some reason, so their treatment of them was nothing short of brutal if any of them stepped out of line, not that it was much less forgiving towards the British and French. The allied senior officers had agreed to help each other where they could, which meant that if the French or British could find a way of passing over spare food to the Russians, they would. But in reality, no one was doing more than just surviving and every scrap of food that the Germans gave them was gratefully consumed, even though its quality was meagre and increasingly questionable.

Discipline was instilled rigorously in the camp and there were regular raids on billets, where the Germans arrived without warning and in numbers, literally turning everything upside down in one or two billets, looking for whatever they were looking for. The billets occupants were made to stand to attention at gunpoint outside, waiting to go back in and clear up the mess when their captors had finished. Their German guards now neatly divided into two types: old soldiers who were long past fighting age and young lads who were just too young to go off to the front and fight. The prisoners all preferred the old soldiers, despite some of them being quite mean in their approach and attitude. In the main, the old soldiers had been pulled out of retirement to save using men of fighting age. They understood military ways and largely worked along ethical lines while doing their job, and there was sort of a respect between them and the prisoners. The young guards, or the 'kids' as the prisoners called them, would usually be okay as long as they had an old soldier with them. It was when you had one or two 'kids' together with no old soldiers around that things could get out of hand, as it had when the poor Russian was shot. Had there been an old soldier present, the poor chap would probably be alive, but psyched up and panicked, one of the young guards had opened fire on the Russian prisoner when the situation could probably have been defused by a more experienced hand.

Amongst the prisoners, military discipline was strictly maintained in the camp. Soldiers were expected to be well turned out every single day, clean-shaven and with clean uniforms, so the odd tiny bar of soap sent from home was a godsend. Will's navy uniform with its white trim was a real problem to keep clean as compared to a khaki uniform; the white trim showed every mark. He had largely been wearing the same uniform for well over a year now and apart from looking worn and tattered at the edges, it hung on him in places as he had lost so much weight in captivity. The camp had a small store of spare uniforms, but senior officers were funny about men keeping to their own rank and uniform where they could. As Will's navy attire was in the minority, they did not want navy crew wearing army uniforms, but it was turning into a problem as time dragged on and Will was getting thoroughly fed up with it all.

"I want to work now, Terry, and spend my days with a bit more purpose to them and besides, it would be good to have a few bob in my pocket to buy a few essentials."

Terry looked at Will sternly, "Well, I can understand that, Will, but whatever you do don't come down the salt mines with us, mate. It's bloody purgatory and some of the guards there are pure sadists; they like to see us suffer. The work is physically hard for one thing, but added to that, we don't see daylight at all, and look at the state of our hands and knees," he said, holding out his hands to Will. Terry's hands were full of deep cuts and cracks where the salt had dried out the skin and turned it to leather. "Try and get yourself a job outside on the land, Will. At least you'll have the sun on your back when it's shining."

Will went to see the British commander who was now liaising with the Germans. Within two days, he was told to report for a working party that next morning at 06:30. He slept fitfully that night, and woke himself up shouting long before he needed to get up, running in sweat as his nightmare evaded his conscious memory once again.

CHAPTER TWENTY-SEVEN

The wound was healing nicely on Tom's hand, just leaving thick scars on both sides. The scar tissue itched though, so that he had a habit of scratching the palm of his hand without realising he was doing it. Physiotherapy at the hospital consisted of an old, used, wooden cotton bobbin that Tom had to squeeze and rotate in his injured hand to build up the strength in his fingers. It had been painful at first, but when he reported back to Ashton for duty the second time, he was 'fighting fit' as he put it.

As before, his farewell to his family had been short. He hugged Harriet in the privacy of their kitchen for one last time and slipped quietly out of the front door with his backpack slung over his shoulder, this time not expecting to come home in the near future. By the afternoon, he was on a train to London with a hundred and fifty other soldiers and onward to Dover, with his papers all stamped and in order. 'No going back this time,' he thought to himself. He was to join a regiment of Royal Engineers bound for somewhere in France and then, as soon as they could arrange it, make his way back to his old unit. He was something of a novelty to his new colleagues. All raw recruits heading out to the front for the first time, Tom inwardly smiled to himself at their youth and bravado. He had seen it all before when his unit had travelled over months ago.

'The innocence of youth,' he thought to himself and as before, he appeared to his new colleagues as more of a father figure to them, especially as he was returning back to France after an injury. "What's it like out there?" they all took it in turn to ask, some intrigued and some clearly nervous.

"You'll find out soon enough for yourselves," Tom told them in turn. "Just keep your heads down and remember that most heroes end up dead far quicker than the smart ones, so don't go getting yourself a posthumous medal."

The journey to the front line took a different route to that before and Tom had no recognition of the area. They camped overnight in the grounds of a lovely old farm outside of Bar-le-Duc. Their commanding officer gathered them together during the evening. "Our camp, gentlemen, is on what the French call the 'Voie Sacree', their 'Sacred Road'. Fifty miles up this road is the town of Verdun, strategically important to the war effort and even more important to French moral. Verdun has special significance to the French and they will hold it at all costs. Two miles away from here is the Bar-le-Duc depot, the main supply line to Verdun. Our job is to ensure that the road to Verdun is kept open and problem-free for troops and supplies to get through at speed and without any issues. Most of the problems with the Germans are nearer to Verdun, as the Bosch likes to pepper the road with shells, so make the most of a quiet night here and we will set off first thing after dawn."

"Will we get to fight the Germans?" one of the enthusiastic youngsters enquired.

"Not immediately. Verdun is being defended by the French for now, but they have been taking a bit of a pounding over the last month, so what you will be doing is vital work. The road must stay open at all costs."

The next four months was spent doing just this. They didn't see the nice old farm again over that time but were billeted in a village ten miles back from Verdun. They did, however, see a lot of shell holes that needed filling in quickly. Most of the time, they were drafted in immediately after dawn after overnight shelling, but the Germans switched tactics the closer one got to Verdun and shelled during the daytime, using spotter planes to try and catch troops and transport on the road. The accuracy of their shelling was impressive and depressing for everyone having to fill the holes in. The Germans could run a line of shells down a half mile stretch of road like they had placed land mines on it, making it very difficult to keep the road open. The work was physically very demanding and dangerous, and Tom and his pals had been caught several times in 'death alley' as they nicknamed it, just as a German salvo started. There was nothing to do but get the hell out of it when the Germans opened fire and Tom had been lucky several times, missing a direct hit by just enough to escape. Twice he was blown off his feet though, and one time, was left severely deaf for several days after a blast. When the shelling started and they were on the road, all the engineers had to run like hell and get a hundred yards off the road, then they would normally be safe. Such was the accuracy of the German shelling. It was depressing though, filling in what they were sure were the same holes time after time.

When Tom got back to camp after the close encounter that had left him deaf, he just wanted to be alone. He pulled out Harriet's last letter (still written by Annie) and reread it, this time with shaking hands. The letters from home painted a picture of Bristol, as winter came and Tom meticulously transcribed the scene back home in his own words, picturing it all for himself as autumn turned into winter, missing it as he wrote to Will. Carefully, he folded the pages and addressed the envelope to Will in Doberitz, then he placed his own letter to Harriet in with it and put them inside another envelope addressed to 25 Saxon Road. Harriet's letters usually caught up with Tom roughly every two weeks, and he would set about rewriting each letter to William and write his own letter back to Harriet as soon as his work allowed.

For two or, if they were lucky, three days a fortnight, they would be sent a few miles back from Verdun for rest and recuperation as they called it. They were all grateful to get a break from the back-breaking and dangerous work and it was stressful having to dodge bombs almost every day. Tom had worked out the Germans' pattern of shelling though. They were a regimented lot, the Germans, and liked to keep a routine up, so once he heard the first wiz bang (as they called them) coming in, he knew there would generally be a sequence of eighteen to twenty shells laying a pattern on the road before a break of five to ten minutes when they would launch another salvo of ten to twelve shells. Then after another five to ten minutes, they would drop another five shells, trying to catch anyone back on the road off guard. So as soon as the first shell came, there was nothing to do but to get well off the road for around forty minutes until the shelling had finished. Some days, this sequence would happen two or three times and other days, six or seven times.

Filling in shell holes was always done in relative silence with one ear eagerly cocked for the first sound of incoming fire. The moment anyone heard the familiar but dreaded sound, shovels were discarded at the run while legging it off the road. It was no place for loitering, but the worst of it was when there were horses and mules on the road. When the shelling started, they had to get them off to the side quickly and some of the mules, in particular, just dug their heels in and refused to move, so had to be left. Most of them bolted when the first shells landed and they would be gone up or down the road at high speed, their loads swaying madly on their backs as they ran. Tom got just as upset when he had to clear away the remains of a dead horse as he did when picking up what was left of dead people. That was when life was at its worst. The first time it happened, he found himself holding the head of a dying horse, stroking its face and talking to the animal quietly until an officer came and shot the poor creature to put it out of its misery. As he held the poor animal's head in his arms, his thoughts went back to his life in Bristol, looking after the coal horses. The memory of looking into that horse's desperate eye, as it looked back at him, upset Tom then and for a long time after.

As the months passed, the Germans got cannier and waited for troop movements on the road before the shelling started. The French moved as much as possible, up and down the road under cover of darkness, which was thankfully longer as autumn arrived, but such was the volume of traffic up and down the road that they had no choice but to travel in daylight. Every six or seven days, a battalion of French soldiers would travel away from Verdun to give them a break from the shelling. The forts around the town were taking a real pounding still and the troops coming away looked haggard and worn out, so different to their replacements who passed them going the other way. Many fresh-faced young soldiers often sang as they marched, keeping their spirits up in their innocence of what lay before them.

When they had first arrived on the Verdun Road, it had been busy with refugees leaving the besieged town, and what a sorry sight they were! Families, often with everything that they could possibly fit onto handcarts, would walk alongside with fathers and grandfathers pushing. The British soldiers had made a point of stopping them just before they got to 'death alley'. If they thought that the Germans were about to start shelling, then they would usher them through the most dangerous stretch of road as fast as they could, helping them to push their carts over the well-pitted road. Usually, this worked pretty well if there were not too many refugees trying to pass at any one time, but any large group of people on the road was fair game to the spotters and twice, Tom had to help remove the bodies of dead refugees after they had been shelled and taken direct hits. That's when it hit Tom the most, and even the hardest-faced trooper was brought to silence or tears when the bodies of young children and women had to be gently picked up and carried away.

When they did get a chance to drop back a few miles for a break from the road, there was always inspection and drill to do, the army insisting strictly on ensuring military values at every opportunity. After four months with the same group of engineers, Tom was almost giving up on returning to his original unit. As before, he largely tried to keep himself to himself for fear of gaining too close a friendship, but in truth, it was impossible not to forge a strong bond with the men around him, especially when they all placed their lives on the line together and relied on each other so closely. They were a good bunch of men, the West Middlesex Engineers, and coming originally from London, Tom felt a sort of affinity with many of them anyway. After four months, they were pulled back to Bar-le-Duc and once they had left Verdun ten miles behind them, it was quite a pleasant journey, despite light rain having set in. A chill November wind was starting as they arrived back and their bully beef was well appreciated that evening, Tom cupping his hot mess tin gratefully in his hands to warm them through.

"Well done, men," their commanding officer congratulated them. "A good job well done but it's time for someone else to take over now. You've a two-day break here to rest up and then we will be moving off to the British sector."

"Can I ask where we are going, sir?" one of the engineers asked.

"You can, lad. We are going to the Somme."

"Never heard of it," came the reply.

CHAPTER TWENTY-EIGHT

It was dark and bitter cold. Will pulled his greatcoat up around his ears as best he could and joined a group of around twenty fellow prison workers. "Where are we going?" he whispered to one of the men who he recognised. "Silence!" The order barked back from one of the older prison guards. They were marched out and into the darkness flanked by six prison guards, walking until the dawn started to break. As it did, they turned left down a long lane and into a farm courtyard flanked by a row of empty stables. Silence was maintained all the while as they walked under the watchful eye of the guards. An older guard could speak broken English and with an accent so heavy that Will struggled to make out what he was saying. The gist of it was that this poor farmer's best horses had been taken by the military to support the war effort, so we were now to replace the horses. Each man was given a spade and between them, all had to push a heavy cart full of manure up to the edge of a rough-looking field. The farmer appeared out of a barn, putting his coat back on and came across scowling and cursing under his breath. He grabbed a spade from the first prisoner and pushed him roughly back, barking something unpleasant in German. He dug a short trench two rows wide and then went back and dug the first row a spade depth deeper, piling up the soil in front. He stopped to point at his eyes, then the prisoners and then the ground before filling in the deeper layer with manure and covered this back with the soil.

"Ziss you now do!" the guard ordered.

"It's double digging, lads. A piece of cake," one of Will's new colleagues commented.

"Silence," the guard barked back again.

The 'piece of cake' continued for four back-breaking hours before they were allowed a break. Will's now soft hands had callouses and blisters building up, and when they were finally allowed to stop, they all literally collapsed at the side of the field before being marched back to the stables. In groups of five, they were taken under guard to the farm kitchen. Will sat exhausted on a bale of straw in the stables and was in the last group to go. He was full of anticipation now though, as each group came back still in ordered silence. They had smiles and one of them winked at Will as he threw himself back on the straw. Will and the last four were marched off to the farmhouse. The kitchen was wonderfully warm, with a large 'Aga' at one end under a great inglenook fireplace that belted out enough heat to fill the large kitchen and to give the whole house a glow. The farmer's wife was a kindly looking woman in her fifties, with great podgy fingers and a shy smile that defied her husband, who stood in the corner puffing on an enormous pipe. Five large earthenware bowls and wooden spoons had been laid out around a large and well-used wooden table, each with a quarter loaf of dark rye bread that still had the smell of the oven in it. It was heaven. Will hadn't tasted soup like this since his own mother had made it back at home. It was wonderfully thick and actually had real vegetables in it, unlike the soup at the camp. And the bread was real, no sawdust or mites baked into it, and it smelt beautifully fresh. 'Baked that morning,' Will guessed.

He held the first mouthful of soup in his mouth for an age, closing his eyes to focus his concentration even more on the moment, rolling the bread over his tongue to savour its rich flavour. Heaven unfortunately did not last long and with the meal over, the men were ushered out as soon as they had gratefully scoffed the lot. Every bowl was wiped clean by the last morsel of bread, without a single mark or smear on it, and every crumb of bread was devoured gratefully. Will was the last to leave the kitchen behind the other four men and broke step briefly to give his hostess a warm smile and to whisper 'Danke Schoen'. The woman looked surprised and quickly whispered 'Bitte Schoen' back, smiling awkwardly back in return.

Will's thoughts of food was soon lost to the digging again, and they continued all afternoon until darkness started to fall. The walk back to the camp was completed in silence again, largely because each man was too exhausted to talk anyway. Will, in particular, was dead on his feet. The others were clearly more hardened to the enforced work than he was and at one point, he wasn't sure if he would make it back, stumbling several times to be caught by the man next to him. "It will get easier, lad," he whispered to Will quietly as he picked him up.

When he got back to the billet, Terry and the others had already returned and Will stumbled in and almost collapsed onto Terry's bed, his hands shivering on his chest, a line of blisters on each hand, like glistening, white beads. His friends gathered around concerned. They covered him in a blanket and someone fetched him a hot mug of water to sip on.

The following morning, Will was forcibly woken having been too exhausted to dream anything that night. Every movement hurt as he dragged himself out to join the work party. Yesterday morning's routine repeated itself. It was a huge field and every spade he dug was back-breaking. Alfie had given him a pair of leather gloves and they at least helped his hands, though the blisters had now burst inside each glove and he could see feint stains of dark pushing through the leather, but each time he paused for a few seconds to straighten his back to ease the pain, one of the two guards lounging on the edge of the field would shout at him threateningly. Four of the six guards were in the warm kitchen and they rotated the two guards to be outside in the cold every hour on the hour. The change of guard at least gave the diggers an idea of how the day was passing, and besides, there was usually some moments during the change of guard when Will and the others could grab a few moments rest.

As the hours passed, it was the thought of lunch that drove Will on. His stomach churned with hunger and he felt his strength ebbing as the morning passed. He wasn't disappointed with lunch though when it came. As yesterday, they were ushered into the stables where they threw themselves down onto the straw before being escorted into the farmhouse in groups of five. As before, the soup was heaven and the bread freshly baked and tasty. He ate heartily, and once again was last to leave the table and smiled politely at the farmer's wife and whispered "*Danke Shoen*" that was returned with a faint smile and "*Bitte Schoen*". Without notice, the guard that Will had walked past swung his rifle butt and in one sweeping action, caught Will a glancing blow to the back of his head. Will didn't see it coming and the first he knew was when he came in the stables, his head thumping and his ribs searing in pain. "The teenage thug of a guard heard you say something to the farmer's wife, Will. Gave you a good kicking too I'm afraid, when you were outside," one of the other prisoners told him. That would explain his painful ribs, Will thought. With Will conscious again, both men were marched back to join the others and the digging restarted. He clutched his ribs as he walked, and the pain caught him with every sod that he turned and every time that he breathed in deeply.

When Sunday came at last, Will woke almost crying with the joy that he had a day away from the digging. His whole body ached, with his back and ribs being the focal point of the pain. He was in the army now it seemed. His navy uniform had finally given up the ghost, the bell-bottom trousers having been caked in mud and dried out so many times that the ends were in tatters, and his tunic was in an even worse state, so he had been given a change of uniform and now had a khaki uniform with brass buttons to be kept clean and shining. Every night, he left his pals in the billet to sleep away from them and disturb as few people as possible with his nocturnal shouting. Still, most mornings he would wake bathed in sweat, with the faintest glimpse of a nightmare screaming at him through the grey fog of semi-consciousness. He sometimes had other dreams, almost always of home, but they just made him sad when he awoke, as they reinforced the fact that he wasn't home at all. Those were the days that he prayed for a letter or parcel from home the most, not for the food or cigarettes, but just for the reassurance of contact.

CHAPTER TWENTY-NINE

It was raining hard when Tom's regiment moved again arriving the next day at a section of the front line they called the 'Somme'. The rain fit the desolation of the place well and Tom stared in disbelief at the scene before him. He had never seen anything like it in his entire life, nor could he have ever imagined it. The battle had been raging here for months in a dreadful stalemate, both sides fighting for a stretch of ground that had long been blown out of all recognition. Where there had once been a patchwork of green fields with neat hedgerows, where butterflies had played in the sun surrounded by the dulcet melodies of songbirds from every hedgerow, now there was nothing but an indiscernible brown as far as the eye could see. Months of bombardment from both sides had rendered all the fields and hedgerows into nothingness, with everything churned up time after time by explosions that pitted the earth with thousands of holes. Nothing had survived save a few sharp splinters pointing skyward dotted around that had once been tree trunks, now rendered into shards of wood whose roots defiantly clung on, waiting for the day when man would desist. "It's how I imagine the moon," someone said aloud and Tom couldn't disagree. Arriving here was such a shock to the senses that the moon would seem quite a pleasant place compared to this, he thought.

Tom rarely spoke about this part of his war in the future. It was like he couldn't get what he saw and experienced here to make any sense in his mind. Three long years he was in France and Belgium in total, except for the one time when his injured hand had sent him home to recover. The rest of his time there was spent either at the front or taking breaks behind the line, knowing that he was only ever a few days away from being back to the horror and the mud.

He shed silent and private tears when he and a band of five men fought for over thirty minutes, failing to save a poor frightened and stricken mule as it desperately sank into one of the mud pools that lurked like traps almost everywhere that didn't have a wooden walkway. The poor beast had strayed just a foot or two from the half-sunken wood and stumbled within a few paces into a pit of mud that almost instantly consumed him. The creature fought desperately to free its legs from the liquid mud, but his every movement inching him down ever deeper. He brayed loudly, shaking in fear while Tom and the men around him fought to pull him back to the boards, heaving with every ounce of strength that they had to save the desperate overloaded beast. The mud won, engulfing him until even his ears and nostrils sank out of view, a few muddy bubbles rising where once the doomed creature had been. Tom felt desperate, though his tears stopped after he had seen the fifteenth poor mule drown in this way. They could try any number of things to get the animals out, but it always seemed to happen so fast, and unless they were very lucky, once a man or a horse had stepped off the wooden boards, it was curtains for them. The mud was so wet that it was more liquid than soil, and the rain just made sure it never dried out.

Exhaustion is a word now often over used, but when you are walking, tired from physical exertion and lack of sleep, and the man in front of you accidentally misses the half-sunken slats of the wooden path and plunges suddenly chest deep into liquid mud, one's own exhaustion momentarily disappears in the chaotic activity of trying to save the poor man's life. You only know what exhaustion really is in the minutes after a man has been lost to the mud in front of you. Watching him sink rapidly down, the brilliant flame of life that burnt within him moments before extinguished. Helpless, you watch as he flounders and gasps his last desperate lungful of air, wild desperate eye staring before his head slips beneath the mud, his extended arm waving like a limp flag before it too disappears beneath the bubbling brown mass. Personal tiredness then receives a canopy of depression to carry, engulfing everyone around the scene in a chasm of hopelessness, exhausted bodies wrapped in a dark shroud of utter sadness as they share the sombre last moment of a good man's unnecessary death.

Every time Tom received a letter from home, it was the best tonic ever, and a letter would put a spring in his step for hours. Annie and Harriet wrote once a week but sometimes letters would not arrive for ten days or more and then two might come within days of each other. When they came in a parcel with some socks or something inside, it was a real bonus. Tom was meticulous in looking after his feet, but his boots were often under water as he trudged backwards and forwards. A lot of men had been succumbing to the dreaded 'trench foot' that could become not just extremely painful but a genuine problem. Clean dry socks were heaven to put on, even though they knew they would not stay dry for long. Tom Vaselined his feet every night and tried to keep them protected from the wet as best he could. Keeping everything dry was a nightmare at times, and Tom kept his kitbag wrapped in a waterproof sheet to keep the worst of the damp out. It was particularly important to him to keep his writing paper and envelopes clean and un-creased as they had to look like they had come from home. Still he wrote two letters every week, one to Harriet and another one enclosed to Will. Writing letters to his son was a challenge sometimes, crouched in the corner of a trench or squashed in a dugout, pretending to be relaxed and comfortably sat at the kitchen table at home. In a way, he found it a mental release, finding that he could sometimes read Harriet's letter with its mundane tales of what had been happening back at home and escape for a few minutes while he pictured the scene back in Bristol. Other times though, it wasn't so easy with the interruptions of war going on around him.

There was no such thing as really having a day off here; you just had different days. When they were 'in reserve', they would be either cleaning kit, drilling or working to repair or build something and it was either that or be at the front, where the pressure and tension of being constantly in danger of death made days in reserve a pleasure. Their 'days on' in the trenches became a routine that they just did, without question. The battle had become such a stalemate that both sides would take it in turn to attack and counter-attack, but Tom and his unit were mainly working more as engineers than soldiers, which wasn't in itself without its dangers for sure. Snipers were a constant danger, so they learnt to walk with a bowed head, even in the deeper trenches. And shelling and incoming mortars were a minute-by-minute fear. There were two sorts of shells, and you prayed you wouldn't get too close to either of them. The heavy shells you heard coming and your ears got so tuned to them that you knew if they were destined for somewhere close to you or not, in which case you got your head down pronto and threw your arms over your head to protect yourself as best you could. Tom's prayers worked, as although he was showered with earth several times from a big shell landing nearby, it never 'got him' but boy, did they shake the earth, literally. He would be crouched down as low as he could moments before they hit and was momentarily fascinated to see small grains of soil 'dancing' on the surface as everything shook. The smaller shells, the ones they nicknamed 'whizz-bangs', came over quicker, so you didn't get a lot of notice from those and often you didn't know they were coming they exploded with a great white fluorescent flash.

Living with the constant fear of death takes its toll and a genuine fear it was, so three to four days on the line were enough to test any man's resolve. Sleep was snatched in bits and more often than not sat in a corner of the trench somewhere, head leaning awkwardly to one side or cupped in your hands. Sleep would be lost to the flash and noise of a shell or one of the countless enormous rats that scurried over your legs or head as you sat or lay there. Night time was often a busy time at the front with much activity from both sides in no-man's-land, repairing barbed wire, picking up the wounded and laying down communication wires.

The time that gave Tom the most sleepless night came from being sent out in no-man's-land in a work party. He had been out a dozen times before, but this night, it just went all wrong. He was one of a party of four men who slipped out over the top under the cover of darkness to repair the defensive line. The width of no-man's-land wandered in and out along the length of the front line but this particular night it was almost at its widest point, which was a blessing. Tom hated barbed wire with a passion. It was terrible stuff that cut and tore at everything it touched and just handling it was a nightmare. What made it even more dangerous was that it was noisy to lay, and noise often spelt death out in no-man's-land. This night, the moon was covered by cloud, which was perfect. The four of them had blackened up their faces and hands to avoid any light reflecting off their skin and crept out as silently as possible, bending low and moving one at a time in slow motion, stopping every few yards to avoid detection. Each man carried a skein of barbed wire over a padded shoulder and wore leather welder's gloves, moving carefully so as not to catch the barbed wire on anything as they moved. They worked silently in pairs, unrolling the barbed wire as quietly as they could to repair a gaping hole that had been torn by a shell. Every noisy 'ping' from the wire brought them to an instant stop, holding their breaths and crouching lower before waiting a few moments to peg down the wire and slowly unroll the next section of the dreadful stuff again.

Things were going well and they were almost done, which was good as the dawn wasn't that far away now, and this was one place that you didn't want to be in first light. All of a sudden, there was a flash of light as a German flare burst above them, illuminating the entire scene in a brilliant phosphorous light. Instantly; all hell broke loose. A German machine gun chattered, sending bullets fizzing through the air that Tom could tell were close and two mortar shells burst behind them. Tom scrabbled to his left a few yards and dived immediately into a wide shell crater and threw himself to the ground, face down, motionless.

Two of his comrades dived in moments before him and the fourth man fell in almost on top of Tom. They all lay there panting for breath, whilst hell was unleashing itself around them. For an hour, they played a deadly game with the Germans. A flare would extinguish as it hit the ground and the firing would stop a few seconds after. But each time the stranded men tried to make a move, a sniper would send a bullet whistling by very close to them, followed by another star burst above and a burst of bullets from a machine gun. They tried to move back to their own line, splitting into two groups and dashing a few yards to the left and right, finding the next depression in the ground before throwing themselves in, waiting a few minutes and then trying again. They didn't get far before the two men to Tom's left were literally blown to pieces by a mortar so accurate that it must have had both their names written on it. One moment they were there and a split second later they were gone, as arms and legs were blown in different directions. No scream, no time to reconsider, no time to call for their mothers, nothing. They were just gone.

Tom prayed like he had never prayed before, as he waited for the next mortar, hoping that the Germans had not seen his last position. Despite the cold, the sweat ran off him as his heart thumped loudly in his chest. Suddenly, the next mortar landed on the other side of the crater and blew him off his feet, the percussion from the explosion sending his world from a brilliant flash of light into darkness. As he came too, he wasn't sure what had really happened. He was very groggy as he took in his surroundings. He didn't seem to be injured, but as the stupor left him, he realised that he must have been knocked out for at least a few minutes as the first rays of dawn sent shafts of light through the early morning sky. He was sitting in a large shell hole. His neck hurt like hell, but as he moved his head slowly left and right, he was aware of another man sitting next to him. He gestured to Tom with one finger to his lips, to stay silent. He nodded in acknowledgement, giving his own brain time to take in his new surroundings. He was slumped against the wall of a twenty-feet wide shell hole which was thankfully deep enough to hide him and his colleague from the bullets that pinged with regularity overhead. On the far side of the crater lay a corpse, its face down with its head to one side, a German trooper long dead and completely stripped of flesh by rats. Bony fingers extended from the one visible arm. The corpse's jacket moved slightly, a bulge making its way across the man's back and out of the arm as the biggest rat Tom had ever seen appeared. It stopped for a moment to look at the two men, no doubt eyeing its next meal, before scurrying around the side of the hole and over the top, disappearing from view. "Nine days," the man whispered to Tom. "Our German friend has been here around nine days. That's how long it takes the rats to completely strip a man's flesh here."

Tom cringed at the thought. "The rat's not going to have me," he whispered back and the other man chuckled quietly. Tom's faculties were coming back fully now, and he took a great gulp of air into his lungs and ran his hand through his hair, checking himself for injuries, but apart from a very stiff neck, there did not appear to be any. He recognised the other man now, Captain Pearce, a likeable and affable man in his late twenties who asked more than ordered his men around, which went down well with them. "We're in a bit of a hole, literally," Pearce whispered. While you were unconscious, I took a peep over the top and Gerry has us pinned in here. I don't think he actually knows we are here or he'd be giving us a few more mortar shells, but while we have daylight, we don't have a chance of getting back I'm afraid. The ground between us and our trenches is open and exposed, so we will have to wait the day out and slip back as soon as it's dark.

Tom nodded in agreement. "How far are we from the Bosch front line?" he whispered.

"Difficult to tell. I can't hear any talking, but I do know we are closer to their front line than ours, so we need to keep down and stay quiet. I suspect we might be within reach of a grenade if they knew we were here, so we don't want to alert them to our presence."

Tom moved to carefully get up, crouching low as he did. He had been sitting on wet soil and the dampness was getting through to his bones, making him cold. They had travelled light, so were not carrying food or drink and he crawled over to the dead German who was laid partly on a tarpaulin sheet. He started to carefully ease the tarpaulin out from underneath the body, and there was a screech as a rat leapt out of the trouser leg and disappeared over the rim of the shell hole. Tom dropped the tarpaulin and instinctively jumped back. He had seen rats at home but the ones here were monsters, fed and fat on human fresh and the casualties of war. Every soldier hated them and dreaded being killed anywhere where the rats got to you before your own stretcher bearers did. "Sorry, old mate," Tom whispered apologetically to the dead German, "we need this more than you now I'm afraid." As he gently pulled at the material, the soldier's hidden hand pulled out from beneath his body and the bones that had once been a hand were half wrapped around some photographs. "Poor blighter," Tom whispered. "He must have lain here wounded, knowing he was dying and wanted his last moments to be with his family and friends." Captain Pearce came over to help Tom remove the tarpaulin quietly, though the corpse was literally a bag of bones and offered no resistance or weight when being slid off the sheet. "Stick the photos in your jacket, Tom, or the rats will eat them. Once there's no flesh to eat, they will eat anything they can get hold of." It was a decent-sized tarpaulin and between them, they were just able to both sit on it and take some shelter from the cold. The September sun was insipid, shining through a thick veil of cloud and a chilly morning breeze bit deep into their bones.

The morning passed slowly and both men dozed from time to time, lulled by the cold. Hunger was starting to grind at them, so Pearce carefully examined the dead Bosch and found a water bottle and a small pack of hard biscuits in a tin that had beaten the rats. 'Better than nothing,' they thought, as Pearce shared them out with Tom equally. He started to talk, still in a whisper. "Okay Private Payne, here's the deal. We are stuck out here for at least another four or five hours, I guess, and we are both in the same boat, so for those few hours, I am happy to drop the Captain and private bit. As soon as we get back to our lines, then I shall be your superior officer again and you will call me 'sir'. Are you in agreement with that?"

"I'm happy with that," Tom whispered back, liking Pearce even more. The young officer had an easy way about him, and Tom extended his hand towards him. "Thomas Payne," he said. "My friends call me Tom."

Pearce shook his hand firmly. "Ted Pearce. My friends call me Teddy, but you can call me Ted," he said with a grin, and both men chuckled softly under their breath.

"This is a bloody war," Pearce whispered, "and this battle is a complete mess between you and me. We've been scrapping over this blasted strip of land since July now and getting nowhere. Haig is tactically inept, and we are paying for it with a lot of lives."

"I know that. I just want this war over now. I've seen enough rats and dead bodies for one lifetime."

Two of the photographs Tom found on the dead German in the shell hole.

"I can't tell you how long this war will last, Tom. I wish I knew. Don't mind me asking you, but what are you doing here? I don't mean to be rude but well, you must be one of the older chaps at the front and you must be, how shall I say it, at the top end of the age limit and you don't strike me as the natural soldier type."

"Are we talking in strict confidence, Ted?"

"Of course. What's said out here stays out here, Tom."

"Well, I am officially 'at the top end' of the age limit and no, I'm not here looking to be a hero, far from it, but somewhere out there (he pointed roughly with his index finger), the Germans have my son in a prison camp near Berlin and I want this war over so I can get him back."

They talked at length and for the first time since being away from home, Tom opened up to someone. He felt at ease with this young officer and as his words poured out, he felt the pain of missing home and his old family life even more. "But my son thinks I'm at home still," he whispered. "It was a promise I made to him when he went off to fight that I'd stay at home and look after his mother, but when he was captured, it changed everything somehow. For weeks, I carried on at home, going to work, coming home, trying to get on with life, but I could not just sit back and wait the war out and hope we would win and my lad would come home. I had to do something. So now, I'm on the same soil that my son is, and although it might sound daft, it's a comfort to me to be on the same patch of land as him. I know that I could be with him within a day or two if this war ended, so every day I wake and hope that this will be the day that it all ends."

"Sadly, I don't think there's much chance that the war will end in the next day or two, Tom," Ted whispered. "The whole thing seems to have bedded into a bloody stalemate."

Tom wanted to change the subject, so he asked about Ted's life before the war. Ted reached inside his tunic and produced a bent photograph from his wallet, proudly showing two young children sat on a young woman's lap. "This is my son who is another William by the way. He's just turned five now and my daughter, Victoria. She's two and a half and the spitting image of her mother. I can't wait for this war to be over so that I can see them growing up for myself rather than be sent photographs to see how much they've grown while I've been away."

An hour passed as they talked easily to each other, both opening up in a way that neither man had done since they had left for war those years ago. Despite Ted being the senior officer, he felt relaxed in the company of someone old enough to be his father. "I don't understand this war," Pearce lamented. "I worked for six months in Berlin when I finished my education and found the Germans charming people, educated and refined, and I got to like them a lot. I just don't understand how we have got..."

As Ted whispered, an explosion shook the ground behind them and a barrage of shells landed around the German line in front of them. It broke the moment and Ted hurriedly put the photographs away. As the shelling continued, there was a deep rumbling from behind them and the ground shook. Both men shot out from under the tarpaulin and crouched low, looking behind them as the rumbling suddenly got louder. The tracks of a mechanical monster appeared just to their left.

"Bloody hell! It's a tank," Ted cried out loudly, not worried about whispering anymore as any sound was now drowned out by the noise of the engine. Another tank appeared to their right with British soldiers huddled in tight lines directly behind the two great machines. An attack was being launched. German bullets pinged off the metal casing of the tanks as they churned onwards. Tanks had been used earlier but not on this stretch of the line, so these were the first ones that Tom had seen, and he was quite amazed. The noise of the engine alone was frightening. Smoke billowed out of the top from the engine and its guns fired in turn. The Germans were throwing everything they could at the tanks, so there was no chance of escape for Tom and Ted stranded in their shell hole. The tank to their left suddenly sounded different, the engine coughing and spluttering like an injured animal before it suddenly ground to a halt just ten yards in front of them. The solders behind it swarmed around it and onward as it continued to fire at the German line. More British soldiers poured past, some being cut down as they ran into machine gun fire but it was clear that a full scale attack was under way. The battle raged and the German gunfire had reduced in this part of the line, so Tom and Ted decided to make a break from their shell hole and back to their own line. Just before they did, Tom laid the tarpaulin over the German soldier and thanked him, which was of course a useless gesture but still one that Tom felt he had to make.

They ran back, crouching low and zigzagging left and right as they ran, eventually jumping down into their own trench, grateful to have made it in one piece. Ted shook Tom's hand and smiled at him. "Well done, Private Payne."

"Thank you, Captain Pearce. It's been a pleasure."

"Follow me, Payne. Let's see if we can rustle up a cup of tea and something to eat."

"Yes, sir. My stomach is telling me that it thinks that's an excellent idea."

CHAPTER THIRTY

Will huddled under his coat and stared out of his billet window, watching a limp and watery dawn rising. Christmas Day 1917 was a melancholy affair for the prisoners of Doberitz camp and it was no different for Will as he watched the day start and listened to the camp coming alive, just as if it was any other day. Like Will, many of the men had been captured in the first year of the war, so the camp had been filled to beyond capacity relatively early. He almost didn't want Christmas to come, as somehow it emphasised his years in captivity, this being his fourth Yuletide in Doberitz. The new year would be even less welcome as what news they had from the war didn't fill them with cheer or optimism that 1918 would bring an end to their misery. Their German captors told them constantly that the glorious fatherland was winning the war as every month passed, whilst news from home was heavily censored, so reliable news was less common than hen's teeth, and when news did arrive, it sounded like the allies were holding their own, but no more. The entire war seemed to have bogged down in the mud as a bloody stalemate.

Will was, however, looking forward to the Christmas show that the 'entertainment's department' was putting on this year. They were a real boost to moral and put a buzz about the camp as preparations were made. The German commanders even came to watch the shows and were seen to laugh at one or two of the more visual antics 'on stage'.

On Christmas morning, everyone had queued up in the freezing cold for their post, hopeful that their parcel might contain something a bit extra for Christmas. Any parcel that had arrived in the past few days had been taken and opened immediately though, as any really special treat, like a sponge cake wouldn't improve for being left another few days, but anything resembling a Christmas present was carefully hidden away. There were the usual disasters for some, with the smell of strong tobacco leaching into bread or a cake within the parcel during its journey from home. Terry had had one such 'disaster', as he shared his modestly sized fruit cake out with Will and his mates. The smell of 'Old Holborne' was unmistakable on its outer, dark, fruity edges. Alfie jokingly trying to strike a light to his finger-sized slice like a cigarette, which gave them all a laugh until the cake broke apart and fell onto the bed which made them roar with laughter as he frantically found every last raisin and crumb to devour eagerly. Will's parcel came on

Christmas Eve afternoon, so he decided to wait and open it on Christmas Day morning. The neat little brown paper box contained sixty of his favourite Woodbine cigarettes, vest and underpants, a small sponge cake, some writing paper and most importantly, a letter from Dad and home with another from Annie. Little did Will know that his father had written the letter on the same soil as him, with the letter going back to Bristol before the army mail redirected to Doberitz.

Dear Son,

We are hoping that this will reach you before Christmas Day. We especially wanted you to know how much we are thinking of you at this time of year, and we are sure that by the time next Christmas comes, we will all celebrate it together at home. Hold on to that thought, son.

Your mother and I are with Annie, and your two favourite ladies are busying themselves putting the final touches to this parcel. It has been put together with all the love that these two wonderful ladies have for you. With each passing week, we grow fonder of your, Annie. You chose well, my son. She is a lovely girl and, you will see from the cake enclosed, quite a decent cook. Rationing is getting very tight now, so both households have been collecting the ingredients for this cake, so you will have to thank Mr and Mrs McGrath when you come home. Annie has just finished it now and baked it in our oven, so it would be as fresh as possible for you. Lucky boy.

It is getting more difficult to buy things in the shops now and the damn German U-boats have made a right nuisance of themselves sinking supply ships, so some foods are becoming harder to get hold of. But we are struggling on and just wait for the day that you will walk in through the front door. I can feel it's coming, son, so hold on and we will all pray that it will not be long.

Your ever loving, Mum and Dad xx

He reread the letter and then read the one from Annie. He missed them all, which somehow felt even worse with it being Christmas Day. The letters he had written to Annie had changed a lot over the years, and now he openly talked of his love for her. He knew that German sensors at the camp read his letters but he had got so that he didn't care anymore. He loved Annie, and that was it. He didn't mind who else knew. She had enclosed a new photograph of herself in the letter and he gazed longingly at the small black and white face that smiled prettily back at him. He gave out a great sigh, and was just about to sink into melancholy when Terry burst in. "Hello, Will. Merry Christmas, mate. What you got there? Not hiding some nice cake, are you?"

Will grinned and showed him the sponge that had been carefully wrapped in grease-proof paper that was thankfully free of tobacco smells. "Morning, Terry. Merry Christmas to you too. I was just finishing reading my letters from home and was going to bring the cake to share with you hungry lot."

Even the Germans were carrying a lighter mood than usual today; they too would clearly have rather been at home with their families. On Christmas Eve, the sound of Carol singing had come from the German barracks and the food that evening seemed to have been slightly better for the one meal. In many ways, December the 25th was just another day though. Their bread ration was still half a loaf of dark sawdust tasting rye bread to last the day and the soup that went with it was still foul and thin, with the leftover vegetable stumps from the German cookhouse being boiled for hours until every possible last vestige of flavour had been transferred into the water.

The men working in the salt mines always made sure that it had salt for flavouring as they could not escape coming home with pieces of rough salt crystals caught up in their clothing or pockets and used to joke that it was a shame that there wasn't a pepper mine around to introduce another element of flavour to their range. Food was as dire and boring as ever, and the food parcels were still the difference between near starving or surviving. Many men shuffled around the camp looking gaunt, and they were the lucky ones. The poor Russians still received nothing other than what the Germans gave them, which was woefully inadequate, so they skirted on the edge of malnutrition and slunk around their side of the camp wearing uniforms that, after years in the camp, were in tatters. They would glance up from sunken eyes and occasionally offering wistful smiles from toothless mouths. The British and French would still help them where they could, and bread was commonly sent over if it could be spared. New Year's Eve came and went without a fuss on the British side of the camp. The passing of another year could not be 'celebrated' anything like Christmas, and was greeted with general silence and sadness. Many of the men in the camp had seen 1914 turn into 1915, then 1916 and 1917. The arrival of 1918 just added a feeling of ever-deepening despair to their captivity, incarcerated in a war that seemed to have locked itself into a desperate stalemate. Surviving the winter here had become a dreaded battle against the cold. Will shuffled around, the cold biting deep into his feet in particular, and he found it strange that all his ten toes ached badly, with the five missing ones giving him particular invisible pain. He would sit on his bed trying to rub some warmth and life back into his feet through his socks, and when he closed his eyes, he could swear that his missing toes were back. They throbbed and pained so much.

CHAPTER THIRTY-ONE

Harriet stared at an old photograph of her Tom and Will, as she waited for the tea to brew, looking deeply into the faces of the two men in her life, studying every contour of their lovely faces. Lost back to the time when the photograph was taken, she was only brought back to the moment by the rising whistle of the kettle. The photograph had been taken just before Will went off to war, with the three of them posing politely for the camera. She remembered how Tom had joked ventriloquist-like through barely open lips about how long they had needed to stay absolutely still in their pose, before the photographer replaced the cap over the camera lens to allow them to finally move. It had been a good day, with the three of them walking down Stapleton Road in the spring sunshine together to see Will's photographer friend. Tom and Will had stood in their suits and Harriet in her new best dress that she had made herself just the week before.

It was Harriet's third Christmas without her Tom and almost four and a half years since she had seen her beloved son. It frightened her sometimes how she struggled to remember Will's face in absolute detail, and she sometimes wondered how his face might have changed over that time. She kept the photograph taken of him in captivity on a shelf in the kitchen so that she could look at it as she passed by, but it wasn't enough. Worryingly, she struggled to picture him in anything other than a photograph now. His letters were kept neatly tied in a pink ribbon in her bedside drawer and regularly taken out and the most recent ones reread. She didn't read his earlier letters anymore as they were full of pain and anguish and upset her, but Will's most recent letters had been less tense and more descriptive of his surroundings and friends, more encouraging somehow. At least she knew that he had some good friends around him and that they all looked after each other.

As with the last three years, she had spent Christmas Day with her parents, which had been a joy for them but reminded Harriet more than ever that she was without her own family. Lots of prayers were said before and after the meal and after Harriet had helped her mother clear everything away and had one final cup of tea with them, she had thrust herself underneath a large black umbrella and battled against light rain and a gusty wind to walk home, calling into the shoe shop on the way to sort a few things out ready for work tomorrow.

Annie sat at home with her parents and went to her room mid-afternoon to reread Will's last letter. She had remained faithful to him since he had left and had politely rejected the smiles of any men at work who appeared to take a shine to her. There were less now though, as month by month, the young men at work disappeared to either enlist or be conscripted. Everyone was overworked at Mardons, who were staffed largely by men too young or old to fight, with women doing increasingly more responsible jobs. In a way, the war had been liberating for women, as many of the men's jobs had been filled by women and girls, so some of her friends had changed jobs to take on new skills. As they almost exclusively printed cigarette cartons, they were working flat out as the nation was smoking more than ever as the war progressed, and one thing that the government ensured the country never ran out of was tobacco.

As the months had turned into years and William's letters had mounted up, Annie had come to realise that she had fallen in love with this gentleman who was now a prisoner of war. When they were walking out together before he left, she knew then that she had a growing affection for this funny, likeable man, but as time had passed, her feelings had deepened, with his absence only being filled with his letters, and they had grown more affectionate to the point that she knew that he craved to be with her, not somebody else, but with her. She glowed at the thought and couldn't wait for his return. She missed him. She loved him.

CHAPTER THIRTY-TWO

The fighting didn't stop on Christmas Day. Fewer shells rained over than the days before, but there was certainly no playing football with the Bosch in no-man's land like the stories that Tom had heard about from an earlier Christmas. General Haig had squashed any idea of fraternising with the enemy on Christmas Day quickly and as far as the senior generals were concerned, it was 'business' as usual. But it wasn't in reality and both sides took it steady, sending over the odd shell just to please the Generals and remind themselves that there was a war to be won. On the stretch of front that Tom had learned to call home for more months than he cared to remember now, they had almost taken it in turns with the Germans to attack each other over too many months, gaining a few hundred yards to lose it again a week or two later. It was bloody senseless, he thought, a stalemate that constantly saw young men turned into corpses to be taken away and buried somewhere, all to be replaced by fresh-faced young lads that to Tom seemed to be getting ever more youthful-looking. Every day at the front, Tom increasingly woke up thinking that it could be his last. Life and death spun a coin high into the air, with his living face on one side and the face of death on the other. So far, he had been lucky and the coin had landed with his face upwards and smiling, but he knew that it was only luck that kept him alive.

His experience did help him at times. His ears had become so finely tuned to incoming shells that he ignored almost every whine as shells were fired, gauging that they were far enough away and not to panic. When his ears detected a minutely different pitch, he knew to dive for cover damn quickly, and pray. So far, his praying had worked. When he was at the front, he habitually walked with a slight crouch, keeping his head down even when there was good depth in the trench. Numerous times, he would wait for a few moments as he moved about the communication trenches, anticipating a shell or rattle of a machine gun and nearly always, he was right. He had developed a sixth sense and prayed every night that it stayed with him. At times, he even wondered if he had a guardian Angel watching over him, as certainly his luck had held so far. His wounded hand reminded him regularly to be careful, especially in cold weather. His early shrapnel injury had left a very neat scar on the back and palm of his hand, which was hardly visible now, but this hand in particular seemed to feel the cold more than the other one, and he had developed a habit of opening and closing it rapidly during the cold weather to beat off the dull pain from the injury.

Stress was something that no one talked about, but months of going backwards and forwards to the front line weighed heavy and in different ways on the men. Tom had seen so many cheeky young lads arrive with fresh faces and vivacity for life, only to then disappear on a stretcher, that he had lost count of them. He countered the grief of losing people around him by trying not to get too close to anyone. It had become just too painful to make a real friend and see him shot down or just blown to such small pieces that there was nothing left to pick up or mourn over. He increasingly retained his status as the 'old man' of the trench and had several times politely turned down commissions. He was happy being a 'private thank you' and keeping his head down. But the stress was beginning to tell on Tom as it was on many of the old soaks that had survived a number of years close to the front. Gaunt faces with deeply embedded strained eyes often stared back from under steel helmets, with a haunted look as they shuffled past. Tom had seen one man go 'over the top' on his own and without orders, running out alone screaming, his arms flailing wildly in the air as he ran towards the German lines. He hadn't even taken his rifle. I think the Germans were so surprised to see one man running at them that it took them quite a while to react, before he was shot down in a hail of rapid fire that stopped as quickly as it had started. A sombre silence cast its shadow over the scene as the poor demented soul dropped to the ground. Three men that he knew of had absconded and just started walking in the opposite direction towards home, the stress being just too much for them. They were caught, of course, and it automatically meant a Court Marshall and in one dreadful case that Tom witnessed, a firing squad. Tom didn't know the man really, but his execution was brutally advertised and clearly done to send a message to the other men.

To some of the men, Tom had become something of a father figure, but he did not encourage it at all. In fact when someone told him this, he dismissed it and walked away quickly, almost angry at the comment. There was only one son he wanted to be a father to, and he missed him dreadfully. He calmed down quickly though and started to see it from the younger soldiers' angle. Some of them were just kids and a lot of them were frightened out of their skins, shaking uncontrollably under fire, so he appreciated that they needed a steady older influence at times and someone to look up to. But behind Tom's calm and controlled demeanour, the strain was telling. Being given leave to visit home was almost unheard of. It just didn't happen. It was mid-March that Captain Pearce pulled Tom aside and told him he was to join a party of men to take a turn well away from the front line. "You'll still be working, Tom, but you will be well away from the line for a few weeks."

Tom looked concerned though. "Excuse me asking, sir, but news is thin and is there any chance that we might make a breakthrough soon? I don't want to be away from the front line if we make a breakthrough, sir. If I can be at the front of the push into Germany and be there to release my son, then as you know, that's where I want to be."

Captain Pearce smiled faintly and put his hand on Tom's shoulder. "Take a break, Tom. The war will wait for you to take a little time away and I honestly don't think we are about to storm into Berlin in the new few weeks I'm afraid. I don't know the whole picture but the Bosch seem to be as stubborn as ever and seem rather reluctant to give it up, which is jolly discourteous of them I have to say. Take a break. We'll see you back here in a few weeks' time. That's an order."

When Tom wrote home two days later, he realised that he had developed a slight tremor in his hand. He took a deep breath and steadied his hand against the table as he wrote. He was billeted in a small farmhouse with around forty other men from several regiments, and in the quiet of the Belgian countryside, he suddenly felt a surge of guilt at being there and not at the front with the other lads. Some of his new colleagues were carrying real outward signs of stress and several were very jumpy and their behaviour was erratic. All the men were given 'light duties' around the farm and the commanding officer took a very relaxed attitude towards them all. It turned out that he had medical training in the relatively new branch of psychiatry before being drafted into the military. This was a 'fatigue and rest camp', and he made sure it was.

When Tom arrived, the first thing he was presented with was a great porcelain bath filled with hot water in an outhouse on the farm. He couldn't wait to get in it and attack the lice which irritated his hair and skin to the point that he, like most men, was constantly scratching. His uniform was whisked away to be fumigated when he stepped out of it, and a new outfit laid out for him to spend the rest of the day in. He felt like royalty being waited on like this and just being properly clean made him feel good.

Meals were served in a big room that had four long trestle tables with ten men seated around each one. They were served by several local ladies old enough to be Tom's mother and just being seated around a proper table, with real plates rather than their mess tins, and a knife and fork, being served wholesome food, seemed almost odd. It was such a long time ago that Tom had not eaten from his bully tin that looking down at his plate, with steaming hot food neatly arranged on a porcelain plate instead of being dumped into his tin, felt wonderful yet strange. He was becoming dehumanised and he hadn't realised it.

Then, each man was served a pint of beer in a tin mug. Cold and foaming, the froth clung to Tom's moustache as he took the first sip. It was wonderful. Sure they all had their daily ration of rum, which was so badly needed at times, especially in the winter or to give Dutch courage, but taking a cold beer was rare and he had forgotten how pleasant it was. It quenched his thirst in many ways, and each man sat in silence and with his own thoughts until the food and drink had been hungrily demolished.

For ten wonderful days, Tom enjoyed the sheer relaxed attitude of the farm. Military standards were not eased with regards to cleaning uniform and boots etc., but the pressure was definitely off and he could see the men around him responding to this as he felt himself do too. The postal system worked well here and a new letter arrived for him after he had been there for a week. He eagerly digested each word, feeling less pressurised than usual to write home:

My dearest Harriet and of course, Annie,

Well, here's a thing. Would you believe that I have been given some time off for good behaviour? Unfortunately, it will not allow me enough time to come home to see you, but I am in a beautiful part of the country on a lovely farm. Of course, I am not allowed to say exactly where, but what I can say is that it reminds me of Queen Charlton a bit, with similar walls and some lovely orchards mixed in with fields of sheep and cattle. One of my jobs, would you believe, is to help bring the cows in for milking twice a day. I haven't progressed to actually milking them yet and leave it to the farm hands, who are clearly experts.

It is a real tonic to take some time out and think. It's too early to smell the roses but there is a lovely wisteria growing up the west side of the farm house wall that has just come into flower and it is wonderful to see. It reminds me of your parents' house, Harriet, so that is a happy thought for me. Give them both my regards by the way, and the same to your parents, Annie. Tell them all I am thinking of them.

Many thanks for your last letter. I have enclosed a letter for William as usual and am genuinely writing this one with a spring in my step, such is how I feel. I guess you will be sending the letter off with the usual food parcel? I have written it so. The rumour here is that German prisoners are saying that the blockade against Germany is working and that food is becoming scarcer there, so we had better make sure the boy is eating well. Every night, I pray for this war to end so that we can all go home and start life anew. I will certainly be asking William if he wants to come into the family business again, though I suspect he will want to go back to Mardons and all his old friends. We shall see.

I have been here nine days now and have all the luxuries of home and some more. Can you believe that I have had two lovely hot baths since I arrived here? My skin feels like a baby's! The food is lovely, all home-cooked by the army cooks who have taken over one of the outhouses and it's lovely to have something different from bully beef for a change. We actually get farm fresh vegetables, which is a real treat I can tell you. Nowhere near as good as your cooking though, my love. Now that first meal home is something, I am really looking forwards to. You will find me running up Mina Road, I can tell you, when you get the oven on. News is sparse from the war, but I am sure that we will prevail in the end. God is on our side and that means that we shall always prevail.

Well, I had better finish off now and of course, send my utmost respect and love to you all at home. Keep your chin up and think of me taking it steady here for a while.

God bless, your ever loving Tom xx

Tom then enclosed this letter with its Doberitz-addressed envelope neatly inside.

Dear Will,

Enclosed are a few things to hopefully make life a little easier for you. Spring is around the corner here and your mother and I have been planting a few vegetable seeds in the back garden and are already looking forward to eating the results of our efforts. Home-grown vegetables are always best. We pray that you will be home by then to share them with us, but meanwhile, there are a few things to hopefully give you a smile and remind you that you are always in our thoughts.

It has been a wet few weeks here and the old river Avon has risen a bit higher than usual, with the spring tides higher this year. The docks seem busier than usual for this time of year, and your mother and I took a walk down there recently to catch up with things. It was good to see lots of people walking around there, all wearing their shoes out! That's one thing about our trade; people will always wear their shoes out from time to time, so the shop is ticking over nicely at present. As the war has gone on, there have been more repairs than new shoes sold, but it still keeps the till ringing, so we are not complaining.

Can you remember Michael Jay from down the road? Well, he has come home with a limp and a smile and won't be going back to the line anymore. He's getting around on crutches for now, but it seems that his injury will heal alright but he will be left with a permanent limp.

Annie came over last weekend to help your mother and I put together this little parcel for you. I know I've said it before but she is a lovely lass, Will. You are lucky to have her at home waiting for you to return. We pray that it won't be too long now, son, so keep your spirits up and look to the west. We are there waiting for you.

Your ever loving, Mum and Dad xx

Tom had barely finished his letter when everyone was called to assemble in the courtyard and stand to attention. An officer told them briskly that the Germans had made a big push and broken through part of the line and every fit man was required to return to the front line to help hold them back, so they would set off at first light. During the early evening, they saw a remarkable thing as thousands of American troops arrived and set up camp in the fields around. They made enough noise to be heard miles away and watching them in their fresh new uniforms that had never seen a battle, with fresh innocent faces beaming back, Tom couldn't help but think that they were in for a shock. But it was a real tonic to see them and one of the old lags alongside Tom announced with confidence, "We'll win this bloody war now. This is just the impetus we needed to beat the bloody Germans." Looking at the fields of new troops, Tom knew that he was right and suddenly couldn't wait to get back to the front line.

CHAPTER THIRTY-THREE

Will had noticed how the mood in Germany had changed over the last few months. Every morning, his work party was marched to the farm which took them through a couple of small hamlets on the way. The mood had visibly changed amongst the locals and even though spring was well under way, everything looked darker and poorer. Food was becoming terribly short everywhere, and they noticed it even at the farmhouse. Over time, the bread had become less tasty and smaller in size and the soup had become much thinner and bland. It was still far better than the coloured water that they called soup back at the camp, but it had noticeably reduced in quantity. The number of labourers that the farm took from the camp varied with the work needed, sometimes twenty men and sometimes just five. Will was lucky though in that his name always seemed to be on the list when it came out. In addition to him being a hard worker, he still thought that the farmer and his wife had taken a shine to him, but he had no extra soup dished out now and everybody's rations had reduced in size. He was still lucky though. Terry and the other lads down the salt mine regularly complained as to how harsh their treatment was and how the food was barely edible there. Will's guards were now just the old men, all the younger lads having been drafted to fight on the front line, something Will and the others were delighted to see. Even to the end, one of the youngest soldiers in particular had been verging on being vicious as his confidence gained and would use his rifle butt on any prisoner for the slightest excuse.

Despite the poor food and ill treatment, Will was feeling stronger. He still had his bad dreams but they had reduced in frequency but as always, he couldn't remember the details or the horrors that plagued him when he awoke. The food parcels were still coming, thank God, and were always eagerly shared around his little group of friends. Everyone usually got a parcel every few weeks, but it wouldn't have mattered if one of them had not, as they all shared everything down to the last broken biscuit. It was this friendship that had seen him through. Terry, Alfie and the boys were special mates and lifted his spirits when he inevitably felt gloomy from time to time. As time went on, Will had gained a bit of his old strength and character back. He was still the 'quieter one' of the group, or more thoughtful, as Harold used to say. The mood generally in the camp was that, despite the false news that they received from the German guards, somewhere out there, the tide was turning. Whether it was or not, it was hope that they clung on to. Food was very short in Germany; that was clear, with everyone that went out on working parties saying the same thing, that the Bosch must be taking a hammering somewhere.

When they were not working and were able to get together, there was always someone in the group talking about what they were looking forward to doing when they went home, or what they missed the most. It was a natural way for them to keep their spirits up. Will thought about some things now that he had avoided contemplating before, for fear of raising his own optimism too high, but even he was starting to dream of home again. And so often now, his dreams had Annie in them. It was on July 24th that he wrote to her:

My dearest darling Annie,

I am pleased to report that all is as well as can be expected here in Doberitz. I have been working hard on the farm and I think I might be a bit of a gardener when I come home with all this practice. I have certainly learnt a lot about growing food, or more truthfully, digging! And food has not been the only thing growing in my thoughts, my dear, and I have something to ask you.

As you know, I was very, very fond of you before I went off to war and it has been very long and lonely four years for us both since I saw your lovely face. I owe my very existence to the love and support you have shown me over those years, and through our letters, I feel that I have grown to know you so well. My hope on hope is that you feel the same towards me. One day soon, I hope, this awful war will be over, and I believe more than ever now, that I will one day be coming home, and when I do then I pray that I will come home to you and will be with you always.

This is not the way I had planned to ask this, my love, but may I beg the question as to if when I return, would you please do me the honour of marrying me? I will, of course, ask your father and mother's permission, but I would hope that they would agree. It is to you that I want to ask the question first though, as your feelings mean everything to me. It is such a difficult situation, I know, and I would fully understand if you turned me down, but through our letters, I have grown to love you even more and with such a power and force that no German or mountain will keep me from finding a way to you even if this war never ends. But it will end, and I want more than anything to spend the rest of my life with you and to make you the happiest woman on earth. This is my dream, as I shall dream of you once more again tonight and every night until we meet up, my love. I love you, Annie. I love you more than the stars above that I pray to every night to be with you again soon.

All my love,
William xx

When Annie came home from work ten days later, the letter was waiting on the kitchen table for her. She didn't know why, but she was always slightly embarrassed when she picked up a letter from Will with her parents around. It was silly really. She went to her bedroom to change out of her work clothes but opened the letter first, her heart thumping as she carefully peeled back the gum on the envelope. She was standing by her little bed as she opened the letter but sat down on it as she got to the part of Will's proposal. She felt a wave of heat engulf her as his words unfolded. Her mind was a blur of emotion as she reread the letter from start to finish again. She wanted to shout out with happiness but she couldn't. She so longed to see him right now and say 'yes' to him in person. She reread the letter a third time, before doing a little dance around the room. She couldn't wait to write back to Will and tell him that she would love to accept his proposal, subject of course to her father and mother agreeing, which she thought they would, as it was clear that they both liked Will and could see how sweet she was on him. Her father in particular was very supportive of Will in his predicament, so she was confident that they would agree. Now more than ever, she wanted this horrid war over and to have her man home.

She knew that she was lucky, as several of the women at work had lost boyfriends and husbands in the war. It had been awful when the bad-news telegram had been delivered to one girl at work. She had been asked to go to the foreman's office where the telegram boy was waiting and the poor woman broke down as he solemnly handed the brown note over. The other girls could not help but watch the silent scene through the glass windows of the office. The poor girl's legs gave way as she read the stark text and she fainted on the spot. It had been awful to watch. Whilst Annie knew that her William was not in a good place, at least he was relatively safe, so she would one day get him home.

CHAPTER THIRTY-FOUR

When Tom reached the frontline, it had moved several miles backwards since he had left and he was shocked to see how ferociously the Germans had attacked and how far they had pushed the frontline back. There was almost a desperate atmosphere as the British fought to hold the line where it was and stop it slipping back even further. Trenches were being dug furiously in front of a dense wood to hold the line, and Tom and dozens of others were immediately put to work digging frantically. The soil here was hard though, two feet down they hit a deep layer of blue clay which slowed their digging down. It was dreadfully hard work, each full spade weighing heavily on tired arms and the clay stuck to the spade like glue.

As they dug ever deeper, groundwater started to gush in from the sides just above the clay layer in floods and soon, they were ankle deep in water. In front of them, the firing was intense and seemed to get closer by the hour, which focused the mind and sped the urgency of digging even more. They had barely dug the minimum depth to give men shelter when their own soldiers appeared from in front of them and jumped into the half dug trench to escape bullets that were suddenly flying in all directions. "We hold them here," the cry went out as Tom and others continued to dig. The men around them crowded into the confined space and started firing at shapes that appeared in front of them, running fast towards them across the open field. Tom glanced up and was shocked at how many Germans were attacking. They must have had two or more battalions running towards them, and he frantically dug, waiting the moment when the order would come for the diggers to also start firing. It was only when two machine guns were set up on either side of them that the shapes running at them started to diminish.

The battle raged for hours and at its height, everyone was ordered to cease digging and fire, so against his better wishes, Tom grabbed his rifle. It was very clear that there was a real chance that the Germans might overrun them at one point as hundreds of them poured forwards towards them across the field, falling like ninepins under the constant fire from the now three machine guns. It seemed like madness to Tom that the Bosch kept coming and it was pitiful to see them falling with each sweep of the guns, like their knees had suddenly given way. When Tom took aim and fired, he deliberately aimed low at the legs of the attackers and when one fell, he wasn't sure if it was his bullet or someone else's that had struck the man. The air was so thick with lead. Still, they kept coming and suddenly, the urgency of the situation became apparent as the order rang out down the line to fix bayonets in two groups so that the firing would not stop completely while men fixed on their clumsy weapons. Despite having so many men cut down, they still kept coming and were now just sixty feet away. Tom's mouth was dry at the thought of fighting hand to hand with fixed bayonets and the intensity of firing seemed to increase. From Tom's left side, a forth newly positioned Lewis gun suddenly opened fire and the shapes in front of him seemed to disappear, falling mercilessly under the increased fire. Tom was sweating heavily as he reloaded and fired so many times that he was in danger of running out of ammunition. He hated it. He hated the bloody war, and had always thought that it was the bloody politicians that should be out here in the trench, not tucked up snugly in their beds in London. He did not want to be here, but he thought of Will again and it steadied his nerve.

Almost as quickly as it had started, the flood of Germans reduced to a trickle and knowing that the attack had failed, they turned and started running back. The defensive line had held and for now, the tide had turned. Tom raised his head from looking down his rifle barrel and blurted out loudly. "Bloody hell, I thought we were for it for a while then."

The man next to him said nothing, and just stared out with his head resting on his rifle butt. Something didn't look right. "Are you alright?" Tom asked and as he put his hand on the man's shoulder, his head lolled forward and his tin hat slid sideways. Tom instinctively caught it, and it was unusually heavy. His finger caught on a jagged piece of metal at the front of the helmet where the metal had splayed inwards around a perfect hole. At the back of the helmet, a section of the soldier's brain and bone had collected, white and bloody in its metal container with a clump of matted hair sticking out the front. The poor chap had a near perfect hole at the top of his forehead but the back of his head had been blown out and lay in the back of the helmet. Tom dropped it instinctively, shouting out "Medic, medic" at the top of his voice, though he stopped after his second shout, realising that no doctor in the world could save the man now. He had gone.

What occurred only later to Tom was how relatively un-phased he had been by the incident. He had seen so much blood and gore in this war now that he had partly become immune to seeing body parts and dead men. It was just another day.

When the inevitable counter-attack was rapidly organised, Tom and a handful of men were kept behind and assigned stretcher duties. What was shocking was the sheer numbers of young Germans that had been killed in just a hundred yards. In some places, the bodies were almost piled on top of each other and some of them were so young. 'Just young lads,' Tom thought to himself. These were definitely not the 'old soldiers' of years gone by, some looking barely older than fourteen or fifteen. The wounded were pitiful, often carrying a look of frightened despair in their eyes as they fought for life, spitting out blood and gasping for air through gurgling lungs. There was no difference between the nationalities when they were seriously wounded; Tom thought to himself. The Germans often just called for their mothers in their own language as their last moments arrived. So bloody sad, such a waste! Tom did his best to comfort the wounded, no matter who they were, British or German, they were still men, or now more often, boys. Some of the injuries were beyond belief, and it was difficult to imagine how a single bullet or piece of shrapnel could inflict such injuries on a man. If anything kept Tom awake at night later, it was thinking about the wounded, not the dead. The dead had escaped. They had been freed from all pain and in a way, were the lucky ones. But the wounded were real and their injuries were real, and they now had the job of staying alive, contending with injuries that would have made their mothers weep and wail if they could have seen them laid in that field. It was amazing that some of the injured men were still alive at all, gaping holes could be anywhere on a man's head or body with some big enough to put a football inside, yet still they lived, and still they breathed, and still they shouted and boy, could some of them shout, poor blighters.

By the time the slow clear up was over, darkness had fallen, so it was not until the following morning that the men were sent forwards to catch up with their units. What was immediately noticeable then was how much ground had now been made. It seemed that the German resistance had collapsed in the area and instead of hundreds of yards; it was a good three miles before they started seeing any fighting and then it was in old trenches that had swapped ownership twice over recent weeks. The ground was just still recognisable, with an old bank of trees now blown into some strange shapes, with twisted shards of wood reaching into the sky where branches and leaves had once waved gently in the summer breeze. The Bosch were on the run and only a delay for munitions, food and men made for a temporary halt in the allied counter-attack. Two Sopwith Camels flew overhead, spying the situation unchallenged in the sky.

Over the coming weeks, the advance was remarkable compared to the last three or more years. There were pockets of localised resistance but the word was that the German line had collapsed and they had largely retreated back behind the Hindenburg line. Captured prisoners now openly spoke like they were already beaten, with stories of frustration at not having enough to eat, yet alone enough ammunition to fight with. Things were collapsing behind the German lines and their resistance was crumbling.

"Payne, is there a Private Payne here?" Tom heard his name being called and made himself known to the young, fresh-faced soldier. "You've to go with me to divisional HQ, Payne. Captain Pearce says you are to report as quickly as you can, please."

Tom made his way back to the old chateau that was the temporary allied head-quarters, wondering if he was in trouble and trying to work out what it might be for. He saluted briskly as he met Captain Pearce again. "At ease, Payne. Let's go for a walk, shall we?"

Tom followed him out down the corridor, glancing left and right as he went, noticing several large rooms full of activity, as men poured over large maps laid out on tables. They went outside and into the brilliant September sunshine and started walking slowly now through a large orchard that had quickly been stripped of apples. Tom noticed the change in Pearce's uniform as he walked alongside him. "Congratulations, sir. I see you've been promoted."

"Thank you, Payne. Yes, from a Captain to Major and four months later to Brigadier," he glanced at Tom and smiled wryly. "That's what happens when you are lucky enough to survive longer than average, Payne. You stand in dead men's shoes I'm afraid. We took quite a hit when a stray Gerry shell took out a divisional HQ a month or so back, so here I am. Two promotions in five months." He chuckled as he turned to face Tom. Pearce looked much older and more lined than he had before. Tom noticed. "Right, down to business, Payne. I don't have much time to talk and I'm putting you on trust. Okay? What I tell you now must, I repeat must, remain absolutely confidential."

"Of course," Tom replied, straightening his back and standing to attention as he spoke.

"I haven't forgotten your story about your son being held in Germany. In strict confidence, we believe that the Bosch is darn near finished. They have fallen back behind their old defensive position at the Hindenburg line but behind that line, we believe that things are pretty much collapsing. Once we break through their defence there, then we believe we will drive them fairly swiftly all the way back to Germany. We are not there yet, but our intelligence makes us think that perhaps we might be able to bring this business to a conclusion sometime this year or at the latest, early next. What we don't know, of course, is how and when the Germans might throw the towel in, or if they intend to fight to the last man but we don't think that they will. There's still a lot we don't know, but what we do know gives rise to some optimism at last.

"You told me Tom that you were out here to get your son back and wanted to be at the front to be first in when the time came, right?"

"That's right, sir."

"So that's why I'm talking to you now and I repeat, in total confidence. When the time's right, the plan is that I will be leading one of the first units into Germany. My language skills and my knowledge of Berlin means that Haig wants me out front when the final push comes. I believe you said that your son is in near Berlin, so I am offering to assign you to my unit so that you can be one of the first into Germany with me and, the moment we have Berlin secure and under Marshall law, I will give you six men to go and find your son. How does that sound? But there is a negative for you though, in that I would need you to swap your shovel for a gun. Being out front going into Germany is likely to be dangerous, even if they have thrown the towel in by then, so consider it carefully.

"I'm also offering you a promotion. You're a natural leader, Tom, in your quiet way, and it's clear that the other men look up to you and respect you. You are wasted as a private, so I'm offering you a commission in the field."

Tom's heart raced as he listened to the news and though inside he felt like jumping for joy at the thought of getting to Germany, he remained calm. "Thank you, sir. I'd like to join your unit very much, though I'm happy to remain a private, sir, if that's alright with you. I do have my own reasons, but thank you all the same. But I would be honoured to serve with you, sir. Thank you."

"Good man. I'm sorry you don't want a commission but it's your choice. I'll make arrangements for your transfer and your commanding officer will get the papers tomorrow. I'll be seeing you soon, Private Payne."

Tom turned and snapped to attention, saluting smartly. Brigadier Pearce saluted in return, smiled and turned, heading briskly back to the chateau.

Tom walked back to his unit with the broadest smile that he had worn since he last saw Harriet. When he wrote home that evening, he could say nothing of the day's events, but both his letters to William and Harriet were now bursting with optimism for the future. He just could not reveal why.

CHAPTER THIRTY-FIVE

The sheer venom with which the old woman shook her fist and swore at Will and the prisoners working party was quite frightening. Despite her long years, her hatred was made clear and over the last months, the prisoners in Doberitz had noticed the change in mood amongst the locals when they were marching to work outside the camp. The blockade encircling Germany was gradually squeezing supplies and now almost everyone in Germany was hungry, with the supplies of even the most basic things from food to soap being in short supply. Faces scowled back now with sunken eyes and bitter looks and the guards accompanying work parties were needed to protect the prisoners from groups of locals as much as to stop them escaping. They need not have worried about escapes as the prisoners had the clear understanding that any prisoner found wandering through the German countryside would be set upon quickly, so whilst there had always been some talking of escaping, the mood outside the camp made it unthinkable. It would not only be the German Army that one had to contend with.

It was harvest time at the farm, and Will and the other men were digging out the potatoes crop, with every single spud being watched over and counted jealously. The instruction to ensure every single potato was lifted was made very clear and every prisoner was searched roughly at the end of the day, and they all knew that woe betide anyone who was found with a spud in their pocket. They would be beaten for sure, and each potato was guarded before being placed in its wooden crate to be whisked away by the farmer. The lunchtime soup had become thinner over time and the slice of bread smaller, but it was still better than the food they were given back at camp. The working party at the farm had varied in number, depending on what needed to be done there, but Will was always in that party and despite the language barrier, he had built up a rapport with the farmer and his wife. The farmer's wife was a lovely lady and even the farmer had softened in time towards the men. Will was always conscious that they had a son fighting, so had their own pressures to bear and his 'pleases' and 'thank you's' in German were well received to the point that even the old guards were now more relaxed around the men. As the war dragged on, it was clear that the German people were suffering too, and despite public resentment towards allied prisoners, those working close to them for a period of time understood that they were actually very similar to themselves. It was still tough though, and episodes like earlier today with the old woman cursing them brought it home again. 'They all want this bloody war over as much as we do,' Will thought.

When he got back to camp that night, the parcel and letter waiting for him from home cheered him up a treat. There were cigarettes and two tins of bully beef and biscuits as well as a small bar of *Fry s* chocolate which was carefully divided up amongst the lads as usual. Despite clubbing their resources together to make a better meal than the camp's meagre rations provided, only one of the five lads only received a parcel every few days if they were lucky, so even after home food, they still went to bed hungry as usual. But Will went to bed grinning all over his face that night and couldn't wait to tell the lads once he had read his post. Annie had said 'yes'. She had broached the subject quietly with her mother at first, who had then chosen her moment to ask Cornelius what he might think if Will asked for Annie's hand. Cornelius understood what was going on immediately and called Annie in.

"What's going on then, girl? Come on out with it. You know I like plain-speaking." Cornelius still carried a heavy, southern-Irish accent which softened as he spoke to Annie and he carried a faint smile now. It had been tough for him leaving Ireland with his wife, but with the potato blight ruining the crop and literally starving the nation at home, he'd had little choice but to leave for England to do the best for his family.

Annie was the apple of his eye, as his wife used to say, and he could never talk harshly to her even if he'd wanted to.

"Well, father, Will would like to ask you something when he gets home, but he wants to do it right, so don't make a fuss about it. William will ask you in person."

"Marriage is it then. Is that what's on his mind? So if that's the question that Will might be asking me, what is your thinking on the subject, Annie? Do you want more time when he comes back to get to know him again, or are you happy at the thought of marrying the man? It's a big step, girl. You'll be a wife with all that goes with that."

Annie went as red as a beetroot, as her father spoke and sat down at the kitchen table, rather embarrassed by the conversation. "Well, father, I don't think I could get to know Will any better than I do now really. We have written to each other so many times that I think I know him as well as I could do. I can't wait for him to come home and here with me. He has had such a dreadful time of it these last years that I just want him home. I do miss him so."

"I know, girl. We know," Cornelius said, taking his wife's hand as he spoke. "Why don't you write to Will and tell him what you think on the subject and say that I'll be happy to receive his question whenever he wants to ask it?" Annie jumped up and threw her arms around her father, who was immediately embarrassed.

"Ah, well... Enough there, Annie. You know I don't like all this emotional stuff. Get off and write to yer man."

CHAPTER THIRTY-SIX

The shelling in the distance seemed nonstop. Before Tom eventually drifted off to sleep, he could hear it continually pounding the German lines and every time he woke, which was frequently, it was still hammering away. On the fifth time of waking, he gave up thoughts of sleep and sat up, rubbing his eyes. Still dark, he thought he could detect dawn's first rays in the distance and the morning air had more than the hint of winter's bite to it now. He pulled his greatcoat collar tighter against the cold that had dug deep into his bones as he slept, and he moved to alleviate the ache in his back. The Hindenburg line had been broken in a number of places weeks back but thankfully, they had not been directly involved in the fighting, waiting slightly in reserve and following through one of the gaps in admiration and dismay as to how this seemingly impenetrable defensive line had been literally smashed by very precise heavy artillery.

Brigadier Pearce's division had been held in reserve waiting for this moment, but now began the big push, the drive to finally push the Germans back through France and Belgium. The cracks in the German resistance were everywhere now and their men were literally fighting for their own survival. Tom had never seen so many prisoners taken as in the last week. Their spirit was clearly broken now, though when the Germans fought, it was still as dogged as ever for a while, before self-preservation took over. They typically fought like hell for a while before a white flag would wave in surrender. They were low on food, ammunition and spirit and had clearly had enough. Their morale had gone, so the fighting was now largely one-way as the German resistance crumbled away.

It was in the woods around Bousignies-sur-Roc close to the French border with Belgium that Tom's war took a dramatic and unexpected change. The Bosch had dug in deeply, and fighting in amongst the trees was difficult and at times near impossible. Pearce's brigade had withdrawn once severe resistance was encountered in the woods to let the artillery give them a pounding to soften them up, but apart from uprooting and tearing down a lot of trees that had once stood proud and tall, it did not seem to deter the Germans' resistance much. When the British attacked, they were surprised how the shelling had failed to dent the resistance, which was fiercer than they had seen in weeks. 'They must have a stubborn commander,' Tom thought.

As they cautiously entered the woods, they quickly had to drop to the ground as bullets flew past them. Tom's heart was pounding in his chest as he dropped quickly and crawled forward inch by inch alongside everyone else. After fifty yards of crawling, he was breathing hard.

'I am getting too old for this,' he thought to himself, rolling over onto his back for a minute behind a fallen tree to get his breath back.

The ground was full of fallen leaves and the leaf litter had piled deep in places against fallen trees, having been whipped into mounds by either the wind or explosions. The recent rain had made the ground wet which, added with the cold, made crawling on the ground extremely unpleasant.

There was a sniper out there somewhere in the shadows and he had already shot two men to the left of Tom, so every movement was measured and tense, fearing the Sniper's attention. Brigadier Pearce lay six feet to Tom's right and he swung his arm out, indicating to the furthest two men over to the right to try and swing around and get behind the sniper. They both shuffled off, staying low and trying to work their way up behind another fallen tree for cover. A large beech tree lay about eighty yards up ahead that had been partially felled by shellfire. It lay awkwardly now, propped precariously against another tree with its roots half exposed. Tom peeped cautiously around, straining his eyes, trying to detect the slightest sign of movement in the dark shadows ahead. It was difficult to tell what he was looking at until a single flash of light erupted in the shadows, defining the end of a rifle. Within a millisecond, Tom heard the familiar thud of bullet meeting flesh. Brigadier Pearce rolled over clutching his throat with his right hand, his mouth wide open in a shout that didn't come. His left arm flayed at the air, writhing in pain as he rolled onto his back. Shots rang out in the half light from the men around them who had also seen the flash. Tom rolled over quickly to where the Brigadier lay. His eyes stared wildly as he gulped for air that would not get past the blood entering his lungs. Tom forgot the sniper in the urgency of the situation and got up and knelt beside him, risking the next shot as he frantically tried to stem the blood that now gathered on the ground around, soaking quickly into the soft earth. The bullet had gone straight through the Brigadier's throat from just under the chin at a downward angle, exiting through his back near his shoulder in a mess of a wound. The brigadier writhed around, desperately hunting air where none would pass the wound. He looked deep into Tom's eyes imploringly for a moment that felt like a minute to Tom before his arms dropped limply beside him and all movement stopped. His mouth gaped open and his eyes stared coldly ahead but he had gone. Still kneeling, Tom swung around and lifted his rifle, firing into the darkness at the exact spot where he had seen the flash. He reloaded, swinging the bolt backwards and down and back again and fired again and again, moving his shots to the left and right, anticipating that the sniper would have changed his position by now. For the first time in this war, he wanted to kill. No leg wound, no mercy; he wanted to kill. By the fourth shot, he could not see where he was firing, his eyes had flooded with tears and he swung back around to Ted who lay there motionless, staring coldly into the canopy of trees above. Tom closed the Brigadier's eyes and gently closed his mouth, but there was nothing he could do for his friend. Men were now up on their feet around them, firing as they ran forwards, sensing that the German resistance was now just a few snipers put there to hold up the advance. Tom put his hand on his friend's shoulder for a moment. "God bless and take you, Ted," he whispered, before he rose to his feet and turned, charging forwards with the other men. For the first time in the entire war, he joined the attack with venom and with a savagery he had never possessed before, but their attackers had fled. He saw several dark shadows running between the trees in the far distance, but by that time the red mist was passing, and he could shoot no man in the back.

By the time they had driven the Germans out of the woods, Tom was physically and emotionally exhausted. When the order came to halt the attack and regroup at the edge of the wood under the cover of the trees, he walked back through the woods to find the brigadier, but as he got close to the spot, he saw two men walking away with the Brigadier's body on a stretcher. He didn't chase after them. He knew that he had lost his friend and he slumped down exhausted and sat on the tree next to the stained patch of leaf litter where Ted had given his blood to the earth. He suddenly felt a wave of emotion engulf him as he stared up through the trees to the sky above. He had spent the entire war guarding himself from forging strong friendships with the men around him, keeping his emotions in check. Although Ted had not been so close as to call him a close pal as such, he felt an empathy and friendship built from trust forged in iron between them when they had been marooned in no-man's-land together. Ted was a thoroughly decent guy, a good man, a family man.

The sky above was a dark grey like his mood, and he felt his bottom lip quiver as tiredness and sorrow washed over him. From the hours he had spent marooned in no-man's-land with the Brigadier, he had counted him as close a friend as he had allowed throughout the entire war. As he stared back at the ground, he heard footsteps and looked up. A runner was jogging towards him and slowed down to get his breath back.

"Alright, mate, where's the unit?" he asked with a strong northern accent.

Tom pointed behind him. "Keep going. You're on the right track. They're about another quarter mile up ahead."

"I've got news. The Kaiser's gone, resigned and legged it," he said, puffing out the words.

"What? Abdicated?"

"Eye. That's the word. I'd forgotten it but yea, he's abdicated, mate. Won't be long now. The whole of bloody Germany is collapsing by all accounts." He started running again and Tom was left trying to take the news in.

CHAPTER THIRTY-SEVEN

Something was wrong, different. There were far less guards around than yesterday and no escorts to take the men to work, so the prisoners milled around inside the camp confused. "May as well go for breakfast. Anyone for bacon and eggs? Or will it be sausages this morning," some wag called out, giving everyone a laugh. Will's missing toes shouted at him painfully. The cold got to him every time and today was no exception. After an hour, several guards appeared, rifles in hand and shouted at them to assemble in the parade square. By the time they had filed through, there were already hundreds of prisoners milling around, a sense of excitement now buzzing through them as they sensed something had changed. When the old Commandant came out looking flustered to address them, there was already speculation amongst them that something big had happened. As he mounted the steps onto the raised podium, his limp seemed more exaggerated than usual, taking each step with his working right foot and letting his left foot catch up with it one step at a time. He looked crestfallen, his face grey and haggard looking against his dark blue Prussian uniform. He had hardly finished his first sentence and had said nothing of consequence when a group of men started shouting in excitement, anticipating what was coming. "Quiet!" The order barked out from a British officer and the Commandant continued.

"We have received news from German high command that all hostilities will cease at eleven o' clock today. From that time, our nations will no longer be at war and all prisoners will in time be exchanged."

"We've bloody won!" somebody shouted out from the crowd.

"You have not won!" the Commandant barked out indignantly. "A truce has been agreed and fighting will stop. No more than that," his face reddening as he spat out the words. "Arrangements will be made for you to return home but this may take several weeks, so you are to stay here until there are further orders. The camp will remain locked and you will be fed as normal. Bad behaviour will not be tolerated. Now, I will meet with senior officers in my office in five minutes to discuss details. That is all."

As he turned, a roar of cheers erupted as hundreds of men jumped up and down, hugging and shouting with the men around them, like an excited assembly of skeletons. Will couldn't believe it. He didn't join in the shouting but leaned against the hut behind him in shock, trying to take the news in. Bloody hell, it was over. It was finally bloody over. He needed a cigarette.

In the woods at Bousignies-sur-Roc, the excitement was just as loud at eleven o' clock. Men danced around in sheer joy, swinging each other around by the arm as they took in the news that the war was officially over. Tom stuffed some tobacco into his pipe and with a big grin leisurely pushed out the smoke, for once not worrying about it being seen by a sniper. He closed his eyes for a moment to take in the news with more focus. Four long, long, painful years they'd been fighting, but it was over. It was finally over. He thought of Harriet and a wave of joy washed over him at the thought of going home.

In the first hours, there were still a few explosions and shots heard in the distance, but they quickly ceased. 'Somebody was late hearing the news,' Tom thought. They walked back through the woods to the village and spent the day awaiting orders. As they marched back into town, the villagers were out on the street waving and clapping. There only seemed to be old people left now but everyone seemed to be out on the main street, handing out bottles of beer to the troops and singing the French anthem loudly. Tom had one very satisfying beer before walking back in the woods to be alone and get his thoughts together. Alone, there was an eerie silence amongst the trees and for the first time in ages, he could hear no noises of explosions or shooting in the distance, just the sound of his own feet trudging through the fallen leaves. It was lovely, and he sat on a fallen tree just enjoying the calm. He stood up briskly after a few minutes though and turned. 'Right. Let's go and get Will,' he thought to himself as he marched back to the village.

"Excuse me, sir," he asked as he saluted the Major who had taken over the Brigadier's command. "When will we be going to Berlin, sir?"

The Major looked surprised at the question. "I don't think we will be going to Berlin just yet, Payne, if ever at all. I haven't got details yet but the armistice suggests that fighting will stop as from now and everyone will go home in time, so I don't think we'll be marching into Germany or anything like that. The Germans have just packed it in and will leave France and Belgium. If I hear anything different, then I'll let you know but my orders are to stay here and await further instructions."

"But what about the British prisoners in Germany, sir?"

"Our POWs? Well, I haven't heard anything about them as such, but they will be going home as soon as it can be organised. We certainly don't want to have to feed the ones we've captured for long; I can assure you. There's hardly enough food to feed our own troops yet alone them. It will be the same, I suspect, for our men in prison."

It took Tom a few moments to digest the news. Since the Brigadier had spoken to him, he had pictured himself marching into a beaten Germany to find Will and let him out of prison. Now as he thought, he didn't care what happened as long as Will got home and quickly. But then the thought occurred to him that Will might then get home before he did. Now that was something to think about.

CHAPTER THIRTY-EIGHT

Most of the guards deserted Doberitz and most other prison camps within hours of the armistice being announced. The guards looked devastated and no longer wanted to be there. Knowing that they would never be paid, they deserted their posts in favour of getting back to their own families. The first out of the back door were the guards who had, shall we say, been less kindly to the prisoners in the past and now feared retribution. Even some of the decent ones slunk off quietly, and who could blame them? The gates to the prison remained closed but the locks had been removed and within two hours of the announcement, a large group of half-starved Russian prisoners left, shouting abuse at their German captors as they left. They carried blankets slung around their shoulders and anything else they valued, as they marched out of the front gate, breaking into a rousing Russian song that could be heard for ages as they walked eastwards. The Russians could eat no less outside the camp than they would within it and would take their chances on the open road, but many of them came over to the British and French as they left, shaking hands and giving thanks for what food and support they had managed to give them over their years in captivity.

Monday, the eleventh of November, was a day that Will would never forget all of his life. British and French prisoners stayed inside the camp, roaming around with a new feeling of freedom as they awaited orders. Despite this greater freedom, nearly any relaxed attitudes of the last years dissolved immediately. They were soldiers again and would be until they were officially demobbed.

On the Tuesday morning, a delegation from the Red Cross arrived and went into a long meeting in the commandant's office with him and senior French and English officers. After several hours, they emerged and the British were called to attention. Will would not forget the commander's opening words: "Men, we're going home." His next sentence was halted, drowned out by the roar of noise from the prisoners. Some danced, some shouted, some just stood there in shock and there were a few who sobbed on hearing those four words. Will stood there in silence, not moving, just trying to take the words in as memories of his last four years flashed through his mind. It was only when he pictured 25 Saxon Road that he realised that he was quietly crying, the tears rolling down his face. He was going home.

People were out, celebrating in the streets of Bristol as soon as the news broke. Harriet, Alfred and Anthony shut the shop and walked briskly down to the city centre, the three of them chattering excitedly. Church bells were ringing out all over the city, and groups were gathering on every street corner. They could hardly take it in. Four years of worry, four years of sacrifice, four years of tears, hardship and loss. The war was finally over.

William was in the first group of men from Doberitz to be repatriated because of his injuries. None of the men saw the posting of names for repatriation until the Thursday evening and the first group were to be taken to the railway station before dawn the next morning. There was hardly any time for farewells but it was very emotional for Will and his friends as they said goodbye. Terry, Alfred, Harold and William had been more than friends and as Will reflected afterwards, they had probably saved his life on more than one occasion. They sat around on the Thursday evening, chatting and laughing, nibbling the last of someone's cake from a food parcel, all trying not to become melancholy. They were all going home. Bloody hell, just the thought of it made Will have to fight back a tear at the thought. *Home.* They exchanged addresses with firm handshakes before settling down for what Will knew would be a sleepless night.

Will sat on the train staring out of the window, as it made its way westward and remembered that he had wanted to say goodbye to the farmer and his wife but hadn't had time in the melee of recent days. He felt a little sad at that. They had not been bad to him and he would have liked to have wished them well, but there had just been no guard to go with him and the streets outside were still potentially hostile. For that reason, they had been taken to the station early and put on a special train with just POWs on board. The train was absolutely packed with British and French soldiers, but Will had got a seat and couldn't help but think back to the train that had taken him into captivity those four long years ago. God, what a different journey that had been! He tried not to think of it and just concentrated his thoughts on going home. He had to look forward now, and he pictured his mum and dad sitting at the kitchen table as he walked back through the door for the first time in a few days.

The train only stopped at a couple of stations where bread and cheese was brought on board along with jugs of water for the men. Nothing had changed with the rations then. There was still barely enough to stave off the hunger pains from meal to meal until they arrived in Paris, but once there, they were allowed to get out of the train to stretch their legs. As they stumbled off the train after being cooped up for hours, they were greeted by spontaneous applause from Parisians boarding other trains. That gave Will and all of the men a real boost, as for the first time in years, they actually felt appreciated.

Within an hour, they were back on board the same train bound for Calais where they had to change trains for the short run up the coast. So after nearly two days of travelling, they arrived in Dunkirk and were loaded onto a ship bound for Dover. Will felt weak as he leaned on the rail of the ship but the smell of the salt air felt good despite it being bitterly cold. They set sail within two hours and Will was impressed with the organisation until they got to Dover, where it seemed to break down in the melee. The quayside was packed with troops standing around in the cold, waiting to be moved out of the docks and for a while, nobody seemed to know what was going on. The word went around that they were going to a dispersal camp in Canterbury but nothing seemed to happen for an age. Meanwhile, Will couldn't stop looking around at the distant hills and then down at the ground beneath his feet as he waited in the cold. Despite the confusion, it just felt so, so good to actually be back in England.

CHAPTER THIRTY-NINE

It was a mess. 'How long will it take to return France to what it was before the war?' Tom asked himself as he looked around. The fields around him that had once been flat and full of wheat, sheep and cattle now contained not a single blade of grass. Huge mounds of mud, where explosion on explosion had torn the earth in gigantic lumps and thrown it out, had rendered the once beautiful landscape into something resembling the moon. And there was so much of it, mile on mile of it, looking even more desolate now in the frozen grip of winter.

Every soldier could now walk in confidence, without fear of being put on a charge because they did not immediately have their rifle right by them. They were all working flat out to repair the road so that horses and vehicles could pass without falling into the numerous pot and shell holes. It was a mess. There was no talk of going home yet, though as the days passed, it was becoming clear that hostilities had now definitely ceased. They had just finished a section of road one afternoon when a huge group of returning German prisoners filed passed them, five wide and filling the road as far as the eye could see, heading eastwards. They were still under escort, and passed with a range of expressions, some looking hungry and beaten, sullen faces with no hint of joy in them as they half marched, half shuffled past bound for the next station. Most of them just stared at the road in front of their feet but some of them glanced around with a look of hatred and anger burning in their eyes. 'It didn't pay to look at them,' Tom thought. They all had their own demons to battle and he wondered if Will was making some similar journey home. He put a cigarette to his lips, fumbling inside his pocket for matches when one of the Germans broke from the group and stood in front of him. "Please," he said, looking at Tom and the cigarette.

Tom gave him a cigarette and seeing just three left in the packet, he struck a match and lit the German's cigarette before lighting his own, and then placed three matches inside the cigarette packet and handed them to the German. "There you go. Good luck, mate."

A faint smile grew on the man's grubby face as he re-joined the marching line. "Danke," he said, fixing Tom with a nod of appreciation as he turned.

"You silly sod," the man next to Tom said. "He's just had your last fags."

Tom turned to the man. "I can get some more and he needed them more than me. I just hope someone's showing some kindness to my son in Germany at the moment."

Back in Canterbury, Will was taking his third hot shower in a row. The delousing process was certainly thorough and the chemicals he scrubbed into his scalp on the first shower had smelt overpoweringly strong, but he didn't mind. Having hot water running over his scrawny body was just such a wonderful feeling and by the end of the third shower, he felt cleaner than he had done for years. That was just a wonderful feeling in itself. He was given a great big towel to dry himself and wear as he was taken into a long wide room where as he passed, people handed him underwear and socks, a pair of rock hard boots and finally a brand new army uniform, shirt and tie. The people sizing him up as he passed did an excellent job as everything fit nicely. They must have had a size marked 'half starved' that would fit most of his company.

He then had a long session with two uniformed doctors, one of them saying nothing but making copious notes sitting at a large table. The first doctor started with a thorough physical examination, taking Will's weight and height before running through a lot of tests on his heart and lungs etc. Stripped to his underpants, Will's level of malnutrition was clear, as was his missing toes, which was the last thing the doctor examined. "So what's the story of your feet?" he asked quietly. The whole examination was handled with kid gloves as was the entire process in Canterbury. The doctors looked more civilian than military and were clearly not used to examining men of such physical and mental damage. Will told them of the frostbite during the first winter but nothing more. He certainly wasn't going to tell them about his 'problems' or his dreams or electric-shock treatment; he just wanted to go home.

That night, he slept in a camp bed that had a thin mattress on it and a proper sheet and blankets. It was wonderful, or so he thought, though it was too soft to be comfortable and he could only sleep once he had dragged the blankets onto the floor and slept there. His body had clearly become unaccustomed to comfort. Thankfully, his demons did not visit him that night and it was a real treat to wake and be given a breakfast like he had dreamt about for so long. As he chewed on the hot toast, he could not fail but to grin. It had butter on it. He had forgotten how good simple toast with butter and marmalade tasted. He spent a leisurely hour sat in a large hall that had been hastily kitted out with a lot of chairs and sofas and read the *Daily Mirror*. He must have read every word of every page; much was the novelty of being able to read a newspaper in a relaxed manner. He had almost finished when his name was called and he found himself sitting in front of what he was told was a debriefing team made up of a Colonel, a Captain and an orderly taking notes. He saluted briskly as he entered, but quickly realised that the process was rather more relaxed than that. "Sit down, Payne, and relax. It should be us saluting you, not the other way around. The good news is that for you, the war is most definitely over and you will be going home shortly. Our job now is to do two things: to talk through your experiences as a prisoner of war and then to assess your condition to ensure you are fit and ready to go home. You can be proud of your service to your country and I can confirm that the government has granted that all returning POWs have two months' fully paid leave coming in addition to your back pay."

The interrogation was probing but gentle. As they explained, now that the war was over, they would be looking for cases of malpractice for the examination of war crimes.

The Colonel explained, "War is bound by strict rules of conduct and we are fully aware that those rules have been broken both collectively and by some individuals, and her majesty's government is determined to pursue any case of mistreatment thoroughly." Will's left hand still had a slight tremor which he was adept at hiding now by forcing it against his body but thankfully, all his other problems had largely left him. He was quite proud of how he had mastered walking without the aid of a stick and had worked on it for hours back in the camp.

All his physical scars had pretty much healed but it was just his nightmares that still haunted him deep into the night. Gradually, pictures of them were momentarily retained sometimes now as he woke, and it was always the same image and face that he saw as he woke in a breathless panic. But he was not about to tell them about that. All he wanted to do now was go home and see his mum and dad and his Annie. Telling the military of how he had been subjected to electric-shock treatment would, he could guarantee, raise a lot more questions and take more days here being debriefed. No, he had had enough. He just wanted to go home now, so he skipped over the questions of mistreatment and wrapped his nightmares tightly in silence and locked them deep down within himself. The following day, he was given his discharge papers, a travel warrant and a large cup of tea. The tea was lovely, but his discharge papers from military service were far better beyond words.

When Will stood outside Temple Meads Station and looked back at its grand façade, he had to lean on the wall there and take a moment to gather himself. The last few weeks had been quite a shock to his system and just getting off the train and arriving back in familiar old Bristol had suddenly made him feel quite emotional, and he hadn't expected that. Across Temple Way, the red brick factory, where his old job was, stared back at him and he slung his lightweight kit bag over his shoulder and hobbled his way in his new painful boots over to the factory gates. "Excuse me, sir, you can't come in here." Old Charlie still manned the gates as he had done before Will left and Will greeted him with a smile.

"Sod off, Charlie. I'll want my old job back in a few weeks' time but for now, I've just popped back to say hello."

Charlie looked unsure for a few moments. Then recognition came. "Blimey, Will, you're a sight for sore eyes. Welcome back. I didn't recognise you. You've lost weight, lad."

"Look after my bag, would you, Charlie? I'll be back in a few minutes."

He stepped through into the factory and was immediately hit by the familiar sounds of the machinery clattering noisily. He made his way past some surprised faces through the factory until he saw Annie working at the far end of the room. She hadn't seen him and was busy at a long table, working feverishly as he came up behind her quietly. He then spoke loudly to be heard over the noise. "I asked you a question, Miss McGrath, but I'd like to ask it again in person if I may."

She swung around, startled by his voice, her mouth now wide open in disbelief. Will held onto the table with one hand and stepped awkwardly forwards down on one knee. "Annie McGrath, would you do me the honour of marrying me, please?"

She stood there in total surprise. "Will, oh, Will, you're home." She grabbed his hand and pulled him up, falling into his arms and nearly toppled him over in her enthusiasm. For a moment, they just embraced and stared into each other's eyes. "Yes," she said. "Yes, I will." And the half a dozen girls that had quickly gathered around them broke into a cheer and clapped loudly as she answered. "But you'd better go and ask my dad first," she said, beaming back at him.

Will walked back to the station and took a carriage to the shop, leaning forwards, half out of the cab to take in the scene that he had missed so much. Nothing had changed much and he got out at the end of the road as he wanted to walk the last few yards to the shop. He glanced in to see his mother serving a customer. He waited just out of sight until the customer came out, and he held the bell with one hand and the door with the other as he quietly closed it behind him. His mother looked up from the till as he came in grinning. "Any chance of a cup of tea, Mum?" he asked. She rushed out from behind the counter and hugged him for a full two minutes, saying nothing. When she did pull back, he could see that she was crying. "There's nothing to you, son. You're as skinny as a rake. You will need some food as well as a cup of tea!" she grinned.

They went through to the workshop, with Will eager to see his father again. He was confused when he saw just Alfred and Anthony. They greeted each other warmly with handshakes and Alfred looked awkward when Will asked where his dad was. "Come and have that cup of tea, Will, and I'll explain," Harriet said. "Your father went to find you, Will. Went to get you back, as he thought. As it turns out, you have got home before him, but he's fine and will be back home before long."

Will stood there in disbelief. "So when did he go? He's only just gone, right? The last letter I got was only two weeks ago and he wrote it from here."

"Not quite, son. He, well, we...we all didn't want you to be worrying about him. You had enough things going on."

Will sat down and sipped his tea in silence for a minute or two, just staring into space. "But he's alright you say. You've heard from him since the war ended?"

"Today, Will. His last letter arrived at the shop this morning. He was in some village with a long name in France, sharing a bottle of beer with some villagers. He's fine. It was all done to save you from worrying. Please don't be angry."

"The lying old sod," Will said, lighting up a Woodbine and as his left hand started to shake. He thrust it deep into his pocket, out of sight.

CHAPTER FORTY

The question was on everyone's lips, but it had already been made clear by high command that everyone would be going home in time, but everyone had to be patient and obey orders. There was a structure and organisation in place for getting everyone home and they were working to a set of priorities, so everyone had to be patient. Tom had written home twice within a few days, but as he had been moving around, any post from home since war's end had not reached him. It was frustrating, not that he had much time to sit around and dwell on it. Everyone was put to work helping the villagers get straight. Some of the houses had been shelled during the fighting and were dangerous, with walls at strange angles holding up roofs that might fall at any moment.

Tom was sent with four other men to check out a stone cottage which had been hit by a shell and looked precarious with part of its front wall and roof blown out. One of the younger engineers went straight for the front door which had been partly wedged open by the blast, but Tom grabbed his arm, stopping him from going inside. "Wait, lad. It doesn't look safe," and as he pulled him back, the entire front section of the cottage suddenly folded outwards in the middle, sending large stones flying in all directions and revealing an unexploded bomb wedged by its fins between an inner wall and the ceiling. Disturbed by the falling masonry, it dislodged and fell its last seven feet with the ceiling on top of it. A second later, it hit the ground and completed the task that it had been designed for, exploding less than fifteen feet away from where Tom and the young lad were standing.

Back in Bristol, Will was greeted enthusiastically by Annie's mum and dad when he arrived and Cornelius had immediately opened a bottle of his 'special' Whisky as he called it. "Here's to Annie's hero, our hero. Here's to you, William," he pronounced, raising his glass high into the air. It was only after a few minutes of Will looking uncomfortable, answering a tirade of questions that Cornelius pulled him onto the punch as it were with his burning question. "I hear you've something to ask me," Cornelius McGrath said to Will, making him feel very uncomfortable. Will felt embarrassed, knowing he was expected to react, but he pushed his embarrassment behind him quickly. "Um, yes sir. I know I've only just got back but I've been waiting a long time to ask this, sir. Would you please allow me to marry Annie?"

"I think you know I will, lad, and I'd be proud to call you my son-in-law. You're a good lad. Just you look after her properly, mind you," he said, slapping him on the back. "Come on, let's have another drink!" Will had hardly taken a sip of his first one and it had already gone to his head. It was years since he'd tasted anything alcoholic, and it had made his face glow as he felt his head swimming.

"And when did you want to be wedding our Annie?" Cornelius asked, as he poured himself a large one.

"Well, sir, I do have paid leave from the navy and Mardons have told me to take the two months off but that my old job is waiting for me. They've been really nice and sent me two hundred cigarettes and a crate of beer, courtesy of the Mardon family. And then I do have my back pay to come from the navy, so I do have some money to give us a start. We have both just lost four years of our lives so, well, if you are happy, then I would like to marry Annie as soon as possible really."

Cornelius sat down, careful not to spill his near full glass. "Agreed. You go with Annie to sort out the church and all that stuff and we can take it from there. Come on, lad. Let's drink to that. We've now got two things to celebrate!"

Will woke next morning with a headache and a very dry mouth. He still slept on the floor despite the comfort of his own bed. His mum knocked gently on the bedroom door, determined to make a fuss of her only son. "Cup of tea, Will?" He gathered the bedcover around him and got up and sat on the end of the bed. Harriet came in and carefully put the cup on the bedside table. "You look awful, son. It either says it went well or badly with old Cornelius but I can smell the whisky on you now. You're not used to it, are you?" she said, with an understanding smile.

"It went well, Mum. They are happy for me and Annie. Mr McGrath just wanted to start the celebrations a little early, that's all."

"Are you alright, son? I don't mean the drink. You're entitled to let your hair down after what you've been through, only you were shouting out in the night. I did come in and you were in a fever and had stopped shouting then, but is everything alright?"

Will couldn't remember a thing, but he knew he must have had one of his nightmares. "I don't remember, Mum. I haven't had a strong drink for a long, long time, so I guess it didn't agree with me. I have decided I don't like whisky though. It's given me a headache."

"You had it rough out in Germany. I know that, son," she said, looking painfully at his feet and his missing toes. "If there's anything you ever want to talk about, then I'm here, son. Okay?"

"Thanks, Mum. I know that. I'll be just fine. Thanks. It's wonderful being home. It's just a bit strange adjusting to being back and having proper food to eat and all of that, but I'll be fine. I'm loving it. But I miss dad. Have you had any word from him yet?"

"Not yet, son, but the postal service from France seems to have got worse since the war ended. I think the post offices aren't taking their jobs as seriously anymore." Quietly though, Harriet was worried. It had been an unusually long wait now for a letter from Tom to arrive. Annie was coming over this evening, so the three of them would write a letter and see if he knew when he was coming home.

Will went to the shop with his mum most mornings. It was just lovely being back in Bristol and he wanted to spend as much time with his mum as he could. When the letter arrived for him, marked 'Strictly Confidential' and with a Buckingham Palace Stamp on the envelope, he was out in the workshop talking with uncle. Harriet came through, holding the envelope, looking slightly worried. "It's a letter for you, Will. It looks official."

Will opened the envelope and unfolded the single page letter and read it carefully. "Blimey, take a look, Mum. I've had a letter from the King." Sure enough, written in his own hand was a letter headed 'Buckingham Palace' and signed 'George R'.

Harriet took it and looked at the letter, still unable to read the words fully. "That's wonderful, Will. That really is something special. I bet you can't wait to show Annie." It flashed across her mind that she would have been happier to have received a simple letter from her husband. She was increasingly getting concerned by the lack of contact from Tom. That same afternoon, William and Annie went to see the vicar and set a date to marry on the 4th of January. 'Dad will be home long before then,' Will thought.

Two soldiers were killed in the explosion at the cottage in Bousignies-sur-Roc, two men whose families had thought that as the war had already ended, they would be seeing their loved ones home soon and for good, two families that were planning celebrations and homecomings befitting their returning heroes. Both families would now get the one letter that throughout all of the war they had dreaded receiving and, since the war had ended, thought that they would never receive.

When they pulled Tom out from under the rubble, he was barely breathing. The young lad that he had pulled back from the door was dead, killed outright by flying masonry, as was the sergeant stood behind them, who had also taken the full force of the explosion. They took Tom to the nearest civilian hospital and he stayed there on the edge of death in a coma for four days while his brain and body fought to survive. On the fifth day, he slowly opened his eyes and started speaking rubbish, and it took another week in which he slept most of the time before his head started to clear and he could remember bits and pieces but nothing about the explosion. He had been hit by a number of pieces of masonry during the explosion and taken a blow to the head from one of the huge stones that had made up the front wall of the cottage, but the French doctor told him, "You are one lucky man."

For the next two weeks, he struggled to recover, but as the jigsaw, that was his mind, started to slowly put the pieces back together and his fuzzy memory returned, he knew that he had to do something urgently; he just wasn't sure what it was. When he had a visit from his old sergeant who brought with him several letters from home, instant realisation came to him. He needed to write home and let Harriet know that he was alright. Everything was just such a damned blur.

He wrapped himself in the hospital-issued dressing gown and took the three letters through to the empty patient's recovery room. The large windows there gave good light and looked out over the lawns still white with frost to the front of the hospital. He arranged the three letters by order of their date and opened the oldest one first. As he finished the last one, he was in a panic. William was home, bless him, and picturing him there brought a tear to his eye. He had gone to such extremes to get him back and there he was, at home, waiting for him instead. The panic set in when he got to the last letter and discovered that William and Annie were getting married on the 4th of January. He scooped up the letters roughly and hobbled quickly back to the ward. The doctor was at the end of the ward, just finishing talking to a patient. "Pardon Monsieur Doctor, can you tell me what day it is?"

"Oui, Monsieur. Tomorrow will be the eve of Noel."

Tom's head was reeling and he was confused. "The eve of Noel. Noel?" 'What was that?' he thought. Then the penny dropped. "Christmas. Tomorrow is Christmas Eve? So today is the 23rd of December?"

"Oui, Monsieur. It is the 23rd today."

"I've got to get home," Tom said in a panic, and went back to his bed, looking for his uniform. It took an hour for Tom to get the hospital staff to understand, but the doctor was reluctant to discuss discharging him there and then.

"You 'av' had a serious blow to the head, Monsieur. You need more time to recover."

"I am recovered," Tom said urgently. "I need to get back to my unit and get home quickly."

"We will contact the British military, Monsieur. Until then, please get back into bed. You must rest."

Tom was reluctant, and insisted that they call someone right away. When the officer arrived at the hospital the following morning, he told Tom that his unit had moved days ago and was now near Paris. Tom implored him to let him get back to England quickly and explained that his son was getting married. It was clear that the officer wasn't impressed. "Everyone has a good reason to be at the front of the queue to go home," he said, smiling broadly.

Tom, not to be deterred, found the third letter and showed him. "Here, sir. Look, my son has been incarcerated in Germany all through the war but now he's home and getting married on January the 4th."

The officer took the letter and read it. "Okay, first let me first talk to the doctor here and make sure that you are fit to leave and then I'll see what can be arranged. We are basically mopping up here but there is a large backlog of troops going back to England, so I will need to get your papers in order. I warn you. Getting home for January, the 4th, is going to be tight, even if I can get your papers sorted."

Christmas Day was a very special one in Harriet's house, but it came with mixed feelings for her in particular. She had slipped away from the shop yesterday to the war office to ask about Tom and they had no information but said they would make enquiries. There were so many troops on the move at the moment that there was a lot of confusion as to who was exactly where at any one time. The system was overloaded with troops waiting to come home but it still didn't stop Harriet from worrying. She knew her Tom and he always wrote as regular as clockwork.

Weeks had gone by now without word and although she made light of it in front of William, she confided in Alfred as to how worried she was.

But she had her William home and was determined that she would make it a special Christmas for him. She had been saving up her rations for months and made every effort to put together a Christmas dinner that she hoped he would never forget. Annie and her parents came, as well as her own parents and Alfred and his wife, but Harriet kept looking at the spot where Tom would usually sit.

It was a good opportunity for everyone to discuss the wedding arrangements and with food so tight and rationed, they would have to pool their resources to be able to put together a simple wedding plan. Harriet and Annie were already working on Annie's wedding dress, working in the evenings over the sewing machine and they would all muck in with the food.

CHAPTER FORTY-ONE

Tom was treated to a festive meal in the hospital on Christmas Eve along with the other patients, but he ate fast. He was hungry but also hoped that a doctor would arrive to give the 'okay' for him to leave. When the doctor came in the following morning, saying that he was being discharged, he was out of his bed like it was on fire. His uniform had been cleaned and he dressed quickly and bade a quick farewell to the hospital staff, grateful for their help. Then he marched out into the chill afternoon air, clearly on a mission.

Back at the local army headquarters, he tried to find the officer that he had seen in the hospital, but it was Christmas Day and he was not there. All the troops were in a festive mood and were looking forward to their Christmas dinner, so Tom walked into an atmosphere that he had not felt in all his time in the army. No one was in the mood to deal with Tom's pleas for paperwork and information and frustratingly, he sat down to his second Christmas dinner in two days, though he would have gladly given up his meal to be travelling towards home. It took another frustrating day to find an officer that would sign his papers and allow him to travel to Paris to meet up with his own unit. He had to wait until the following morning when transport would be going to the capital, so he spent another frustrating night waiting. During the evening, he sat and wrote a letter home that he hoped to beat. "I am on my way" was the main thrust of a short letter. Now the race was on, to beat the postal system and get home before it arrived.

Back home, Annie's wedding dress had been finished and William had been banished from the house while she tried it on with her mother and Harriet, making small adjustments to the length of the dress with pins. Annie looked beautiful. William had written to Terry and asked him to be his best man and he would be getting the train up from Dorset the day before the wedding. Harold was getting the early train up from Plymouth and both would be staying over. Will was looking forward to seeing them both. Although he didn't tell anyone, he was finding it difficult to settle back into his new life. It was wonderful being home, but he was only starting to realise how being incarcerated for four years had affected him. He decided that he needed to go back to work sooner than originally planned. He needed something to occupy his mind and distract him from the flashbacks and memories that regularly haunted him. He kept wondering if the poor Russians he had seen flooding out of the camp on foot had made it to their homes yet. They had looked such a sorry sight, humanity starved to skin and bone inside rags shuffling out of the camp bound for an uncertain journey home.

Tom's heart sank. He sat in the back of the lorry and they had barely gone two miles and joined the main route to Paris when they met a flood of humanity. In both directions, there were thousands of people on every conceivable form of transport. The displaced of war were trying to go home. It took the convoy of army lorries the entire morning to travel ten miles and they still had another one hundred and fifty to go to get to Paris. Tom got out of the truck and walked around to the driver. "Can't we do anything to speed up the journey? Isn't there another road we could take?" he pleaded to the driver. I've got a wedding to get to."

The driver laughed. "Well, they tell me that every other road is the same, mate. It's a waste of time me honking my horn as all I'll do is frighten the horses and then it will be even more chaotic than it is now. I'd say your best bet is to get a train, to be honest, but I hear they are just as full. Everyone wants to go home, mate. Me included."

"Permission requested to use the train, sir?" Tom asked the officer.

"Denied," came back to sharp reply, but as they crawled past Peronne, Tom quietly grabbed his kitbag and slipped discreetly off the truck, disappearing into the sea of people. He'd never disobeyed an order before, but this was not his unit and he now had his own mission. His heart sank when he saw the queues at the railway station though. There were hundreds of people milling round outside the small station. He joined the throng, making his way down the side of the crowd as best as he could. He heard someone up ahead blowing a whistle and looked up to see a French soldier standing on top of a wall, who seemed to be trying to direct affairs. The man started pointing at Tom and blew his whistle frantically. He stopped his blasts to shout in French at the crowd, waving his arms side to side as he did. Tom found that the crowd parted ever so slightly in front of him, and called on by the man's waves, he was able to make his way through the crowd. He was either in trouble or his luck had changed, he thought.

"Monsieur, you are going to Paris?" the French soldier asked.

"I am, sir, trying to make my way home," he said, handing over his travel papers.

The Frenchman waved his papers away.

"Go to Platform One. There will be a train in about forty minutes. You take priority Mon Amie. Bon Journey." He shook Tom's hand and went back to directing the crowd.

Tom's spirits lifted and he made his way through the crowded station to find Platform One, fingers crossed for a swift journey back to England.

CHAPTER FORTY-TWO

Harriet had hardly slept and had crept downstairs in the early hours, lighting her way with a candle and sat huddled in her dressing gown in the kitchen. In a few hours' time, the house would be a hive of activity as everyone arrived for the wedding. With no word from Tom for weeks and no news from the army, she had been worrying long past her ability to sleep. Something was wrong. Will was also getting concerned, but Harriet had told him that the post from the continent often didn't work and such long delays had happened before, but she knew they had not; she just didn't want Will worrying. As she sat there with her candle, she felt a tear forming in the corner of her eye and wiped it away quickly. 'I must hold it together,' she thought to herself. 'It's Will and Annie's big day.'

When the postman came at eight o' clock, the house was already a buzz of activity. The postman didn't normally knock, but today, he rapped his knuckles loudly on the door. Harriet answered it, distracted from frantic sandwich-making in the kitchen. He handed over four letters with a big grin on his face. "Morning, Mrs Payne. Hope all goes well for today," he said, beaming. Harriet thanked him and went back to the kitchen. She hurriedly shuffled through the letters but saw nothing resembling Tom's handwriting. She sat down back at the kitchen table and could not stem the tears any longer. The strain of the last four years seemed to break through in one rush and at that moment, Will came in, half dressed in his uniform.

She stood up quickly and hugged him tightly. "Ignore me," she said, smiling to distract his worried look. "It's a mother's prerogative to have a tear on her only son's wedding day."

All through the service, Harriet kept glancing around, hoping the door would open and that her Tom would breeze in, but the door stayed closed. When the moment of the service came, where they took their vows, Will and Annie faced each other in front of the congregation and as they did so, Will glanced at his mother and gave her a smile of comfort before looking back at his Annie. "I do," he replied to the vicar.

Back at 25 Saxon Road, they lined up for the wedding photographs. When they formed the wedding group, no words were spoken but they deliberately left a space next to Annie, where Tom would have been standing. Harriet tried to smile for the photographs but was distracted that her Tom was not with them as her worries mounted. The wedding party went back inside the house after the photographs to warm up, squeezing into the kitchen and lounge to enjoy the food and drink that had been laid on. Cornelius had already started on the whisky that he had brought himself to be sure of a good supply and some of the women were modestly sipping on sherry until in twos and threes, they all drifted off home.

Harriet was washing up at the kitchen sink, reliving the day and relieved that everyone, but Will and Annie, had now gone home. She looked through the kitchen window and smiled as she saw Will and Annie standing in the garden, holding hands. The look of love in their eyes for each other was as clear as the crisp afternoon air. As Harriet washed up the last of the plates and rested them on the draining board, she did not hear the front door open. Tom laid down his kitbag quietly and tip-toed down the hall to the kitchen. He stopped when he saw Harriet standing at the sink, humming to herself as she looked out into the back garden. It was a scene that Tom had longed for so many times over the last four years. He quietly stole up behind Harriet and gently placed his hands around her waist. "Sorry, I'm late, my love," he said softly. "Any chance of a cup of tea?"

THE END

POSTSCRIPT

Immediately after what soon became known as 'the war to end all wars', everyone in this story went back to the lives that they'd had before the war started. Almost. Thomas went back to making boots and shoes and although the wound in his hand quietly pained him, especially in the winter months, he continued to work with his brother in their little shop in Bristol.

In the Second World War, Tom, who was now 67 years old, served as an air raid warden in Bristol. On the 16th March 1941, the Luftwaffe unleashed the heaviest bombing raid on Bristol of the entire war. Two hundred and fifty-seven people were killed and three hundred and ninety-one injured that night, with the bombing starting at 8:30 pm and continuing until twelve minutes past four in the morning. Between seven hundred and eight hundred heavy bombs and thousands of incendiaries were dropped on the city that night and hundreds of fires broke out right across the city. Tom was assigned with four other wardens to tackle a fire at St Thomas boys' club in town. The building had taken a direct hit and was already blazing fiercely by the time they arrived. A guardian angel must have been watching over Tom that night, as the four other wardens were killed outright by falling masonry as the building collapsed, with Tom being struck a glancing blow which fractured his right shoulder and left him severely concussed. He was taken to St Martin's hospital in Bath and stayed there until the 9th April. After recovering at home, he resumed his air raid duties by night and continued making shoes by day.

Harriet started using her skills in millinery and became a seamstress, which brought in a better income than working in the shop. They both continued to live at 25 Saxon Road and delighted in their grandchildren and then great-grandchildren as the years passed. Some marriages, they say, are made in heaven and this seemed so for Thomas and Harriet. They joked that there had never been a crossed word between them in all their years of marriage, but I guess there must have been. But their wonderfully kind and giving natures made for a relationship that spanned sixty-eight years. Harriet passed away in hospital in February 1958, aged 86, and Thomas, lost without his beloved Harriet, died quietly in his sleep at his grandson Sid's house just five months later. As was their wish, Thomas and Harriet were laid next to each other in Greenbank Cemetery in Bristol, so that they could share the rest of eternity together.

William and Annie both went back to work at Mardons after the first war. The scars and horrors of the conflict sometimes revisited Will, often coming in the night, waking him and the household to his persecuted screams. But he battled on largely in silence, and life became complete for them both as first Ernest, then Sidney, William (always known as Bill) and Irene were born.

Will was a good father, who instilled the same moral values in his children that he had been brought up with, always starting with family values. He would delight in taking the three boys cycling around Bristol and spending as much time with his four children as he could. William would today almost certainly be recognised as a very talented artist, for his skill as a photographer and painter in watercolours. In the days before colour photography, William would take black and white photographs and develop them in the spare bedroom at home. He then hand-painted over the black and white images in watercolours with such skill that the images were brought back to life. In this and for his time, he was a genius, and it is wonderful to see his talent as an artist resurface today in his great-grandson Vincent Brown.

But as the years passed, Will's demons increasingly resurfaced from time to time. Like so many of his generations, the official war ended in 1918, but Will had to fight another darker war for the rest of his life. Lost toes and bodily scars could be seen, but the wounds buried deep in the mind were far harder to see. Shell-shock was a new phenomenon in 1918, and had never been seen or recorded before. Such was this new level of brutality in warfare. While Will watched his father 'doing his bit' as an Air Warden in the Second World War, he found the thought of war too stressful and could not bring himself to get involved. When German bombs fell on Bristol, painful memories that William had buried deep inside came flooding back. It was a troubled time.

Today, we call shell-shock 'post-traumatic stress', and it still troubles the modern soldier and will always be a man-inflicted curse on the body's most delicate and intricate facet, the mind. In his later years, William's nightmares sometimes resurfaced during his waking hours and finally, his mental issues were recognised as relating to his captivity and hardship in the 'Great War'. Somewhat ironically, he was several times treated with electro-therapy, the doctors never realising that William had seen this all before only under much more frightening circumstances. Until his later years, William's health was largely fine and one would never know that the scars of a war long ago were laying there dormant and suppressed, waiting to resurface many years later. He continued to work at Mardon-Son and Hall until 1952, completing forty-two years' service and it was only in his retirement that old demons resurfaced. Sometimes, he might wake believing himself to be back in 1914, a prisoner once again, fighting off guards. Despite this, he rarely lost his quiet sparkle. My grandfather passed quietly away in the Bristol Royal Infirmary, on December 6th, 1978, aged eighty-two.

Annie raised four lovely children, where mothering came so naturally to her that it was like a gift. William and Annie raised their four children, instilling love and strong family values in them all. As over time, grandchildren and great-grandchildren came along, Annie went from being mother to nan, great-nan and even great-great-nan, and she bestowed the same abundance of love on each and every one of them that she had given to her own children. For many years, Annie lived with her daughter Irene. Diagnosed with a weak heart, she defied the best doctors and lived on for many years, passing away peacefully in her sleep at the grand age of ninety-three.

The legacy of Thomas, Harriet, William and Annie continues. Today, their descendants are still blessed with strong family values, each generation passing down the ethics of the last and helping each other where and when needed. William and Annie were my grandparents and I have fond memories of them both.

Thomas and his brother outside the family shop, taken around 1940

Thomas and Harriet's 68th Wedding Anniversary

William: aged about nine and then on his favourite mode of transport in later life

*William and Annie, with children (from left to right), Bill, Ernest, Irene and Sid
Taken at Weston Beach around 1930*

William and Annie in retirement

William, the artist
A black and white photograph of their eldest Son, Ernest, hand-coloured in watercolours by William

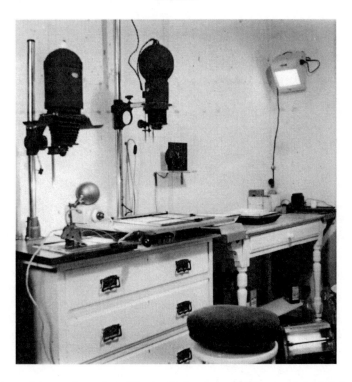

Where photographs came to life, the dark room at William and Annie's home

The artist's imagination. Top: William ties the rope to a large tree and urged his three sons to pull it down. Below: In WW2, in a rare moment when all three sons were home on leave, William recreated the same photograph. Taken at Queenshill Road in Knowle. Note the bomb damage from a German air raid. It must have been a poignant moment for William, Annie and daughter Irene, as all three boys would be leaving within days to return to their units overseas. Thankfully, they were all to return safely in 1945.

January 4th 1915. The only picture of William and Annie's wedding. Thomas did not arrive back in time from France.

SEPIA PHOTOGRAPHS

Sepia faces, gazing back from tattered photographs
Men and boys captured in time, sharing a few rare laughs
Locked away for a hundred years, their eyes still tell a tale
With faces older than their years, eyes determined not to fail.

Trenches deep in water, shared with rats and mice
Wet and muddy uniforms with this week's round of lice
Frozen feet and hands again, companions for the day
Come on lads, chin up boys, let our next salvo have its say.

Dulce et decorum est, take a deep breath and all that stuff
And forget to tell them when you write home that it's very tough
Don't tell them of your facial tic or hands that shake with fear
Or how you nearly lost it when that whiz-bang landed near.

No point in worrying Mum and Dad, so write home with a smile
And let your heart dream better times and the post count every mile
Send that little photo home, the one with your smiling pals
Don't tell 'em how you pray so hard and long to hear home's bells.

One day it will be over lad, so just pray you don't get hit
Or hope you get a Blighty wound, no, you won't mind that a bit
Until that time, best pray some more and trust in fate again
Try and find some dry socks now and keep out of the rain.

Captured so in cellulose, just a photo in a box
But its liberation tells its tale and history unlocks
No one can smell the cordite now or smell the fear in men
But let us always remember them, lest we do it all again.